THE DRYSLWYN CASTLE KILLINGS

THE CARMARTHEN CRIME SERIES BOOK 4

JOHN NICHOLL

Boldwood

First published in 2018. This edition first published in Great Britain in 2022 by Boldwood Books Ltd.

Cover Design by Head Design

Cover Photography: Shutterstock

The moral right of John Nicholl to be identified as the author of this work has been asserted in accordance with the Copyright, Designs and Patents Act 1988.

This book is a work of fiction and, except in the case of historical fact, any resemblance to actual persons, living or dead, is purely coincidental.

Every effort has been made to obtain the necessary permissions with reference to copyright material, both illustrative and quoted. We apologise for any omissions in this respect and will be pleased to make the appropriate acknowledgements in any future edition.

A CIP catalogue record for this book is available from the British Library.

Paperback ISBN 978-1-80426-328-0

Large Print ISBN 978-1-80426-329-7

Hardback ISBN 978-1-80426-330-3

Ebook ISBN 978-1-80426-327-3

Kindle ISBN 978-1-80426-326-6

Audio CD ISBN 978-1-80426-335-8

MP3 CD ISBN 978-1-80426-334-1

Digital audio download ISBN 978-1-80426-331-0

Boldwood Books Ltd
23 Bowerdean Street
London SW6 3TN
www.boldwoodbooks.com

For Roy, Myra, Jack and Doreen, never to be forgotten.

1

Mia ignored his first two emails, deleting them unopened. But the third was different, and it stood out in her inbox as if a spotlight was shining upon it, bright and bold. It demanded to be opened. It screamed to be opened. It reached out to drag her in.

I know where you live

Mia stared at the screen with a growing sense of foreboding that occupied each part of her being. They were only words. Just words. That's what she told herself. But words could frighten. Words could hurt.

She raised a hand to her face and closed her eyes for a beat, as one unwelcome thought after another bombarded her fragile mind. Who'd send such a thing? Someone she'd slighted online, without ever realising the offence she'd caused? A struggling author who resented her writing success? Or just another inadequate lowlife troll looking to boost their self-esteem, like a playground bully targeting the vulnerable? It couldn't be serious, could it? That implied threat and sense of menace... but what if it was? That was the real question. What if it was? Open it, Mia, there may be clues. Just open the damned thing and be done with it. It was time to bring her futile ruminations to an end. Time to silence her overactive intellect. Time to take control.

Mia's finger hovered over the keyboard for a few seconds more, and then there it was in front of her, the message that changed everything:

Tell me you love me, Mia. I'm your number one fan.

Mia thought long and hard as to whether to reply at all, drinking two cups of strong black coffee and taking three prescribed codeine tablets – excessive even for her – before finally deciding to send a carefully considered response likely to silence the sender forever.

She started typing, stopped, and then began again as the words came in and out of focus on the screen. She wanted her reply to sound formal, impersonal but polite. Yes, neutral but courteous – that seemed best. Maybe that would be sufficient to satisfy the mystery man with his abnormal intentions. How could she be expected to create, to concentrate given his unwelcome intrusion? Hopefully he'd sod off and leave her in peace to get on with her day. Her next book wasn't going to write itself.

Mia completed her retort in a matter of minutes. She read it through for the second time and then sent it without further hesitation. There, done – surely that was an end to it. The matter was closed and best forgotten. But why were her hands shaking? Why the feelings of apprehension that wouldn't let go? She took a deep breath, turning her attention to her latest novel and attempting to focus. Anything to stay positive. Anything to remain centred on her work. She typed a paragraph, deleted it, and then typed it again, almost word for word, before finally checking the grammar. She was still dissatisfied with the progression of the story, which wasn't flowing as it usually did, almost on autopilot as if channelled from elsewhere entirely. As if the words were being dictated in her head by some unseen force she couldn't begin to comprehend. Words, sentences and paragraphs, moving backwards and forwards in time, as if recounted from unremembered dreams and appearing on the page. Maybe a glass of wine would help. Perhaps the alcohol would stimulate her creative juices and help her relax as an added benefit. No, no, not with the painkillers, what on earth was she thinking? She just had to unwind, to loosen up and let the words come. They always had before, so why not now?

Mia sat at her computer for another hour before finally accepting that she wasn't in the right frame of mind to write anything worth keeping, not even a single word with which she could be pleased. It was a lost cause, a waste of time and effort. She rose to her feet and headed to the kitchen where she ate a light lunch, cautious with calories, and watched a mildly entertaining American sitcom at the pine table, her thoughts drifting back to that unwanted email with frustrating regularity. How dare anyone write such a thing!

Mia returned to her white-painted lounge just after 2:00 p.m., fed, watered and in a better frame of mind. What on earth was she worrying about? The email wasn't such a big deal, was it? She'd probably overreacted. Why get so worked up over nothing at all?

She relaxed back in her armchair with the intention of writing a chapter or two before collecting her young daughter from school. But there was another email awaiting her as she opened her laptop. One more message commanding her attention that made her squirm.

What were you thinking?
Your response was somewhat dismissive. That displeases me. It disap-

points and angers me. Naughty, naughty, I wouldn't make that mistake again, if I were you. You must do better, as my form teacher used to say before beating me mercilessly with a stick. Respond to my satisfaction or suffer the consequences. Make your choice but ignore me at your peril. Think of me as a malevolent spectre dedicated to you and only you. I think that's the best way of explaining it. I'm your shadow. I'm there with you now, always at your side, watching, listening and waiting to pounce. Tell me you love me, Mia. I'm your number one fan.

Mia swallowed hard, swore crudely under her breath, typed

LEAVE ME ALONE

in large, bold capitals and sent it with the tap of a key, before regretting her impulsiveness almost immediately. Just ignore him, Mia, that was best. Disregard the slimeball. Don't feed his obsession. He was looking for attention, desperate to light up his mundane existence. She'd been stupid. He was of no consequence, insignificant, unimportant. Why give him the validation he so obviously craved?

She pushed events from her mind and began writing, but with only limited success. It was hard to concentrate. Difficult to focus, just as earlier in the day. He'd got to her, whoever he was, and wherever he was. And she knew he'd be back in touch, whatever she said to herself. It was just a matter of time. She was sure of it. She'd never been more certain of anything in her life.

The next email arrived in Mia's inbox as she paced the floor, attempting to control her escalating anxiety as it threatened to drive her to one bottle or another for a slurp of brain-numbing alcohol or a prescribed chemical cosh. Why let the bastard get to her? Why indulge him? Why the hell had she replied at all?

Take a tablet, Mia, maybe take a tablet. Just to take the edge off on a stressful day. That was justified, wasn't it? She shook her head violently. No, no, it had only been an hour since the last one. Count the minutes, girl. Cling on to sanity. Her medication was fast running out and she'd have to wait.

Mia returned to her seat, sucking in the warm summer air in a further attempt to steady her rattling nerves. Breathe in for a count of seven, hold, one-two-three, and out for a count of seven... there, that was better. Hold it together, Mia. Breathe deeply and repeat.

She glared at the screen, fully intending to threaten legal action or to unleash a tirade of heartfelt insults, whatever the content of his communication. But as she opened the message she stiffened, jerking her head back and pressing herself hard against the back of her seat, as if attempting to escape the likely implications. There were six colour photographs in all, six photographs of her: queuing alone at the local cinema, shopping for underwear, walking in the busy high street weighed down by bags, enjoying a coffee and a bite to eat at a popular local café, sunning herself on a park bench with a daily newspaper in hand, and opening her front door. Even outside her house! He'd been watching her. He knew where she lived. Just as he'd said. Oh God, he knew where she lived. Don't freak out, Mia. Best not to panic. What did that achieve? The sender may be harmless. All words and no action. Sticks and stones. Anxiety achieved nothing at all.

Mia stared at the photos, up, down, from left to right and back again, and then read the accompanying text with narrowed eyes that slowly filled with tears:

I'd think very carefully if I were you.

There are things you need to know. Things you need to understand. Crucial factors that should inform every decision you make from this second onwards. Are you ready? Are you paying attention? Yes? Then

I'll continue. I can always find you, but you will never find me. I see everything. If you contact the police, I will hurt you bad. You won't know when and you won't know how. But it will happen. Where would that little girl of yours be without her mummy to care for her as she negotiates life's many dangers? She'd never get over her loss. It would ruin her life forever. Scar her emotionally before her life really began. Think about that when you're considering what to do next. I'd be very cautious if I were you, lady. Your life will depend on it. Tell me you love me, Mia. I'm your number one fan.

Mia picked up her smartphone and stared at it with unblinking eyes, fully intending to dial 999 to summon help. But she put it down again almost immediately, his written words resonating in her mind as if on a loop, like some crazed Eastern mantra that wouldn't let up. *I will hurt you. I will hurt you.* That's what he'd written. It was all there in black and white, unequivocal, unambiguous, as clear as day. It couldn't be true, could it? He'd followed her, taken the photographs. That was real. There was no denying it. Maybe he meant every miserable word.

Mia rushed to the kitchen, drank wine from the bottle and then returned to her computer with tears running down her face and black mascara smudged across one cheek. She gritted her teeth, typed three words and hated herself for it. She'd never felt so stupid, so ridiculous, even in her lowest drug-addled moments, weighed down by illness when the cancer was at its worst. But what else could she do? How else could she answer? She had to do something. Just send it, Mia. Just tap the key and send.

I love you.

His inevitable response appeared within minutes:

Now, that's better, Mia, that's much better. What a compliant and cooperative young woman you are! That's to your credit, top marks. I can't tell you what a pleasure it was to receive your declaration of fondness and affection. You love me and I love you. Isn't that wonderful! It's so good to know. It gives me a warm golden glow. But I want you to make it public. I want you to announce it to the world. Facebook seems like an obvious choice. Publish something bold, something dramatic that stands out with an attention-grabbing, colourful background decorated with symbols of love. And make certain it's not only your friends who see it. Take out advertising. I want many thousands to see it. The more the better. Hundreds of thousands or even more. Yes, why not a million? Let's aim for a million. You sell a lot of books. The cost shouldn't be too much of a problem for a successful young woman like you. Mia Hamilton loves her number one fan. That's all it needs to say. I'll be waiting with bated breath. Do that one thing for me and I'll leave you alone. You'll never hear from me again.

Mia glared at the screen, wiping a teardrop from her cheek with a cotton sleeve and considering his solicitation. It was a simple enough request. Crazed, lunatic, but what did that matter? She could cooperate, give him what he wanted. What harm could it possibly do? It was achieved easily enough, and if it got him off her back, if it got rid of him, well, hooray to that! Oh, what the hell, it may even bring her some publicity, up her online profile, sell a few more books and pay a few more bills in the process. That was reasonable, wasn't it? Or was she being stupid? Maybe she was being stupid. She had to do something. Inaction wasn't an option.

Mia tapped her index finger repeatedly on the coffee table in an attempt to deal with her anxiety. Perhaps one more tablet before collecting Isabella from school? That would help, wouldn't it? That would calm her racing mind and help her think more clearly. Just to feel better, just to feel normal. Go online, place the advert and then the medication. Just like he wanted. Shut the bastard up. It was a case of priorities. Doing things in the correct order. She knew what she needed to do. Why not get it over with?

Mia signed in, typing her familiar password, but she remained unconvinced as to the best course of action despite her internal argument. Oh, what the hell, just do it, Mia, just do it. He'd leave her alone. Just as he said. Just as he'd promised. She was doing the right thing, wasn't she? That's what she asked herself. Of course, she was. Of course, she was! She repeated it, louder and louder, yelling it in her head and drowning out her doubts. Get it written, place the advert. Just get it done. And then a tablet, as a reward. She'd waited long enough. What was there to lose?

2

The man stared at the first of five colour monitors on the shelving unit in front of him and reminded himself that his military intelligence background was ideal for the task. Okay, so the judgemental bastards had kicked him out of the service for no good reason at all. And a dishonourable discharge too, thanks to that interfering bitch who couldn't keep her mouth shut. But so what? Fuck 'em! Their loss, his gain. He'd destroyed her one day at a time before finally signing her death warrant. He'd changed his name and created a new identity and career. Put the past behind him as if it never existed in the first place. That was to his credit, a triumph worthy of a thousand plaudits. It meant more time to watch, more time to plan. More time to dedicate to what mattered most, the things that stirred the senses. The experiences that made life worth living and gave purpose to his very existence. He was on a path to greatness, to infamy. One day he'd be a killer celebrated in the annals of history, alongside other like-minded men who lived life to the limit. Men who broke the rules. Men who rejected society's self-imposed limitations and enjoyed the heights of intense emotion that only the suffering of others could bring. He was the dark-clad executioner, a creature devoid of empathy for anyone but himself. It was his needs and his alone that mattered. No one else counted, not in any real sense, as he did. He was special, and they ordinary and insignificant by comparison, every single one of them. Four had died, and soon a fifth would follow. Mia, that oh-so-self-important bitch who thought so much of herself fitted the bill perfectly. Her psychological and physical destruction would be his greatest achievement yet. A work of art, a masterpiece painted in blood and tears for all to appreciate. One day he'd reveal his methods. Abandon the need for secrecy and cunning. The world would finally see him for the genius he was.

He leaned forward in his seat with his nose almost touching the screen as Mia stripped off her cotton nightgown for her early morning shower, taking full advantage of the limited time available before waking her daughter for school.

He looked her up and down, appreciating her long legs, slim waist, full breasts and prominent nipples, and savoured the moment, imprinting it in his mind for later reference. That's it, my little darling, turn on the shower, lather yourself up, use plenty of soap. Yes, she was moving with sensuous grace, taking such obvious pleasure in the flowing water warming her skin. He was mesmerised, entranced. There was a sheen to her body, a beautiful golden glow that could only be bettered by blood. Such a beautiful woman, and now she was his, all his, to do with whatever he chose and whenever he chose. Mia, lovely Mia, a creature led to the slaughter yet unaware of her impending fate. Maybe he'd use a knife this time, to slice open her gullet from ear to ear and watch it gush red, or perhaps a hammer to smash her skull to pieces with blow after blow, or even his bare hands or a length of rope to twist around her throat. Didn't that German serial killer he'd read so much about once strangle one of his victims with her own bra? Yes, there was an irony to it, a sense of theatre he'd applauded. But it hardly mattered. There was no cause to concern himself. He'd know what to do when the time came. He always did. A method never failed him. Inspiration would come.

The man unbuttoned his trousers, pushed down the front of his underpants, grasped his engorged phallus and began masturbating frantically, faster and faster, up and down, up and down, as Mia took a pink safety razor in hand and began shaving her legs, starting just above her ankles and working upwards. When she moved on to her bikini line, it was more than he could handle, and he shot his load, spraying sticky white semen over his cotton shirt with a loud and visceral groan of delight as endorphins flooded his system and heightened his senses.

The man relaxed back in his seat, his chest rising and falling as he wiped himself with a paper tissue. He refastened his trousers and watched as Mia stepped out of the glass cubicle and began drying herself with a large, fluffy, blue bath towel taken from the stainless steel rail next to the bidet. He continued watching her every movement for another five minutes as she dressed casually, but he lost sight of her as she stepped out of the room. He waited with increasing frustration as she crossed the small landing, unseen by him, and he sighed with almost over-whelming relief as she reappeared on a monitor to his left on entering her bedroom at the front of the house. He tilted his head at a slight angle and licked his top lip slowly with the tip of his tongue as she sat at the dressing table and began brushing her long auburn hair. Maybe he should install additional cameras on the landing and in the hallway. He'd covered the bathroom, her bedroom, the lounge and kitchen. Why not those rooms too? Yes, yes, it seemed so obvious now that he thought about it. And perhaps in the little girl's room as well. Yes, of course, he should. He had the equipment. He had the skills and inclination. What the hell was wrong with him? He must be tired, jaded, in need of rest. Learn from experience, for goodness' sake. He really should have considered it before.

The man switched off the monitors with the click of a dark-green button and reached for his laptop, cursing what he considered a frustratingly slow wi-fi connection until the desired page finally appeared only seconds later. He stared at the screen with keen eyes and punched the air in silent triumph. She'd done it. She'd only fucking well done it. There it was before his eyes, a declaration of love and affection emblazoned in bold white capitals on a pink background decorated with multiple hearts of various sizes! Just as he'd asked of her. Exactly as he'd instructed. She loved him. That's what it said. She really did love him. It was meant to be, written in the stars, as sure as night and day. And thousands had seen it already. More than even he had hoped. There were hundreds of likes, many shares and various enthusiastic comments: who do you love, Mia? Who's your number one fan? Is it me? They went on and on.

He read them all, taking his time and searching for meaning. It had all gone so very well in the end. Even better than he could have hoped. Mia was providing herself as a sacrifice. It was the only logical explanation. Laying herself at his feet, ready and waiting for that final blow. She adored him. And why shouldn't she? He was her god, her master. Mia Hamilton worshipped her number one fan.

The man switched off his computer and hurried to the rear of the rented double garage located in an unpopulated industrial area on the outskirts of town. He stilled himself, tilted his head first to one side and then the other and focussed on a photographic portrait of Mia hanging on the concrete wall. He stared at it with a burning intensity that made his head ache. The frame wasn't perfectly straight, not entirely faultless. He hoped that wouldn't prove an omen of sorts, a metaphor for life, a condemnation.

Beauty was only skin deep, after all. He knew that better than most.

He stepped forward and adjusted the position of the latest addition to his collection, moving the top right-hand corner of the frame up a fraction of an inch, and then back down again, almost to the exact same position as before. It wasn't a great start. Was she trying to enrage him? Would the bitch dare? Or was he being unreasonable? He should at least give her the opportunity to prove herself worthy of his love and dedication. She'd passed the first test well enough, and now for the next. Maybe Mia would survive for a time as her life slowly disintegrated around her. Perhaps she wouldn't let him down like all the others. The girls who promised much but ultimately disappointed, before being dispatched in one way or another. Death finally redeemed them and made their lives worthwhile. That was his achievement and his alone. They were gone, but Mia was living with the breath of life in her lungs. Maybe, just maybe, it would stay that way.

He turned away from Mia's image and sauntered towards the gradually decomposing body of a young woman, propped up in a seated position in the far left-hand corner of the garage, away from the metal door. He reached out and touched her hair tenderly, before kneeling down and kissing her bony forehead. He was sad to note that the degree of decay had reached a point of no return. He enjoyed the company of corpses, their unquestioning compliance to his every whim and desire. He liked the way the dead looked, the way they felt, tasted and smelled. But things had gone too far now, even for him. He had to accept that unhappy reality. The body was stiff, the flesh breaking down and blackening, the face more a skull than a woman. Their affair was over and never to be rekindled in anything but memory. He'd had his fun, but it was at an end now. It was high time for reluctant disposal. Time to destroy the evidence. Time to move on.

The man dragged the corpse out into the centre of the floor and retrieved a metal hacksaw and cleaver from a shelf to his right. Better put on an overall before starting. Cover his clothes. It was time to start working. Time to send her on her final journey and say his sad goodbyes. If only he could go back in time and kill her again.

He pulled the bloodstained overall over his clothing, raised the cleaver high above his head and brought it down onto what was left of the woman's neck with as much force as he could muster, sending fragments of bone and rotting flesh into the air. He repeated the process once, then again, before rolling the head aside with a smile playing on his boyish face. Wasn't it intriguing how the hair and nails continued to grow after death? As if she was still in the land of the living.

He sat at her side and looked her up and down, a little out of breath from his efforts. Dismemberment was such a demanding process, but he'd learned from experience. He'd honed his skills with each new victim. Now all he had to do was put that knowledge to good use. It was essential to do things in the correct order and with the minimum of fuss. He gripped the hacksaw and began removing her right arm at just below the shoulder, sawing through the bone with repeated rapid movements of the blade. Maybe he should have done it a day or two earlier. The flesh and internal organs were putrid, filling his nostrils with an awful stench that he just couldn't bring himself to appreciate, despite death's certain allure. Just get on with it. That was best. Cut off the arms, remove the legs, bury them, and he'd be done. Another hour or two's work at most. He could manage that easily enough. And there was no hurry. Why not enjoy the process? Put on some music and work to a rhythm. He picked up her head by the hair and began dancing around what was left of the corpse, moving with happy abandon and skidding through the gore when the mood took him. Yes, why not make the most of her company while he still had the opportunity? She'd be in the ground soon enough to join the others. Buried in the soft earth of the inky night-time forest where no one else would see. It was now or never.

He stopped suddenly, his face red and hot with exertion. He dropped her head to the floor, wiped his hands on his overalls, stretched expansively and approached a stainless steel kettle, located on the same shelf from which he'd taken the tools only minutes earlier. He spooned coffee into a porcelain cup, added a splash of semi-skimmed milk and a single spoonful of dark-brown sugar, and waited for the water to come to the boil. Wasn't it strange how long it took when you were watching? Still, his guest wasn't going anywhere. There was no chance of escape. Not now. Not any more. Why not sit back, relax, eat a biscuit or two and switch on the monitors for a time before continuing his work? It would be Mia's turn soon enough. Her opportunity to join him in his garage lair. It was a matter of timing. How much suffering could she possibly endure before she finally broke down in mind and spirit? He wanted her in a state of total mental free fall before capture. It was more fun that way, more entertaining, more rewarding. But how long would it take? Oh, well, there was only one way to find out. Up the pressure, turn the screw and see where it got him.

3

Three days had passed since the sender's last message and Mia was beginning to think that the matter was at an end, nothing but a memory. A part of her felt foolish for acceding to his request, but at least it was over. That was the main thing. And sales had increased somewhat, an undoubted benefit for a relatively minor financial investment. It was always worth focussing on the positives in life. A glass half full as opposed to empty. The enforced online advertising initiative had been followed by a radio interview. The opportunity to discuss her next book in the series. Additional readers were always a good thing. Life was looking up at last. It seemed there'd been a silver lining after all.

Mia sat at the kitchen table writing chapter ten – a particularly steamy bodice-ripping scenario in her latest novel – when the notification of his latest message popped up in the top right-hand corner of her laptop screen, accompanied by an insistent ping demanding not to be ignored. She cursed loudly and crudely as she manoeuvred the cursor and clicked on the icon, and then there it was at the top of her inbox. Every part of her being wanted to mark it as junk, to send it to oblivion never to be seen again. But she knew she had to open it. She had to read it. Whatever it said. Whatever the sick bastard's latest demands. He'd broken his word. Gone back on his promise. And why on earth was she surprised? It was a no-win scenario and she had to put a stop to it before it got totally out of hand.

Mia reached for her medication, never far away, but resisted the desire to take another tablet and pushed the brown plastic bottle aside, before opening the offending email only seconds later. She bit her bottom lip hard and read the contents, as feelings of trepidation and anger sent adrenalin surging through her bloodstream. The bastard! The dirty, sick perverted bastard! There was no way she was doing that. No way at all!

Mia's mouth fell open as she read his message for the second time:

I really did appreciate your declaration of love and affection. Reading it gave me such a warm golden glow. And the hearts, the hearts were a lovely touch which moved me almost to tears. I've decided, however, that you need to prove that what you say is true. Words are cheap. I need actions. Actions that demonstrate just how much you love me. You've completed task one to my satisfaction, which is to your credit. Perform my next instruction to an acceptable standard and I'll know that your love is real. That we have an unbreakable bond born of fondness and mutual admiration. How does that sound? Complete one further simple assignment and it's over. I'll know you're not lying. That your words of endearment are true. So, here goes. I want you to send me seven naked selfies, one for each day of the week, to print and hang on my bedroom wall, to keep me company as I lie awake at night and think of you. And they need to be imaginative. They need to be creative. You need to approach the task with genuine enthusiasm. You have to turn me on. The emotions need to ring true. The various scenarios have to be entirely plausible and convincing. If I get even the slightest hint that you lack passion, you fail. If the pictures don't excite me sufficiently, that's a fail too. And you know what that means. There will be a price to pay. A high price you really don't want to face. I'll punish you when you least expect it and in the worst possible way. Best get a shift on, don't you think? Click, click, off you go. You've got seventy-two hours from now.

Mia began typing frantically, instinctively, from the heart as opposed to brain:

NO, NO, NO!
You said I was done. That was the deal. I'll not be sending pictures, no way, it's not happening. Go away and leave me alone!

Mia waited for his inevitable reply in the certain knowledge that he wouldn't let it go. When his email arrived only minutes later, she read it quickly and then ran to the downstairs toilet where she threw up repeatedly until her gut ached and there was nothing left but bile. There were four photographs in sharp and undeniable focus. Four images of her and Isabella, the two of them strolling together at the park, at the shops, on the beach in Amroth and arriving at school earlier that very day. He'd been watching them for weeks. He knew where Isabella's school was. He'd been there. He knew everything about them. It was the only viable explanation. The only thing that made sense. The bastard! The total bastard! How dare he?

Mia washed her mouth out with copious amounts of cold water from the tap, squirted a generous dollop of spearmint toothpaste onto her tongue to mask the lingering taste of acidic vomit, swirled it around her mouth, spat and then ran back to her laptop to read the accompanying message:

An exam you have to pass

Think very carefully, Mia. I see you and I see your daughter. That four-year-old little girl you seem to cherish in the way mothers often do. And why wouldn't you? Children are so fragile. So easily hurt. Their lives can end in the blink of an eye. Let's see how much she really means to you. Let's see what you're prepared to do to keep her safe. She wouldn't be my first victim. Not by a long shot. Picture that little girl of yours lying cold, stiff and alone in a white coffin lined with pink satin, and you'll begin to understand the cost of failure. Think of this as an exam you have to pass. Do or die, life or the grave. Go to the police and I'll kill her. Fail to send me the photos I require, and I'll kill her. It really is that simple. Make no mistake. You've brought this on yourself. There will be no more chances, no reprieve. Those are my rules, my law, with no room for doubt or ambiguity. Obey or she dies. I can't be any clearer than that. It really is up to you.

Love and kisses,

Your number one fan

Mia shoved her computer aside, leapt to her feet and rushed towards the kitchen, where her mobile was charging on the breakfast bar next to the fridge. What was the number? What the hell was the number? She grabbed the phone, opened the contacts page and scrolled through the contents: P-R-S, yes, there it was, there it was.

She dialled and waited for what seemed like an age but in reality was a matter of seconds. Come on, answer the damned thing. Come on, come on.

'Hello, St Peter's Junior School. How can I help you?'

Mia pressed the phone to her face. 'I need to speak to the head-teacher, it's urgent.'

There was a discernible sigh at the other end of the line. 'Who's speaking, please?'

Mia swallowed hard. 'It's Mia Hamilton, Isabella's mother. She's in Miss Fury's class.'

'Mr Sutcliffe is unavailable, *Ms* Hamilton. Would you like to make an appointment?'

Mia choked back a scream, forcing it down her throat. 'I think my daughter may be in danger. I need to know she's safe. It really can't wait.'

'I saw her not half an hour ago. She's in class. She's absolutely fine.'

'You're certain?'

'Yes, *Ms* Hamilton, I'm sure. I've never been surer. Now is there anything else I can do for you? There are things I need to get on with.'

'Keep her there, please. I'll collect her at three sharp. Do *not* hand her to anybody else, whoever they are, whatever they say. No one but me, is that clear?'

'If you say so, *Ms* Hamilton.'

'There it is again, the implied criticism, the emphasis on the *Ms*. Maybe choosing a Catholic school wasn't such a good idea after all.'

'I have absolutely no idea what you're talking about, *Ms* Hamilton. If you're not satisfied with the school for some inexplicable reason, I suggest you discuss it with the head.'

Mia's entire body tensed. 'Just follow my instructions, that's all you have to do. It really couldn't be more important.'

She checked the diary. 'As you say, *Ms* Hamilton. I'll ask the headteacher to contact you at around eleven-thirty tomorrow morning, if that's convenient?'

'He can't ring before?'

Another sigh, more obvious this time with no attempt to hide it. 'No, I've checked his commitments.'

'Then, I suppose that'll have to do.'

Do you want me to hurt her?

Mia glanced in every corner of the room with nervous darting eyes. What the hell? Another email, and just as she'd ended her call. Really? Was it a coincidence? Lucky chance or informed assumption? Or was he watching her as he'd claimed? She wrung her hands and tugged at her hair. How else could he possibly know?

Mia hurried across the room in three rapid strides, fetching a roll of green parcel tape from a cluttered drawer, before tearing off a piece with her front teeth and placing it carefully over the small camera lens located above her computer screen. He could be watching, couldn't he? She'd heard of such things. Read of such cases in the national newspapers more than once. Deviant voyeurs watching unseen for their perverted sexual gratification. Criminal predators targeting unsuspecting victims for the sick pleasure it gave them. Or was she being paranoid? Her thinking clouded by the medication, her anxiety or a combination of both. Perhaps she was overthinking things again. Then, why didn't it feel that way? Listen to your gut, Mia. Listen to your heart.

Mia pressed the tape firmly with the thumb of her right hand, ensuring it was secure, before slumping back in her seat with her head in her hands, imaginary alarm bells ringing in her ears so loud as to further confuse her thinking. What to do? What the hell to do? A tablet, yes, time to take a tablet. The situation was too much to deal with, too onerous to contemplate. Even worse than the cancer, if such a thing were possible. One of the lowest points of her life.

4

The phone seemed to ring and ring before Mia finally heard her sister's voice at the other end of the line.

'Macauley and Harley. How can I help you?'

Mia chose to ignore the manufactured upper-crust accent that sounded so out of place in her sister's mouth. 'Hi Ella, it's Mia, have you got time to talk?'

Ella glanced to the right and left. 'It'll have to be quick. The boss is in one hell of a mood this morning. His wife's walked out on him. I don't know what took her so long, to be honest. I'd have gone long ago. He's a miserable git at the best of times.'

Mia's brow furrowed as she spoke in hushed tones, as if fearing someone may overhear. 'Can you meet me at lunchtime? I really would appreciate it if you could. I'd like to talk to you face to face. This isn't something I want to deal with over the phone.'

Ella felt a sinking feeling deep in the pit of her stomach. 'Oh my God, you're not ill again, are you? Please don't tell me the cancer has come back. Not after everything you went through.'

'No, no, it's nothing like that.'

Ella blew the air through pursed lips decorated with scarlet lipstick. 'Okay, that's good to hear. You had me worried for a second there. Where do you want to meet?'

'How about that nice vegetarian place in Merlin's Lane? You know, the one Mum used to like so much before moving to Italy. The menu suits me, and it's convenient for you. It's only a five-minute walk from your office.'

Ella grimaced as her line manager of two years approached her desk with a predictable glower on his unattractive face. 'Oh, look out, here he comes.'

Ella looked up at her boss and smiled less than convincingly. 'I'm nearly done, Mr Aitken, promise. It's an urgent personal matter. I can only apologise.'

'Make it quick and get on with your work. You're not paid to gossip.'

Ella ignored the inclination to tell him exactly what she thought of him and returned her attention to her call as he walked away, his oversized backside wobbling like a birthday blancmange with each and every step.

'Is a quarter-to-one any good to you? The quicker I'm out of here, the happier I'd be. I'd take a half day if I didn't need to keep my leave for the wedding.'

Mia looked at the wall clock to her right. 'It's going to have to be one o'clock, if that's all right with you? I need to call at the surgery; my medication's running low.'

Ella hesitated before responding. There was something about her sister's tone that was concerning. 'Are you sure you're not ill again? You would tell me if you were, wouldn't you? I'd really want to know. You know that. I've always hated secrets. Lift the stone and let the light in. I've always thought that's best.'

'I'm fine, Ella, I've never been better. How many times do I have to say it?'

Ella felt a weight lift from her shoulders. 'Oh, look out, here he comes again, the miserable sod. Why she married him in the first place is a complete mystery to me. I'll see you at one. Don't be late.'

5

Mia sat opposite her general practitioner of over fifteen years and uncrossed her legs, attempting to present as relaxed a persona as possible, though failing miserably as tiny beads of sweat formed on her brow. 'I just need some more tablets, that's all. I really didn't need to speak to you. You've got more important things to do. It's not a big deal. I just went through them a little quicker than I anticipated.'

Dr Anne Miller looked back and frowned. 'I gave you a prescription for twenty-eight days. That means there are almost two weeks to go. You should have plenty left. How often are you taking them, for goodness' sake?'

Mia shifted her weight from one buttock to the other, briefly considering saying she'd lost the bottle, but she rejected the idea almost immediately. She'd used that excuse once before. Maybe half-truths were the best policy. 'I've been trying to cut down, truly I have, but I still need them for the pain. I can't cope without them, what with the operation. I've had an awful time. That's reasonable, isn't it? I don't even smoke. I drink moderately, and I've never used drugs in my life. If I had an addictive personality, I'd understand your concerns.'

Dr Miller checked Mia's medical records and shook her head. 'Almost five months have passed since your surgery. You should have been well healed long before now. The tablets were intended as a temporary measure, not as the long-term crutch they've so obviously become.'

Mia frowned hard, deciding that silence was her best option. 'Opioids are addictive and become less effective with time. I've explained this to you before. It's time to start reducing the dose with a view to stopping the tablets altogether as soon as practicably possible. We need to wean you off them. You're putting your long-term health at risk if we don't. You're an intelligent woman, Mia. You understand that as well as I do.'

'But you know I've been experiencing back problems. The pain is horrendous at times.' Mia forced a quickly vanishing smile, suspecting the doctor was far from persuaded. 'It's all the time I spend hunched over my laptop that's the problem. Four or five thousand words a day. It's the writers' curse. The price I pay for creativity.'

'That's all very well, but the consultant said that your back's entirely normal. I showed you his letter. He couldn't find any problems at all. If there is a pain, it's muscular. Tablets aren't the answer.'

Mia visibly stiffened. 'Are you calling me a liar?'

'No, that's not what I'm saying. The pain's real for you, I'm in no doubt about that, but there's a psychological element. Physical and mental stress is playing a significant part. You're tense. You're holding yourself stiffly. Back pain is an almost inevitable consequence, but it doesn't require codeine.'

Mia sighed, buying time and searching for an alternative argument that wouldn't come.

'Have you considered the Thai massage I recommended? Or the

yoga classes? You're obviously under a great deal of pressure. I can see it etched on your face. I really think either – preferably both – would help you get back on an even keel a lot more effectively than more tablets. They've worked wonders for me. Medication isn't always the best option.'

'I haven't got the time.'

'Oh, come on, Mia, you need to make time. There's an excellent yoga class in the library twice weekly. I go myself. What's more important than your health?'

Mia checked her watch, making it obvious. 'I'll start cutting down.'

'You said much the same thing last month. Good intentions aren't enough. It's time for action.'

Mia averted her gaze to the wall. 'Okay, I hear you, enough said. But I still think you're making a fuss about nothing.'

The doctor shook her head again, took a prescription pad and biro from her desk drawer and began writing in scribbled, barely decipherable black ink. 'One tablet every four to six hours, as a *maximum*. Any more than that and you're putting yourself in danger. Mental and physical dependence can occur. I fear that may already have happened in your case. If you're not prepared to take control, I'll have to do it for you.'

Mia's relief was virtually palpable as Dr Miller handed her the slip of paper. 'Thank you, it's appreciated.'

'It's a slightly lower dose than you've been used to. And there'll be no more until precisely two weeks from today. We'll talk again then and reduce the dose a little further. You can make an appointment in reception on your way out.'

Mia clutched the prescription tightly in her right hand and stood to leave. 'I'd better make a move. I'm meeting my sister for lunch.'

Dr Miller nodded. 'I'll see you in two weeks, Mia. Take what I've said on board this time. And stay off the booze. Narcotics and alcohol don't go well together. Have I made myself clear?'

Mia looked back and smiled sheepishly upon approaching the door. 'Thanks, Doctor, I'm glad of your help. I'll see you in a fortnight. Everything's going to be just fine.'

6

Mia looked up and smiled thinly as her much-loved big sister entered the popular vegetarian café, its bright-lilac paint and original paintings by talented local artists festooning the walls.

'Hi, Ella, thanks for coming. I've ordered you an almond milk cappuccino. Hope that's okay?'

Ella joined Mia at a table for two. 'It sounds lovely, are you eating?'

'Just soup and a roll, they do a lovely vegan cawl.'

Ella looked up and glanced at the wall-mounted specials board to her left. 'Yeah, sounds good, I think I'll have the same. I'm trying to lose a bit of weight.'

Mia smiled again, spontaneously this time. 'Oh, come on, you're absolutely gorgeous as you are. I wish I had your figure.'

'Oh yeah, I'm sure I am. Angelina Jolie eat your heart out. I still haven't lost the weight I put on at Christmas. If eating mince pies was a competitive event, I'd be the champion of the world.'

Mia raised her arm and waved as a skinny, pretty waitress with red hair and an unmistakable air of authority manoeuvred herself between the tables, plated meals in hand. 'I'll be with you in a second, guys.'

After the two sisters finally gave their orders, they looked into each other's face, as they had many times before. 'Right, Mia, what's this about? I know it's serious. I can see you shaking from here.'

Mia took a deep breath, her eyes flickering like a faulty bulb. 'There's a ghastly troll targeting me online. A really nasty piece of work. It's doing my head in.'

'Is that all?'

Mia jerked her head back. 'What's that supposed to mean?'

'Oh, come on, it's not the first time you've had some nutter giving you hassle online. Your books are selling better than you could have hoped and your profile's growing. You've said that your-self. Some people are going to get jealous. They resent your success and hit out from the anonymous safety of their homes or work-places. I guess it's one of the prices of fame.'

The waitress reappeared with their order but left quickly on sensing further interruption would be unwelcome.

Mia watched the young woman walk away with a sway of her hips before speaking again. 'Yeah, I've had my share of trolls, I get that, no big deal, but this one is different.'

'Different how?'

Mia took her medicine bottle from her oversized handbag, unscrewed the top and placed a single tablet on her tongue before washing it down with a slurp of cooling coffee. 'He's made threats. Serious threats! I can't think about anything else. I just don't know what to do for the best. He's really getting to me.' Ella's expression hardened. 'Just ignore the scumbag. He's looking for a reaction. Winding you up. Don't reply at all or just tell him to fuck off, and the sicko will move on to somebody else. That's the way those people operate. You should know that by now. Think of all the shit you went through at school when you had the braces fitted.'

Mia shook her head. 'I really don't think he'll back off. He's been watching me, watching Isabella. I'm scared, Ella. I'm not ashamed to admit it. This isn't like anything I've experienced before. There's something about him, something sinister. I know he's dangerous.'

Ella dipped a chunk of crusty bread into her soup and took a toothsome bite. 'It's all talk. He's searching for a vulnerability. Looking for a soft spot to sink his claws into. He sounds like he's full of crap to me.'

'Oh, he's been watching us, for sure. He's been watching us for weeks.'

Ella looked far from persuaded. 'Oh, come on, how can you be so sure?'

'He sent me photographs to prove it – photos of me, photos of Isabella. He's got me seriously worried. The bastard knows where we live. He's even been to Isabella's school. What the hell's that about?'

Ella's expression darkened. 'Photos, really?'

Mia unscrewed the white plastic top, closed it and opened it again, then placed the second tablet in her mouth and swallowed. 'Oh, yeah, if he's looking to frighten me, he's succeeded. There are some sick people out there. You only have to watch the news to know that. You've just got to hope you never meet one.'

'Are you still taking those things?'

Mia tensed, avoiding her sister's gaze. 'They're just paracetamol, what's the big deal? Don't you take painkillers when you need them?'

'What, you're not taking the opioids any more?'

'No, of *course* not! I stopped taking the damn things ages ago. You're worrying about nothing.'

'Okay, calm down, pardon me for caring. You can take too many paracetamols too if you're not careful. You need to take it easy. They can damage your liver if you overdo it. One of the girls I work with ended up in hospital and had her stomach pumped. She was ill for months.'

Mia washed the tablet down with a slurp of soup. 'You're sounding more like Mum by the day. You'll be telling me to get a real job next.'

Ella chose not to pursue the matter, suspecting that Mia would either continue to lie at best or storm off in a whirl of feigned righteous indignation that wouldn't help anyone. 'Have you thought about talking to the police? That's what I'd do if I were you. I'll come with you if you want me to. We could go together when I finish work. Why not collect your laptop, show the police the photographs and leave it to them to sort him out? Job done, nothing more to worry about.'

Mia appeared close to tears, her face reddening. 'He's warned against it. "Go to the police and Isabella gets hurt." That's what he said. He'd hurt my little girl. There's something about the messages, the tone, the coldness... I believe him. I really think he'd do it.'

'Oh, come on, you're not thinking straight. The police could trace the emails, find out who it is, arrest him, problem solved. We'll go together and sort it out. Ella and Mia against the world, the old team back together again, just like when we were kids. What do you think?'

Mia fought the urge to take a third tablet, dropping the bottle back into her bag and silently cursing her growing addiction as it sunk its teeth in a little deeper. 'He says he's untraceable.'

'Well, he would say that, wouldn't he?'

'I guess so.'

'He's a chancer making empty threats. Nothing's going to come of it.'

Mia's face crumpled, her eyelids blinking repeatedly. 'Yeah, but what if it does? What if the police can't trace him? What if he finds out I've reported him? He may follow through on his threats. He seems crazy enough to me. I'd never forgive myself if it all went horribly wrong.'

'That's not going to happen.'

'I'm not so sure. I haven't exactly had a lot of luck lately.'

Ella stalled, beginning to doubt the wisdom of her advice for the first time as Mia fought the impulse to panic. 'Okay, so if not the police, what are you going to do? What's the alternative? You must have thought about it.'

'He wants me to send him photos of myself – naked photos, pornographic photos. He says if I don't, he'll kill her.'

Ella held her hands wide. 'You're not thinking of sending them, surely? You are, aren't you? I can't believe you're actually considering this. It's completely ridiculous. Get a grip Mia, for goodness' sake. This is getting out of hand. I've never heard anything so ludicrous in my life.'

Mia's face twisted. 'I'm just thinking about it, that's all. Obviously, I don't want to do it, but what other choice have I got? Isabella's safety has to come first. What if he does something? What if he hurts her?'

'Oh, come on, Mia, there are always choices.'

Mia shook her head. 'That's easy for you to say. It doesn't seem that way to me.'

'You're not thinking straight. I think those tablets you're taking must be addling your brain.'

Mia raised an eyebrow. 'Oh, thank you *very* much, that is *really* helpful. And that's sarcasm by the way, in case you were wondering. I'm beginning to wish I hadn't told you about this at all.'

Ella reached across the table and gripped Mia's hand, holding it tight. 'Now, you listen to me. If you take the photos, if you send them, if you do what he says, he'll have you hooked. He'll have you *exactly* where he wants you. And that won't be the end of it. There'll be something else. I can guarantee it. Threats to make the images public, demands for money. It'll escalate. He'll never leave you alone. Take my word for it. Sending them is the worst thing you could possibly do.'

Mia pulled her hand free, took a paper hankie from her blue jeans and blew her nose noisily as a tear ran down her left cheek. 'Yeah, I appreciate that, I'm not completely stupid, but what the hell else am I going to do? I've got to do something. Inaction isn't an option.'

'Is there nothing I can say to persuade you to go to the police? It still seems like the obvious thing to do to me. He wouldn't be the first pervert they've dealt with.'

Mia shook her head frantically, becoming increasingly irate with every second that passed. 'No, no, no, it's not happening! I can't risk it. I need you to understand that.'

'Then, there is one option I can think of.'

'What are you talking about?'

'I'm thinking about Mattia. The good-looking dark-haired guy I went out with for a few months before meeting Adam.'

'I know who he is, for goodness' sake. You never stopped banging on about him, Mattia this, Mattia that. I met him a couple of times. He was a bit too much of a charmer for my tastes.'

Ella smiled without parting her lips. 'I bumped into him in the park a few days back. He's in computers, programming, something of an expert. I could ask him to trace the source of the emails, if you want me to? You know, without going into too much detail as to why I'm asking. At least then you'd know exactly who you're dealing with. Maybe the bastard will be a lot easier to track down than he makes out. Hell, it may even be someone you know. Stranger things have happened. As you said, there are a lot of creeps out there and they can be hard to spot sometimes. We could go to the police with a name, give them the proof they'd need to prosecute. Let's give it a go. What have we got to lose?'

Mia nodded twice, her eyes wide. 'I guess it's got to be worth a try.'

'Yes, of course, it is. Mattia knows what he's doing. He did a master's degree at Cardiff University. It's a win-win.'

'Do you really think he'd be willing to help?'

Ella grinned mischievously. 'Yes, I don't see why not. He seemed pleased to see me.'

'Have you still got his number?'

Ella delved into her bag, looking a little sheepish as she searched for her phone. 'Yeah, yeah, I've still got it. Am I going to do this?'

Mia nodded. 'Yes, go for it. It's got to be better than doing nothing at all.'

Ella dialled and waited but got no reply. 'He's not answering. I'll keep trying and let you know what he says as soon as I get hold of him.'

'You will do it quickly, won't you?'

'Absolutely, goes without saying.'

Mia started to eat her soup with gusto, feeling more positive as a light of hope shone at the end of a very dark tunnel. 'Thanks, sis, that's brilliant. I don't know what I'd do without you.'

Ella reached across the table, squeezed Mia's hand for the second time and grinned. 'No problem, what are big sisters for?' She winked. 'And it gives me an excuse to see Mattia again. I still think about him sometimes.'

'Do you?'

'Oh, yes, usually when the lights are out.'

'Here we go again. Adam's one of life's good guys, you should try to remember that. You could do one hell of a lot worse. I wish I could find one like him. Why agree to marry the man if you're still thinking about somebody else?'

'Yeah, yeah, I know.' Ella mock-slapped her wrist. 'I'll behave myself. Are you going to tell Rhys about all this?'

'Why on earth would I do that?'

'You say Isabella's in danger. Don't you think he has the right to know that? He's her father after all.'

Mia scowled and spat her words. 'He hasn't seen Izzy for months. He didn't even bother turning up on her birthday. No card, no present, nothing. I'd like to slap him in the face sometimes. And slap him hard. He does nothing but let her down.'

'I'll take that as a no then.'

Mia grinned despite the conversation's emotive nature but didn't reply.

'It might be an idea to pop to the bathroom and wash your face before finishing your soup, Mia.'

'Oh God, I must look a right mess.'

Ella pushed up her sleeve, checked her watch and stood. 'I'm going to have to make a move. Things will work out. We'll put this behind us. You wait and see. I'll be back in touch as soon as I know something... promise.'

'Thanks, Ella, but please be quick. I haven't got long before the deadline. I'd really love to see the look on the smug bastard's face when we find out who he is.'

'I still think we should go to the police.'

'If Mattia can find out who he is, we'll do it then. Like you said earlier. When I know he's traceable.'

Ella raised a hand to her mouth. 'Okay, if that's how you want to play it. We'll do it your way for now. But if you change your mind, all you have to do is say. I'll be with you every step of the way.'

7

Ella's resolve was slipping long before she knocked on Mattia's front door that evening. She was feeling somewhat conflicted. Guilty about telling Adam that she was meeting a girlfriend for drinks but keenly anticipating whatever the evening may bring. Adam was steadfast reliability, like a loyal lapdog, she liked to think. But Mattia was unbridled excitement. He possessed an animal magnetism that oozed from every pore, and bright intelligence to match. She liked those things and missed him. She missed him horribly, that heady combination of sexuality and intellect that she found almost impossible to resist, even if she wanted to. If only he'd had reliability to match. He was so close to perfect.

Ella told herself insistently that she was there for Mia, there for her little sister, to help, to do the right thing. But deep down she knew the truth. The fact that she'd rushed home after work to shower, change into a matching lacy black thong and bra set and had doused herself in sweet-smelling French perfume, told her all she needed to know. When Mattia opened the door with a gleaming come-to-bed smile on his sexy, angular face only seconds later, she knew that he knew it too. Who was she trying to kid?

Mia's dilemma was just the excuse she'd needed. She was wanton, keen to feel his hands on her body again. It was written all over her face.

'Are you going to invite me in or just leave me standing here?'

He shook himself as the not-so-distant past released its grip. 'Yeah, sorry, it was strange to see you back here again. It's almost as if you never left.'

Ella smiled, her chemically enhanced teeth gleaming, as she followed him into his still familiar lounge, its stylish furnishings and pristine white-painted walls refreshed, but unchanged. 'So, how are things with you? I thought you'd have moved someone in long before now.'

Mattia shook his head determinedly. 'No, it's like I told you in the park. I'm living the single life. There's been no one since we split up. I can't believe it ended when it did.'

Ella giggled like a bashful schoolgirl. 'Oh, yeah, I'm sure that's true. You're living the life of a monk and space aliens have landed in the grounds of Buckingham Palace. I think that's far more likely than you being celibate. You were never short of female attention.'

He lifted his perfectly manicured hands in the air to either side of his head. 'Okay, okay, you've got me. There's been the odd dalliance now and again, but nothing serious. That's what I meant to say. Nothing significant. Just one-night stands, no one like you. And I don't bring them here. It doesn't feel right, not after what we had together. I just can't bring myself to do it. I still think of this as *our* place. It's special.'

Ella blushed crimson. 'Oh, so I won't find any sexy female underwear in your wash basket if I take a look? Or a second toothbrush in the bathroom cabinet? Is that what you're claiming? It seems like an unlikely scenario to me.'

This time it was his turn to laugh. 'Have you got time for a drink? I've got a rather nice bottle of champagne cooling in the fridge, one of your favourites. I can fetch it if you like. It's ready and waiting for you.'

Ella sat herself down and crossed her long, tanned legs, her tight skirt raising just above the knee. 'That would be lovely. You know me so well.'

He looked her up and down, lingering on her low-cut top and enticing cleavage, before finally turning away and heading for the kitchen humming. He called out without looking back. 'Do you want a bite to eat with your drink? I've been taking cooking classes. It's no bother. I could knock something up quickly enough.'

'No thanks, just the champagne will be lovely. I ate before coming out.'

Ella ran a brush through her hair and checked her dark-red lipstick in a handheld mirror taken from her handbag before he returned.

'Oh, about time, I was starting to miss you.'

Mattia popped the cork, filled two fluted glasses to the halfway point, sipped his and handed Ella hers with an alluring grin. 'Shall we drink it in the bedroom?'

Ella slowly crossed and uncrossed her legs, licking her top lip and holding his gaze as her skirt inched up a little further. She could see the Mediterranean in him, his Italian ancestry with his slightly greying black stubble and those golden-brown eyes within which to drown. 'I've missed you, Mattia, I've really missed you. I don't know why we split up in the first place. I must have been crazy to end it. We're good together. There's a chemistry. There has never been anyone like you. We fit so very well.'

He leaned forward, reached out a hand and helped her to her feet as she tottered on her high heels, her heart pounding in her throat. 'I was thinking much the same thing. You're the best I've ever had. No one comes close.'

Ella kissed him on the mouth. Softly at first, tenderly, her lips brushing his, but then more aggressively, her pink tongue probing his mouth as she dropped her glass to the floor. She pulled away, undid the zip of his trousers with urgent fingers, slid her hand into his tight pants and led him towards the bedroom by the swollen tip of his erect penis. 'Come on, big boy. There are things I need you to do for me. We're going to make our wildest fantasies come true.'

He was panting hard now, her aromatic scent filling his nostrils as she tightened her grip and began to move her hand. 'Anything you want, Ella. All you have to do is say. I'm a slave to your desires. Your wish is my command.'

Her skirt dropped around her slender ankles as she opened her legs a little wider and pushed his head down towards her crotch. 'Let's see if you remember how to please me. Make my body quiver, and I'll give you the best time of your life.'

* * *

Mattia lay back on the king-sized bed about twenty minutes later, still slightly out of breath, but smoking a menthol cigarette, blowing toxic grey fumes towards the ceiling. Ella wiped his sticky semen from her abdomen with his white cotton T-shirt and turned her head to face him. 'I thought you'd given those things up. It's a disgusting habit. Your breath's going to stink. Talk about spoiling the mood. I was hoping for an encore.' He took one last long drag before stubbing out the glowing butt in a saucer resting on the glass-topped bedside cabinet to his right. 'Yeah, I know, I'll get round to it sometime.'

'You were saying the exact same thing before we split up.'

He glared at her, his eyes popping. 'Do you fancy another shag before going home to Mr Wonderful? I'm sure he wouldn't dream of smoking in bed. If he's so fucking perfect, what are you doing here with me? Can't he get it up or something? Perhaps he's not man enough for you. You always did like a hard cock inside you.'

She screwed up her face, feelings of culpability invading her mind as the passion faded. 'I think you've said enough for one evening, don't you?'

'Touched a nerve, have I? Mr Limp Dick isn't up to the job. Maybe you should find a real man like me. Someone with a bit of lead in their pencil.'

'Just be quiet, Mattia, you never did know when to shut up.'

He lit a second cigarette and focussed on her prominent nipples as she sat up and reached for her bra.

'Did you check out my sister's emails like I asked you to?'

'Oh, so now you need my help all of a sudden?'

'That's why I'm here.'

He sniggered sardonically. 'Oh, yeah, I'm sure it is. It didn't seem like that when you had my dick in your mouth.'

She fastened her bra at the front and swivelled it around her body. 'Just answer the question and leave it at that. Have you done it, or not?'

'Yes, I did, as it happens. Perhaps I'm not quite as useless as you like to think.'

She chose to ignore the provocation this time, as she stretched out a leg and slipped on her thong. 'So, what did you find out?'

'I'm going to need more time.'

Ella dropped her head, allowing her hair to fall across her face. 'Oh, for goodness' sake, Mattia! My sister hasn't got more time. I made that crystal clear to you. Have you even tried?'

'The sender's identity's hidden behind various layers of security, like an onion. I think that's the best way of explaining it. There are books written about this stuff. The dark web. You must have heard about it. It's not going to be as easy as I'd hoped.'

'Can you do it at all?'

He watched as she pulled on her skirt, relishing one last look at her shapely buttocks, which juddered enticingly with each subtle movement of her body. 'Maybe yes and maybe no, but there are no guarantees. As I said, he knows what he's doing. And that's assuming it's a man at all. It could be a woman. It could be anyone.'

'They read as if a man has written them.'

He nodded. 'Yeah, I guess they do.'

Ella slipped on her shoes, crossed the room and paused at the bedroom door. 'Please try again. And ring me as soon as you know something. Mia's counting on you, I'm counting on you. Don't let us down. We're running out of time.'

He grinned appealingly. 'What's in it for me?'

She looked back, leaned forwards and wiggled her bottom provocatively. 'I think you know the answer to that one. You do your bit, and I'll pay you another booty call. What do you think? Seems like a good deal to me.'

'Promise?'

'Cross my heart and hope to die. I wouldn't miss it for the world.'

Mattia gave a thumbs-up. 'If I find out who's sending them, you'll be the first to know. That, I can guarantee you.'

She blew him a kiss. 'Oh, I know that, Mattia. Are you getting hard again? I can see you drooling from here.'

8

Adam had an appetising meal ready and waiting when Ella arrived back at their two-bedroomed home later that evening. He'd prepared it with care, taking his time and following the online recipe line by line, keen to impress and maybe engender feelings of guilt in the process.

Ella could smell the food cooking as soon as she entered the hall, and she'd already decided not to eat it before Adam appeared from the kitchen and craned his neck to gently peck her cheek. 'Hello gorgeous, did you have a nice time with your girlfriend?'

She looked him in the eye and held his gaze right up to the second it was no longer comfortable. 'Yes, good, thanks. I was planning on an early night. I hope you haven't gone to too much trouble.'

'A quick bite to eat and then an early night sounds good to me. I've got a book I'd like to finish. We could have a quick cuddle before going to sleep.'

Ella took a backward step when he tried to hug her, raising her hands in protest. 'No, I don't think so, Adam. I'm tired, it's been a long day. I've got to be up early for work in the morning, even if you haven't. My boss is a complete nightmare at the moment. I'd like to put the light out and get straight off.'

Adam's face crumbled, his disappointment evident as she turned away, kicked off her shoes and hurried towards the stairs. He mimed slowly cutting her windpipe as she looked the other way. 'Well, at least have something to eat before heading upstairs. It's spaghetti Bolognese, all fresh ingredients, nothing from a jar or packet. You can't usually get enough of the stuff. I thought it would be a nice treat for you.'

Ella felt her hackles rise as she began ascending the staircase, her footsteps muffled by the thick carpeting. 'What's that supposed to mean? Are you trying to say I'm putting on weight?'

He tried not to laugh. 'No, I didn't mean anything by it, I was just kidding around.'

She stopped on the landing and began unfastening her skirt for the second time that evening. 'I'll have it for tea tomorrow evening when I get back from work. I'm not going to my Italian class; I can heat it up in the microwave. Don't trouble yourself, it won't go to waste.'

Adam looked as if he was about to weep. 'Please, Ella, I've really made an effort here. You can spare me half an hour, can't you?'

'I ate while I was out. If you planned to cook, you should have said something in advance. I'm not a mind reader. All you had to do is say.'

'It was meant to be a nice surprise like I said. Things haven't been too great lately. I was hoping we could sit down together, have a heart-to-heart, you know, try and work things out between us. You do want that, don't you? It's been all work and no play, no quality time. I think that's the problem. Come on, come and eat with me, we're supposed to be getting married at the end of next month. It may do us both some good.'

Ella shook her head. 'You can sleep in the spare room tonight. I've got an early start. The boss is on the warpath again. How many times do I have to say it? I can't afford to be late.'

He sighed, accepting defeat. 'So, I'm going to eat on my own again?'

Ella entered the bathroom without replying and closed the door behind her.

Adam sat at the kitchen table enjoying his meal, congratulating himself on his culinary prowess and silently cursing Ella and every breath she took. He pushed his empty plate aside, jumped to his feet, picked up a ten-inch breadknife and pictured himself thrusting it into Ella's body time and again as she begged for mercy. Why on earth were all the women in his life such an utter disappointment? Why did they let him down so very badly? If he tortured them, that was their fault. If he killed them, that was down to them too. He was driven to extremes of behaviour. Women gave him no choice at all. They deserved to hurt, they deserved to pay with their lives. Any reasonable person would understand that. And understand him too, if they knew the full facts. The journey he'd travelled. The upset those bitches had caused with their rejection and indifference, right from the very start. From the moment of his birth. If he was a monster, womankind had created him. He was moulded in their image like soft clay in the hands of a potter. Their punishment was just.

Adam broke into a smile that lit up his face. It would feel so good to end Ella's worthless life, so wondrous to slowly tear her apart as she screamed for clemency, pleading at his feet until she finally accepted her inevitable fate. Maybe poke her eyes out, and pull her teeth one at a time until she was unrecognisable as the bitch he knew only too well. She wouldn't be so pretty then. That would wipe the smile from her disloyal, sanctimonious face. Oh, yes, her time would come. It would come all right, when it suited him, when she'd mourned her sister's loss and shed a thousand tears. She'd suffer as no one had ever hurt before. More than the rest – he'd make certain of that. But Mia first, no deviation from the norm, best stick to the plan. Ella would join her sister in the grave soon enough, but now was not that time.

9

Adam lifted his high-end Swiss binoculars to his eyes and watched from the anonymity of his estate car as Mia and Isabella sat in their comfortable lounge eating buttered toast smothered with straw-berry jam. He checked his watch at precisely 8:15 a.m. and smiled. There were things to do. Batteries to replace. Cameras to install. And now was the perfect time to do precisely that.

He adjusted the blond wig made from real human hair and ran a hand through the false beard applied with spirit gum adhesive, tugging it twice to ensure it was secure. Once satisfied, he added a pair of non-prescription glasses with thick plastic frames and tinted lenses which altered the appearance of his eyes but didn't affect his sight. He examined his reflection in the rear-view mirror for a full thirty seconds before finally exiting the vehicle with a smirk on his face. Spot on, not even a close relative would recognise him. One more thing to celebrate.

Adam opened the car's boot, with its blacked-out window and false number plate, took out the sizeable navy-blue canvas bag he always kept handy and headed towards Mia's front door, a discernible skip in his step. The disguise was one of many he'd

utilised over the years to good effect. The expertly applied facial
adornments and the carefully placed body padding made him
appear two or three stone heavier than his actual weight. He'd
succeeded before and he would again. He repeated it in his mind,
boosting his confidence and raising his spirits. Up the pressure,
that's all he had to do. Just up the pressure and watch the bitch
disintegrate before his eyes.

Adam stood on the front step and took out a laminated faux, yet
convincing, West Wales Fire Service identity card from the inside
pocket of his summer-weight jacket, the sleeves of which reached
his knuckles. He held the card between the thumb and fingers of a
hand covered by a thin latex skin-coloured glove that could only be
noticed on close examination. He began knocking, not too hard for
fear of putting her on her guard, but not too softly either, ensuring
she would hear. Everything had to be precisely right – considered,
planned, measured and implemented. That's what he told himself.
There was no room for complacency. No room for doubt. Military
planning. Leave nothing to chance. Attention to detail was
everything.

Adam took a single step back, not wanting to appear in any way
intimidating or threatening, and only had to wait for about forty-
five seconds before Mia opened the door ajar, the recently installed
security chain still securely on the lock.

Adam looked down and smiled at Isabella who was standing
close to her mother and clutching a favourite rag doll to her chest.
He raised his eyes almost immediately to focus on Mia and nothing
else, peering through the narrow gap between the door and frame,
speaking in a convincing, perfectly practised Glaswegian accent,
very different to his own. 'G'mornin' to you, ma'am, I was hopin' to
catch y'in.'

Mia shifted her weight from one foot to the other, oblivious to
her involuntary dance as Isabella gripped her leg, sensing her

mother's anxiety but not comprehending the cause. There was something about the man that unnerved Mia. Something she couldn't quantify or compute. Or was it recent events? Maybe it was recent events. 'What can I do for you? If you're selling something, I'm not interested.'

He held up his identity card in plain sight and smiled thinly as she took it from his hand. 'I'm visitin' you as part of a fire prevention initiative in the area followin' the unfortunate death of a family in a nearby town. Ya may have seen it reported in the media. We're doin' all we can to prevent another similar tragedy. It's a high priority for the service.'

Mia unfastened the chain with trembling fingers, opened the door a little wider and handed back his card, telling herself she was being silly, worrying about nothing for no good reason at all. 'So, what exactly are you doing?'

'We fit the very latest state-of-the-art fire detectors at key points in each property. They're highly effective, no expense spared, the very best on the market. I'm not being overly dramatic when I say that one of these bad boys could save ya lives.' He tapped his bag with his free hand. 'If the family I mentioned had had these fitted, well, ya know what I'm sayin'. They'd still be alive and kicking and not lying in the ground.'

Mia raised an eyebrow. Just for a fraction of a second, she thought she may recognise the man, that she'd seen him some-where before. But she couldn't remember when or where, or even if she'd seen him at all. It was a small town. Most people were familiar in one way or another. 'One of your colleagues called and fitted some alarms a few weeks back, a guy with black hair.'

Adam smiled reassuringly, revealing lip-stretching buck teeth secured over his own. 'Ah, I, I'm aware of tha'. I'm afraid there have been some problems with that particular member of staff's work. I can only apologise on behalf of the service. Not all the detectors he installed are fitted correctly. I'd just like to check that everythin's working as it should be and to fit any additional detectors as required. He wasn't as expert as he liked to pretend. It's a free service, no charge. It's savin' lives that counts, not money.'

Mia checked her watch as Isabella pulled at the back of her skirt. 'We were just about to leave for school. Can you come back at a more convenient time? I'll be back within the hour.'

He shook his head with the hint of a frown on his face. 'Oh, no, I'm 'fraid that's not gonna be possible. I'll be movin' on t'other parts of the county. It's now or never. I'd love to help, but I'm workin' to a tight schedule. It's more than my job's worth.' He tensed, muscles taut, as Mia hesitated, though he hid it well, before adding, 'It'll take me ten minutes, fifteen at the very most. Better safe than sorry, don't ya think? You'd never forgive yourself if you turned me away and somethin' went terribly wrong at some future date. I can see that you're a proud mum. And, why wouldn't you be? What a beautiful little girl! She's a true credit to you.'

Mia weighed up the pros and cons in her busy mind, then stepped aside, concluding that her earlier apprehension and concern were entirely unjustified. She couldn't panic every time a stranger came to the door. Where was the sense in that? 'In you come, and please do everything you need to do as quickly as you possibly can. I'll be in the kitchen if you need me. Just give me a shout.'

Adam patted Isabella's head and grinned as she peered up at him. 'That's nay problem t'all, I'll be out of your hair before ya know it.' He stopped mid-step and looked back on approaching the stairs. 'I don't s'ppose there's any chance of a cup of coffee? My wife's got serious health issues. I'm spending a lot of time lookin' after her. There was no time for breakfast before the carers arrived. It's a terrible business. You can't plan for that sort of thing. God laughs at our plans.'

Mia felt herself relax, the tension melting away. What on earth was she worrying about? He seemed like a nice guy, kind, thoughtful, no threat at all. She couldn't doubt every man who crossed her path. What would that achieve? 'Yeah, of course, no problem, I was about to make one anyway. Do you fancy a piece of toast to go with it? It's no bother.'

He took an alarm from the bag and began climbing the stairs, which creaked under his weight. 'No, ya all right, thanks, kind o' you t'offer. Just a coffee would be great. I don't usually eat till lunchtime. It's somethin' I've had to get used to. The missus has to come first.'

'Milk and sugar?'

'Both, please. You're too kind.'

He opened the alarm's white plastic lid and checked the tiny wireless surveillance camera and attached microphone, polishing the tiny lens with a soft yellow cloth before securing the unit to the ceiling with two shiny steel screws. He glanced down the staircase towards the hall and listened intently, ensuring Mia was safely out of the way. He opened her bedroom door and moved quickly, searching through the second of three drawers and stuffing a pair of her white cotton knickers into a trouser pocket, before replacing the battery in the alarm secured to the ceiling above the double bed and leaving the room.

Mia entered the hall and stood with a cup in hand as Adam closed her bedroom door with a self-satisfied smirk playing on his lips and thoughts of triumph at the forefront of his mind.

'Do you want me to bring it up to you?'

'No, y'all right, ta. The detectors on the landing and in your bedroom are done. I'll just put one in your daughter's room, replace the battery in the bathroom and I'll be with you in two minutes. A bit of caffeine will be very welcome. It's just wha' I need. It's hard to stay awake sometimes.'

Mia was about to head back into the kitchen but paused. 'I thought it was a bit strange having an alarm in the bathroom. I'd never heard of anyone doing that before.'

He clenched and unclenched his fists, strong feelings of annoyance and displeasure threatening to bubble to the surface. 'Yeah, we never used to do it, but regulations have changed. We try to cover *all* the rooms these days. It makes sense, really. It's surprisin' how many fires are caused by electric shower units just like yours. I've seen it more times than I care to count. Sometimes with unfortunate results.'

'Who'd have thought it?'

'It's a more serious problem than most people appreciate.'

Mia crossed her arms. 'I still can't help thinking that *every* room seems a bit over the top.'

'The more I fit, the safer you are, and there's no charge to you. What's not to like? Take full advantage of the opportunity while you can, that's what I say.'

Mia accepted his explanation without further question and placed the cup on the bottom step of the stairs. 'Your coffee will be here whenever you're ready, but I need to be out of here by a quarter to at the latest. The school is a stickler for timekeeping. I can't afford to be late.'

He glanced at his digital watch and nodded. 'Right, understood, I'll get on with it. That's not gonna be a problem.'

Adam spent a minute or two searching through the laundry basket on entering the white-tiled bathroom, lifting several items of Mia's clothing to his face and sniffing them appreciatively, probing any sweat patches and soiled undergarments with his tongue, before reluctantly putting them back where he'd found them. He met his eyes in the large circular mirror above the sink and broke into a Cheshire cat smile. Mia provided an ideal opportunity. She was an inspired choice on his part. She had the right look, the right smell and the right taste. She was perfect, absolutely perfect! He really couldn't have chosen a better target to watch, deconstruct and destroy. And the fact that she was Ella's sister, with all the shock and distress that revelation would ultimately cause, was a wonderful added bonus.

Adam began gently kneading his genitals through a trouser pocket and thought for a moment that he may kill Mia right there and then, without further delay; kill her with forethought and malice. Put his hands around her throat and squeeze harder and harder until the light of life left her eyes forever. Or take a knife and plunge it into her body time and again, with her warm blood pouring from her wounds like a heavenly fountain in full flow. But what of his plans? The watching and waiting, the glorious anticipation as her life slowly unravelled around her. Was the instant gratification really worth the sacrifice? He'd made that mistake once before when over-impulsive, and it was all over far too quickly in the end. What use was that? He had to learn from experience. Make full use of his knowledge and skills. Yes, but it would feel good, wouldn't it? So very good! Dispatching her when she least expected it. When she'd just started to trust him in that naïve way of hers, so gullible, so malleable and so utterly dull-witted.

Adam stilled himself, deep in contemplative thought, as his erection slowly subsided to be replaced by nagging doubts that just wouldn't let go. But what about the little girl? Children weren't his thing, and witnesses were never a good idea, whatever their age and however effective his disguise. Come on, man, think, think! Stick to the plan. Stick to the plan!

He took a deep breath, attempting to calm his pounding heart, before changing the batteries, attending to the camera as before and heading downstairs to fit an additional alarm in the hallway as he'd originally intended. He had to resist the temptation. Play the long game with all its attractions.

'Is it okay if I add a little cold water to ma coffee? It's a bit too hot to drink as quickly as I'd like. I don't want to keep you waitin' any longer than necessary.'

Mia called back from the lounge, where Isabella was watching a cartoon on the flat-screen telly. 'Yes, of course, help yourself. The kitchen's the first door on your left.'

Adam allowed the kitchen table to support his twelve-stone frame, gulping down his drink, opening one cupboard, then another, and appearing at the lounge door just as the family tabby cat climbed through a three-quarter-closed window from the small front garden bordering the road. 'I'm nearly done. Be outta here before you know it.'

Mia looked up and smiled as the cat climbed onto her lap and began purring appreciatively. 'Any problems?'

'No, it's all lookin' good. It seems my workmate did a better job than I'd anticipated. I'll just check this last one, and I'll be outta ya hair.'

She thought it a strange choice of phrase but pushed it from her mind as Isabella lost interest in the cartoon and began stroking the cat's head a little too firmly for its liking.

'Is it okay if I stand on a chair? The ceilin' seems a little higher in here for some reason.'

'Yeah, sure, please carry on. This is an original part of the house; the kitchen's a fifties' extension.'

He nodded. 'Ah, okay, that explains it.'

Mia lowered the cat to the floor and turned her attention to her daughter as Adam closed the alarm and observed them.

'Okay, that's it, finished. I've fitted extra-long-lastin' batteries so you should be fine for a few years.'

'Really, as long as that?'

He nodded twice. 'Don't touch them at all, that's my advice.

These new ones are extremely sensitive. Leave it to the experts. It's safer that way. They're heat detectors as opposed ta smoke.

You won't have any problems with them going off accidentally if you burn the toast.'

Mia stood up with Isabella's hand in hers as the cat wandered back in the direction of the kitchen towards her food bowl. 'I'll leave them well alone.'

He pictured his hands around her throat, wild eyes bulging as if attempting to escape her skull, and smiled. 'Very wise, I wish all my customers were half as sensible.'

'And you said there'd be no charge?'

He picked up his bag and beamed as Mia's subtle floral perfume filled his nostrils, making his head spin. He'd watch and delay but her time would come. Anticipation was part of the pleasure. The foreplay that preceded the eventual climax, making it all the more glorious for the waiting. 'No, it's all part o' the service. Lovely to meet ya both. Bye for now, I'll let you get on with ya day.'

'Okay, thanks.'

Mia was about to close the front door when Adam turned and spoke again. 'I noticed ya got a gas fire in the lounge.'

'Yes, I tend to use it in the colder months, never at this time of year.'

'I may call and fit a carbon monoxide alarm if I'm passin', if that's all right with you? Better safe than sorry.'

'Of course, no problem, anytime at all. Your help is appreciated.'

He smiled that buck-toothed smile. It was so effortless, so straightforward. Easier than even he had hoped in his wildest fantasies. What a stupid woman!

10

Adam watched on monitor number three and listened intently as Mia and Ella sat in Mia's comfortable lounge drinking red wine from a second bottle and nibbling dark chocolate laced with sea salt. Mia placed her glass back on the low coffee table in front of her and met her sister's eyes with a deep frown on her tired face. 'So, Mattia couldn't come up with anything at all?'

Ella moved to the very edge of her seat and shook her head, wishing she had a different, more positive reply to offer. 'No, sorry, he did his best, but he drew a blank.'

'But I thought he was an expert at that kind of stuff? How hard can it possibly be?'

'Mattia said that whoever sent the messages has hidden their identity incredibly well. "The best I've ever seen," were his exact words. He'll keep trying but said not to hold your breath. He doesn't think he's going to win with this one.'

Mia looked into her sister's face with a pained stare, her anxiety obvious. 'Do you really think he tried?'

'Yes, I do. He's got his faults, but he's not a liar.'

'Then, what the hell do I do now?'

'You're running out of time.'

Mia raised her glass to her mouth, drained it then refilled it to the three-quarter point. 'Do you think I don't know that? I can't sleep, it's almost impossible to concentrate, I've been snappy with Isabella and I haven't written anything worthwhile for days. The dirty bastard's ruining my life!'

'What about the police? I really think you need to reconsider. Maybe they can succeed where Mattia failed. It seems like the sensible choice.'

Mia winced. 'Yeah, but what if they don't? What if the sender finds out? We've already talked about this. He said he's untraceable and it looks as if that's true. You know what he said he'd do. That could be true too. I just can't risk it.'

'You're running scared, Mia. That's exactly what he wants. You shouldn't have replied at all. And why you put that ridiculous statement on Facebook is a complete mystery to me. Loads of people saw it. Thousands, from what I could gather. It's not like you to be so impulsive. You're usually the sensible one. It should be you giving me advice, not the other way around. That's the way it's supposed to work in our relationship.'

Mia smiled, but the expression quickly left her face. 'I was coping, the cancer's in remission, I was feeling more positive about the future, but then all this... it's the last thing I needed. It really couldn't have happened at a worst time.' She emptied her glass yet again and reached for the bottle. 'I just don't know what to do for the best.'

'I've got one more idea.'

'Okay, let's hear it.'

'Do you remember Gareth Gravel, Grav, the nice overweight detective Dad used to go to the rugby club with before Mum and Dad moved to Italy?'

Mia smiled, fond memories pushing her anxieties from her

mind for a few brief seconds as the past met the present and clouded her thinking. 'Yeah, I can remember visiting the house a few times when we were kids. They had two children, a boy and a girl. Grav always used to stink of cigars. I hated that. Why do you ask?'

'I was just thinking, you could speak to him off the record. Ask his advice. I remember Dad telling us that he sometimes bent the rules when it suited him. That he's not your typical by-the-book copper. You never know your luck. He may be able to help.'

Mia remained silent for a second or two, weighing up her limited options before speaking again. 'He's probably retired by now; Dad's fifty-eight in August. Don't most officers give up work early? It's one of the benefits of the job.'

'Yeah, he may be retired, but he may not be too. Make a phone call. It's got to be worth a try. And even if he has left the job, he may be able to point us in the right direction. He's got years of relevant experience, contacts. It's got to be worth a try, hasn't it?'

Mia pressed her lips together. 'Even if I can get hold of him, even if he's still working, he's not a miracle worker. Mattia couldn't find out anything, why should Grav be any different?'

'Just talk to him. Ask his advice. See what he's got to say for himself. Mattia's good with computers, but he's a civilian. There may be methods he's unaware of. Things he can't do.'

Mia visibly stiffened. 'It's too late. Have you seen the time? There are less than two hours before the deadline. What if the bastard does something to harm me, to harm Isabella? I'm scared.'

'Oh, come on, Mia, use your imagination, girl. You need to buy some time. Give the bastard what he wants, but don't compromise yourself in the process. It's easily done.'

Mia's brow furrowed. 'What on earth are you talking about now?'

'You know the sort of photos he wants, yes?'

'Yes, of course, I do. I'm not a complete innocent.'

Ella chose her words carefully. 'Mattia used to be into that kind of stuff. He showed me a few sites he thought may interest me, you know, more creative stuff, female-friendly, black and white, arty. Some of it was quite erotic, to be honest.'

'I don't care how artistic the pictures were. I don't want to be any part of it. Not like this. Not when forced to. It's not my style. What if the bastard makes the photos public? What if he puts them online for anyone to see? People who know me. They'd be there forever. I could never show my face in public again.'

'Not all of the photos I saw showed the women's faces. I think you know what I'm saying. Men are simple creatures. Visually stimulated and easily pleased. We can use that to our advantage if you're up for it. What do you think?'

Mia refilled her glass again and handed Ella the bottle. 'I still don't want to do it. It's just not me. But, maybe if I drink enough... I'd need to be totally legless before getting undressed.'

Ella smiled. 'That's not what I'm saying.'

'Okay, tell me more.'

'Where's your laptop?'

'It's charging in the kitchen.'

Ella crossed the room, returning a few seconds later with the computer already open and on what she considered a suitable website. 'What if we download a series of images from the net, photos of the same woman, someone with a similar build and hair colour to you, but who can't be identified? He gets what he wants and you get the time you need to talk to Grav. Take a look at these. This is the sort of thing I had in mind.'

Mia raised an eyebrow. 'Oh, for goodness' sake, do *all* men look at this stuff?'

'All the ones I've known.'

'What, even Adam?'

Ella laughed, amused by a possibility she considered ludicrous. 'Well, perhaps not Adam. He may well be the only heterosexual man in the world who's never looked at a picture of a naked woman in his life. He's one of life's rare innocents. It's a shame really, he could do with some inspiration in the bedroom department. He's more interested in his true crime magazines than women. I sometimes wonder if we'd ever have sex at all if he had his way. I'd be doomed to a life of clitoral vibrators and dildos, not that that seems such a bad thing at the moment, given some of his recent under par performances. He has got so much to learn.'

'Oh, I'm sure he'll up his game soon enough with a bit of encouragement from you.'

'Let's hope so. I've never much fancied life as a nun. I wouldn't look good in a habit. Black's not my colour.'

The smile disappeared from Mia's face as quickly as it appeared. 'Do you really think we could get away with it?'

'What, sending a few photos and seeking Grav's advice?'

'Well, yes, that's what you've suggested.'

Ella picked up what was left of the chocolate bar and broke off a large chunk before handing Mia the remainder. 'I don't see why not. The manipulative sod isn't Superman. He hasn't got X-ray vision. Let's do it. Let's nail the bastard. How could our mystery man possibly find out?'

11

The tale of the fat detective
This fat pig went to market.
This fat pig stayed at home.
This fat pig had roast beef.
And this fat pig had none.
And this fat pig's daughter got raped and strangled on the way home.
What do you think, Inspector Sick Leave? Do you like my merry rhyme?
Does it conjure up pleasant images in your mind? Images of death?
Images of destruction? I know where you live. I know where your
daughter lives. That grown-up child of yours. Only in her twenties and
already a solicitor, clever girl! A chip off the old block, so it seems.
Wouldn't it be a terrible shame if all that promise came to a premature
end? Life can change so very quickly, in the blink of an eye, the shake of
a lamb's tail. Help Mia and I'll focus on Emily instead. How does that
sound, Mr Heart Attack? Make your choice. Your daughter or a woman
who means little, if anything, to you? Ignore Mia's needs and all will be
well. Emily's life will continue as if I never existed. It seems like an easy
enough decision to make. Let me know when you've reached a resolu-
tion. But be quick. I'm not a patient man by nature. I'm the lord of the

flies, the devil in human form. Killing your daughter would be an undoubted pleasure. Blink and I'll do it. Don't delay.

Grav swore loudly, shook a clenched fist at the computer screen for a second time then flung his half-empty beer can at the nearest wall, spraying a golden liquid which ran down the wallpaper towards the floor. He'd been threatened before. Of course, he had. Threatened more times than he cared to remember and by some of the best too. Hard men, dangerous men who'd served their time. But this time was different, very different. Threaten a copper, by all means. It was part of the game. To be expected. But his daughter? Really, his daughter? That wasn't on. It wasn't on at all.

He opened another can, drank half its contents and continued his ruminations. And who the hell was this Mia, anyway? The name meant nothing to him. Was someone trying to wind him up? Revenge, maybe? Some scrote trying to make his life even more of a nightmare than it already was? Yeah, that made sense. He'd made more than his fair share of enemies over the years. He'd put a lot of people away. Some for a very long time.

Grav sat back on the sofa and tried to relax as his chest tightened and his blood pressure soared to a savage high. How dare he? How fucking well dare he? He'd catch the scrote. Put him in his place. Nail the cunt to a door by his balls.

He looked across the room to where a framed photograph of his long-deceased wife sat in pride of place on top of the television, and he heard her voice as if she were whispering in his ear for only him to hear. As if she were still with him. As if she'd never left. '*Watch your language, Grav my boy. This is my home, not the rugby club. You're not with those foul-mouthed mates of yours now. I expect better of you. Do you hear me?*'

He blinked repeatedly and saw her coming back and forth into focus, hovering above him with an oh-so-familiar look of disapproval on her beautiful face. 'Someone's threatened Emily, love. Threatened to hurt her. I'm too old for this shit. You'd swear yourself in my place.'

The big detective winced as Heather placed her hands on her fleshy hips and glared at him with unblinking eyes that seemed to penetrate his very soul. '*Come on now, Grav, you need to sober up and get your act together. You're being manipulated, that's all. Someone's pressing your buttons. Turning up the pressure to maximum. You just need to figure out who it is and put them straight. You can do that, can't you?*'

He dropped his head and focussed on the multicoloured floral carpet at his feet. 'I'm ill, Heather. I've had three heart attacks. You know that as well as I do. I'm not up to it any more. I'm getting old. Maybe I'll be with you sooner than you think.'

He lifted his head on picturing her placing a hand under his chin and kissing him gently on his forehead.

'*He's threatened our little girl, Grav, that's a game changer. Now, on your feet, take a shower, shave, eat something wholesome for a change, and do whatever it is you need to do. Make certain our little girl's safe and sound. I know you can do it. I'm relying on you, and Emily's relying on you too. Don't forget that. That's your function as her father.*'

Grav lifted himself to his feet on unsteady legs as his overburdened knees tightened and grumbled. 'I hear you, love, I hear you. I'll be back in work before you know it. The scrote's picked on the wrong man this time. Just you wait and see.'

He heard his wife call after him as he stumbled towards the bathroom, every item of furniture an obstacle in his path. '*Come on, old man, hurry up. One foot in front of the other. That's the Grav I know and love. I knew I could rely on you. You've never let me down before, and you're not going to start now.*'

He stopped mid-step and clung to the doorframe. 'Any idea who this Mia is, love? Find her and I find him.'

She faded slowly away and disappeared back into the photo, as he narrowed his eyes and clung to her memory with every cell of his being. '*That's for you to find out, Grav my boy. You're the detective, not me. You need to remember that and act accordingly.*'

Heather drifted back into focus for one final time, wagging her finger. '*I've got things to do up here. Things to get on with. Things you can't begin to understand. It's not all harps and angelic choirs on this side of the veil. You need to get off your fat arse and pull your weight.*' She grinned and looked suddenly younger, as she had when they first met. Long before her illness took its toll. '*We'll be together soon enough, Grav. I can see you've put on a pound or two. But there are things you have to do before then. This one is up to you.*'

12

Emily Gravel met her client's eyes with an apologetic look of regret and picked up the phone on the third insistent ring. 'Harrison and Turner.'

'Hello, love, it's Dad. Have you got five minutes to talk?'

The busy small-town lawyer pressed the phone to her face. 'I'm with a client, is everything okay?'

'We need a quick chat.'

She rubbed the back of her neck and frowned. 'You know what the doctor said. If you have any chest pains, get yourself to casualty as quickly as possible or call an ambulance. I can run you to West Wales General if you need me to. Just say the word.'

'We need to talk, that's all.'

Emily looked across at her client for the second time, smiling thinly before returning her attention to the call. 'I'll ring you back in half an hour or so. As long as you're sure you're okay until then?'

A sigh came down the line. 'For goodness' sake, girl, you're as bad as your mother. I've told you I'm fine. I've never been better.'

* * *

Grav was lying stretched out on the sofa, drinking his fourth beer of the day and drifting in and out of fitful sleep, when his phone rang and startled him at ten past one that afternoon. He emptied the can down his throat, dragged himself into a seated position and fumbled in his trouser pocket to retrieve his mobile. 'Hello, Emily, thanks for ringing back, love. I was hoping you wouldn't take too long.'

'What's this about, Dad? I need to leave for a child protection case conference soon. I've got to be in Llanelli by two o'clock at the latest.'

Grav smiled, remembering the little girl who'd become a woman. 'Look, love, I was in two minds about telling you this at all. It's probably the last thing you need to hear after everything you went through with Turner...'

'Just say it. You're starting to worry me.'

He opened his fifth can with a metallic ping and took a slurp before speaking. 'Yeah, that's why I thought of keeping it to myself.'

She raised her eyes to the ceiling. 'Spit it out, Dad, it's not like you to be so reticent. I can handle whatever it is you've got to say. I'm a big girl now.'

Grav saw his long deceased wife hover over him with a wagging finger, then refocussed on his call. 'Yeah, sorry, love, I don't know what the hell's wrong with me. It's no big deal. I just thought you had the right to know, that's all.'

'To know what?'

He pictured Heather shaking him awake as he closed his eyes for a second, desperate for sleep. 'Some nutter sent me an email. It referred to a woman called Mia. I couldn't remember her at first, but then it came to me: Ella's sister. You used to play with them when you were kids, Roy and Myra's girls, do you remember?'

'Yeah, I do. We were close for a time. I saw Mia in town a few months back, but I don't think she recognised me. She's a successful author now, a bestseller.'

Grav rubbed his eyes with the back of one hand and opened them wide. 'The email threatened you if I helped Mia. I've got no idea what that's supposed to mean. I've had no contact with her. But someone obviously thought it was important enough to try and manipulate me.'

'Strange!'

'I thought so.'

Emily brushed non-existent fluff from both shoulders. 'What sort of threats?'

'Nothing specific. If it hadn't mentioned you, I wouldn't have given it a second's thought. I've been threatened by some of the best. This stuff was amateur by comparison.'

'Any idea who sent it?'

'I can probably find out. I'm not short of enemies.'

'It may not be about you at all.'

He blinked himself awake and smiled up at Heather as she looked down at him. 'You could be right, I guess it's a possibility.' Emily fingered her necklace. 'I wasn't planning on telling you this, but someone sent me a disgusting maggot-ridden rat in the post. Do you think the two things could be connected?'

'Oh, for Pete's sake, girl, you've got to tell me this stuff. I could have done something about it.'

'I didn't want to worry you.'

He frowned hard, feeling he'd let her down for no good reason at all. 'What about the packaging?'

'What?'

'The packaging, what packaging did it come in?'

She exploded the air from her mouth, tasting decay on her breath and wanting to forget. 'It was one of those brown padded envelopes. You know, the ones lined with bubble wrap.'

'Have you still got it?'

'No, no, I threw the damned thing away. I couldn't stand the sight of it. And it absolutely stank. I had to open every window in the house.'

Grav sighed, knowing his best opportunity was probably lost. 'We could have checked for DNA, fingerprints, the postmark.'

'I didn't think.'

'Oh, come on, Emily, you're a lawyer. You understand this stuff as well as I do.'

'Well, it's too late now.'

'Has the rubbish been collected?' He knew it was a long shot, as Heather pointed out.

'Yeah, it has, last night.' Emily looked up and nodded as her secretary opened her office door and pointed at the clock. 'So, what do you suggest we do?'

'If you receive anything else, keep it, and I'll call in a few favours. I should be back in work soon enough anyway. Not that my being on sick leave need delay anything. We'll find out who's doing these things and sort them out good and proper. No one upsets my little girl and gets away with it.'

'Thanks, Dad.'

'You're welcome.'

Grav lay back down and yawned. 'You do realise that whoever's doing these things could be dangerous, yes? I'm not saying they are, but it's a possibility we can't rule out. You need to be cautious, take precautions.'

'Yeah, I do know. I'm not a complete muppet. We've had this conversation before.'

'Just be careful, that's all I'm saying.'

Emily sounded a lot more positive than she felt as she picked up her briefcase. 'I'll keep my eyes open. Thanks for the heads up. I'm a copper's daughter. I know how to look after myself.'

'Of course, you do, love. Are you still doing the kickboxing?'

She talked as she walked. 'Yeah, Laura teaches the class every Saturday and sometimes on a Wednesday. She's a British champion now. There's even talk of a European title fight in Holland. I'd like to be as good as her one day.'

'If the bastard approaches you, give him a good kick in the balls from me. Nice and hard mind, that should slow him down a bit.'

She smiled. 'I'll keep it in mind.'

'You do that, love, and I'll join in when I get my hands on him. Nobody threatens one of my own. I'll batter him senseless.'

13

Mia thought long and hard before dialling Carmarthen Police Station's non-emergency number, and she almost put the phone down more than once before hearing the receptionist's nasal North Wales tones at the other end of the line. 'West Wales Police Head-quarters, how can I help you?'

Mia swallowed hard, sweat patches forming under both arms. 'Can I speak to Gareth Gravel, please? My name's Mia Hamilton, he's a family friend.'

'Detective Inspector Gravel is still on sick leave, I'm afraid. Can somebody else help you? Another detective, perhaps?'

Mia hesitated, unsure of her response, then finally said, 'No, you're all right, thanks. It's not important. Do you know when he's likely to be back in work?'

'I'm told it could be quite some time, but I can't be more specific than that, sorry. There's no guarantee he'll be back at all.'

* * *

Mia parked her small German hatchback half on, half off the wide pavement directly opposite Grav's modest Carmarthen home. She sat staring at the front door for almost five minutes before finally running a brush through her long hair, checking her subtle make-up in the rear-view mirror and exiting the vehicle. She stood motionless on the doorstep for a few seconds, lacking the conviction to knock, but then she raised her hand quickly and did just that, not allowing herself time to change her mind.

Mia sucked in repeated deep breaths of warm summer air to build her confidence as she heard an internal door slam shut and heavy footsteps making their way down the hall towards her. She recognised Grav as soon as he opened the door, his big arms spread wide, a supportive hand gripping each side of the frame. He looked older than the man she'd known, heavier than she recalled, blunted at the edges, as if fighting an ongoing battle with gravity and losing, but there was still an undoubted spark of intelligence and good humour in those tired eyes. A man of whom her parents had been so very fond.

'What can I do for you, love?'

Mia briefly considered making some excuse or other and walking away, but Ella's words of advice and caution resonated in her mind, and she thought better of it. There was potentially everything to gain, and little, if anything, to lose. 'I was hoping you still lived here. I'd like your advice. I need your help. I need your urgent help.'

He stared at her through an alcoholic haze, red eyes blinking, trying to figure out where he'd seen her before but failing to pin it down. 'Do I know you, love?'

Mia was beginning to doubt the wisdom of her visit as he burped at full volume and his beer-soaked breath filled her nostrils. 'You don't remember me?'

'You're not one of Emily's old school friends, are you? Or one of

Dewi's ex-girlfriends? He had quite a few. Your face is definitely familiar.'

She forced a smile. 'I'm Mia, Mia Hamilton, Roy and Myra's daughter. You used to play golf with Dad before they moved abroad.'

Grav broke into a broad smile, revealing uneven nicotine-stained teeth that were, at least, his own. 'Ah, yes, of course. How are your mum and dad doing? I haven't seen them for years.'

'They're living in Italy these days, on the Amalfi Coast. Lovely part of the world.'

'Why Italy?'

'They used to go there on holiday. They fell in love with the place and bought a villa overlooking the sea after Dad retired.'

'Ah, yes, I remember your dad mentioning it over a pint.'

Mia nodded, glad that the ageing detective remembered anything at all.

'How long has it been since we last met, love?'

'Oh, it's a good few years. I'd just left university when they made the move. I did a creative writing degree in London.'

'But now you're back in God's own country.'

She smiled. 'Yes, I am.'

He glanced back as he turned and headed towards the lounge. 'Come on in, love. In you come. Take the weight off. I've been wondering if I'd hear from you.'

Her eyes widened. 'Really?'

He chuckled quietly to himself. 'Call it copper's intuition. There are things we need to discuss.'

Mia glanced around the room with a subtle turn of her head and silently observed that the dated brown furniture and tobacco-yellowed magnolia decoration looked almost as unkempt as the detective. The place could do with a good clean, a bit of female attention. And, of course, he could too. Maybe his wife had left. That would explain it. 'You don't seem that surprised to see me.'

Grav remained standing. 'Do you fancy a drink before we make a start? I was just about to get myself another beer. Water never passes my lips. It's a matter of principle.'

She smiled thinly, thinking he'd had more than enough already but not wanting to offend. 'A cup of coffee would be nice, thanks.'

'You won't have a proper drink with your old Uncle Grav? I keep them chilled in the fridge at this time of year. Sacrilege, I know, but it works for me.'

'Just a coffee would be lovely.'

'Are you certain?'

'Absolutely!'

'Okay, if that's how you want to do things. Milk and sugar?'

'I'll take it black without sugar, thanks.'

'And you're sure you won't have a beer?'

'I drove here. A coffee would be perfect.'

Grav snorted. 'Perfect may be a bit ambitious given my culinary skills, or rather the lack of them, but I'll see what I can do. Heather used to say I made the worst coffee she'd ever tasted.'

Mia bounced her knee up and down, questioning the wisdom of her visit. 'I'm sure it'll be fine.'

He ambled towards the kitchen on unstable legs, reappearing a few minutes later with a mug of steaming coffee in one hand and a can of bitter in the other. 'Refreshments coming up.'

Mia accepted her hot drink and met his inflamed eyes as he slumped onto the settee, as if his lower limbs had suddenly given way under him. 'You didn't seem that surprised to see me,' she said, again.

Grav opened the can with a flick of his nail, lifted it to his mouth and emptied half the contents down his throat in one effortless gulp. 'Some evil git sent me an email, an email threatening my daughter if I help you. Someone doesn't want me to get involved, that's blatantly obvious. I'm guessing you've received something along the same lines. Am I right?'

'Yes, yes I have.'

'I thought as much.'

Her eyes narrowed. 'But why contact *you*? About me, I mean? It doesn't make a lot of sense. I hadn't been to see you then. We hadn't even spoken for years. How on earth did the sender make the link? How could he possibly know?'

'Who knew you were coming to see me?'

'Well, just me and my sister.'

'Did you tell anyone else?'

'No.'

'Sure?'

'Certain!'

'What about your sister?'

'No, absolutely not, no way, she'd know not to tell anyone.'

'Could anyone have overheard the two of you talking?'

'I don't see how they could have.'

'I'll tell you what, love. Give your sister a ring for me, do it now. Ask her if she discussed your intention to visit me with *anyone* but you. Anyone at all. If she did, it may well point us in the right direction. It makes sense to clarify matters before we continue.'

Mia took out her phone and dialled. Within a short time she had her answer. 'Ella *swears* she didn't mention it to anyone. She's one hundred per cent unequivocal on the matter. She said she'd swear to that in any court in the land.'

'Do you believe her?'

'Yes, *absolutely*! I trust her implicitly.'

'Not even the slightest doubt?'

'None whatsoever.'

'Okay, you know your sister, that's good enough for me. I may well talk to her myself at some point, but I suspect she'll tell me the exact same thing.'

'I did contact the police station to ask for you. I gave my name. I said I was a family friend.'

'When?'

'Earlier today.'

'That doesn't help us.'

'Perhaps he knows I know you of old. He could be a friend of Dad's. A lucky guess maybe or an assumption that hit the mark. He could have just *guessed* I *may* turn up. Maybe he didn't *know* I was coming at all.'

Grav took a drink as he pondered the hypothesis. 'Beats me, love. But it's a possibility. Let's see if we can work it out together. It's personal now. He's crossed a line. Nobody threatens my family and gets away with it. I'd beat the bastard to a bloody pulp if I could get my hands on him.'

Mia sipped her coffee, swirling the hot liquid around her mouth before swallowing. 'What do you need me to tell you?'

Grav kicked off his shoes and rested his feet on the coffee table. 'Well, first of all, why are you here with me rather than at the police station? I could make a pretty good stab at the answer, but I'd prefer to hear it in your own words. I usually find that helps. Assumptions aren't always helpful in my world.'

'Well, it's like you said. I've been receiving emails, threatening emails, threatening me, threatening my daughter. Whoever sent them said he'd kill her if I contacted the police. One of my sister's friends, Mattia, tried to trace them for me. He's good at that sort of thing, but no joy. He didn't get anywhere. I've been worried sick. I'm hoping you can help.'

'Has the sender asked you for money?'

She shook her head. 'No, no, he hasn't. My sister thought he would at some point, but it hasn't happened yet.'

Grav emptied the can, burped, fetched another from the kitchen and sat himself back down on the sofa, which creaked loudly, as if in peril of collapsing under his weight. 'Right, start at the beginning, don't leave anything out. Even the most seemingly insignificant detail could prove to be crucial. Tell me absolutely everything and let me decide if it's relevant. Are we clear?'

Mia was beginning to feel more confident, strangely reassured by his world-weary appearance and demeanour. There was more to him than first impressions suggested. An inner strength and a wisdom of sorts. She was even beginning to like him, which surprised her.

'Are you going to tell me your story, love? I'm ready when you are.'

She nodded. 'Yes, sorry, I was deep in thought.'

'Off you go, I'm listening. I may ask you a few questions as we go along if I need to clarify anything.'

Mia spent the next twenty minutes or so outlining events, telling her tale in clear, unambiguous language she thought would best convey both the facts and her level of concern. She was scared, really scared, and she wanted him to understand that. She needed him to treat the situation with the degree of urgency she felt it demanded.

When Mia finally finished telling her story, Grav sat looking at her in contemplative silence for a few seconds before finally speaking. 'So, let me see if I've got this correct. Some demented scrote sends you emails, emails making demands, making threats, and you tell him you love him in an online advert and then send him naked images, telling him they're of you. Am I right? Is that what you're telling me?'

Mia lowered her head, linking her hands over her stomach and studying her thumbs. 'Yes, it all sounds a bit ridiculous when you put it like that.'

'You think?'

She avoided his gaze. 'I've been stupid. I know that.'

'What on earth were you thinking, girl? You're an intelligent woman, a bestselling author, for goodness' sake. Did someone give you a common-sense bypass you haven't told me about? I can't think of any other reason that could explain it.'

Mia raised a hand to her face, an attempt to halt the tears forming in her eyes from falling down her cheek. 'I've had a tough time. Breast cancer, my waste of space partner dumped me by text after Isabella was born, and I've been taking a lot of pain control medication by necessity. I wasn't used to drugs. The tablets clouded my mind. Maybe I haven't been thinking as clearly as I otherwise would have.'

Grav squinted at her. 'You said cloud*ed* as opposed to cloud. Is that significant? Are the painkillers no longer an issue?'

She considered lying but thought better of it in the interests of Isabella's safety. 'Let's just say it's a work in progress.'

He slurped his beer. 'Me too, love, although in my case it's the booze. It tends to take the edge off. I've always liked a drink or two, but since Heather's death... well, I'm sure you know what I'm saying. I don't like to think too clearly unless it's absolutely necessary.'

'I'm sorry for your loss.'

'Me too, love, me too. She was a great girl, my soulmate. We were together for over thirty years.'

'What happened?'

'Bowel cancer, it was a blessing she went in the end. I miss her every second of every day.'

Mia nodded, lost for words as she began to learn there was a more sensitive man beneath the brash exterior he presented to the world. 'I'm sorry.'

He saw the concern on her face. 'No need to worry yourself on my account. I play hard and I work hard. Alcohol has never got in the way of me catching criminals. I know when to stop.'

'That's good to know.'

He cleared his throat, keen to change the focus from past to present. 'Some scrote sending you threats is the last thing you needed after all the crap you've been through. That's the way it happens sometimes. Bad luck comes in bunches. And maybe your sister wasn't the best source of advice in the circumstances.'

'She tried to persuade me to go to the police. She suggested I talk to you when I refused. She's the reason I'm here in the first place.'

'Yeah, but sending the porn to the scheming git, that wasn't a good move. It was the worst thing you could possibly have done. Why feed his fantasies? He's going to feel empowered, validated, more sure of himself than before.'

Mia wiped a tear from her face, surprised by his eloquence. 'We thought it would buy us some time, that's all. We'd had a few glasses of wine. It seemed like the right thing to do. I wish I'd come to see you sooner.'

He reached out and patted her on the shoulder, feeling her distress. 'It's all right, love. No need for tears. We'll get this sorted before you know it. It's nothing we can't put right. You can count on it. You've done the right thing coming to see me.'

'It's just dawned on me. I've always assumed it's a *he*. You seem to be doing the same thing. Do you think there's *any* possibility it could be a woman?'

'Nah, this has got male scumbag written all over it. I'd bet my house on it.'

She nodded her understanding. 'So, what happens now?'

'Are you adamant you don't want to make this official? I still think that's the wisest move if you'll agree.'

Mia looked ready to bolt for the door. 'I don't think that's safe. I really hope asking for your help wasn't an error of judgement on my part. I'm feeling things are out of my control as it is. I need to know you're not going to do anything without my agreement.'

He briefly considered arguing the point but decided against. 'No problem, we'll do it your way if it keeps you happy. I've got a good mate in the technical department. I'll ask him to take a look at my computer, off the record. See where it gets him. We'll have another chat and decide on the next step after that. Best keep all our options open.'

'Do you need my laptop?'

Grav stood up slowly and shook his head. 'No, you hold on to it for now. Let me know if he sends any further messages but don't reply under any circumstances. Just blank him and tell me what's happening. And switch off your smartphone. Avoid using it from now. Don't be tempted to switch the damned thing on. Stick it in a drawer somewhere and leave it there. Buy a basic pay-as-you-go for cash and only use that. And let me know the number as soon as you've got it. We can keep in touch that way.'

'Anything else?'

'Change your routine as often as you can and tell your friends and family not to share any information about you with anyone without your express permission. That's important! He's obviously getting it from somewhere, and that's not helpful. He may well be pumping someone for information without them even realising. Keep everyone in the loop. Let them know what's happening and put them on their guard. Let's keep the bastard guessing.'

Mia nodded her silent agreement, lost in thought, as his advice and its implications sank in.

'How much detail of your personal life is in the public eye?'

'I try to keep my private life exactly that, private.'

'I suspect he'll give up hassling you if he's starved of attention for long enough. Either that or he'll try to up the pressure to draw a response. If that happens, it will make him more visible. Easier to track down. I'll pay him a visit when we find him. Give him a nice surprise. Let's see how he likes me hammering on his door.' He shook a clenched fist in front of him, panting slightly as his breathing became more laboured. 'Stalkers can be notoriously difficult to discourage, but I have my methods. I can be pretty persuasive when I want to be, if you understand my meaning. He's going to be very sorry he ever contacted you in the first place.'

She knew exactly what he meant but decided not to comment. It seemed best. 'Is that what you think this is, stalking?'

'If you want to put a label on it. People usually do for some reason.'

'I can't understand why anyone would behave like that. What on earth's wrong with him?'

Grav grinned. 'If you want my honest opinion, men like him are nutters in need of a good slap. But the more enlightened coppers I know would probably say that stalking is a crime of control. They see their victims as possessions who are rightfully theirs. They feel entitled, as if their behaviour is entirely justified. Some of them have mental health issues and others not. There's no way of telling until our man's caught and assessed. He may think you love him. He may even believe he loves you, even if the two of you have never met in your lives. Bottom line, the guy's fixated on you. That's all that matters. That's what we've got to deal with. And we will, I give you my word on that, we will. It's just a matter of time until we catch him.'

Mia walked towards the hall, with its woodchip wallpaper, feeling a growing sense of hopeful reassurance, despite the detective's more obvious flaws. 'It sounds as if you've dealt with this sort of thing before.'

He opened the front door and stood aside, allowing her to step onto a pavement with grass growing through the cracks. 'More times than I care to count. It happens all too often. A lot of cases around the country aren't even investigated in any meaningful way, that's the truth of it. Far too many victims are badly let down. I like to think our force is different. We treat cases with the attention and resources they deserve. It's one of the advantages of not being in the big city.'

'I'd never even thought about it before it happened to me.'

'Why would you?'

Mia reached for her tablets without commenting.

'Be careful, love. Use your head, don't take any unnecessary risks, suspect any men, even the ones you think you know well, but try not to let it worry you too much. Don't ruin your life on his account, that's my advice. If you do, he's won. Easier said than done, I appreciate. But you've got to give it a good go. You seem like a strong-minded and stoic young woman to me. Make full use of those attributes, for you and for that little girl of yours too. Let's show him what you're made of.'

Mia gripped her medicine bottle tightly in one hand as her heart began to race. 'Isabella's kept me going through some pretty dark times. There's nobody else to care for her. Ella works full time, Mum and Dad are in Italy like I said, and Isabella's father's a total prat who refuses to grow up. When all is said and done, her well-being is down to me. Giving up isn't an option.'

'We haven't really talked about your ex. Do you think there's any chance he's sending the emails? It's often someone close to home.'

Just for a fleeting moment Mia considered the possibility. 'No, I can't see it. I don't think he'd have the imagination or the inclination. Rhys's next to useless but he's not evil. He wouldn't threaten his own child.' She bared her teeth. 'It would be too much effort for a start.'

'You're certain? I need to know if you've got even the slightest doubt.'

Mia massaged her stomach, her gut churning as her need for opioids escalated exponentially. 'Yes, I'm certain. There's no way it's Rhys.'

'Keep your chin up, love. You look like shit all of a sudden. And take it easy on the way home. Put your feet up for a couple of hours when you get there. These things usually come to nothing in my experience.'

As the detective waved his goodbyes with a heavy heart, something was telling him that this time was going to be different. The case was going somewhere. Somewhere Mia wouldn't want it to go. Thirty years of experience dealing with the criminals of this world told him all he needed to know. There was danger in the air and Grav was loving every minute.

14

Mia had taken significantly fewer tablets than was the recent norm, and she wasn't in the best of moods when she contacted Rhys before leaving the house to collect Isabella from school. She dialled and waited, expecting to leave a message, and she was strangely flustered for words when he answered.

She steadied herself, deciding to dive right in despite her crushing withdrawal symptoms. 'Have you been sending me emails?'

He sounded bored, uninterested, as if he didn't care. 'No, why do you ask?'

'It had better not be you.'

Rhys sniggered, contemptuous, dismissive. 'I have got absolutely no idea what you're talking about, you silly mare.'

'This isn't funny. It's about time you grew up. You can't behave like a child all your life.'

'Now look, Mia, if someone has been sending you messages you don't appreciate, it wasn't me.'

'Has anyone been asking you any questions about me or Isabella? Anyone at all?'

'What?'

She clenched her teeth, desperate for a tablet and feeling more irritated than she'd ever thought possible. 'You heard me! It's not a difficult question to answer. Even *you* should be able to manage to reply without too much difficulty.'

'No, Mia, nobody has been asking about you. If you think I spend my time discussing you, you're deluded. I've got my own life to get on with.'

Mia gripped the phone more tightly and stamped her right foot. 'Are you going to even ask how Isabella's doing? You do remember who she is, don't you? Do you need a reminder? Brown hair, blue eyes and a twinkling smile. Remember? That little girl who's your daughter.'

'I was just about to ask if you gave me a chance.'

'Oh, you've had plenty of chances. Do you realise you forgot her birthday again? That's two years running! You're her father, not some stranger, though you may as well be. She asked me where you were. "Is Daddy coming to my party? Is Daddy going to buy me a present? Did Daddy send me a card?" What the hell was I supposed to say in response? I'm tired of making excuses for you, Rhys. It's getting boring. As she gets older she's going to realise she's not very high on your priority list. That's not something she's going to find easy to come to terms with. If you don't change soon you'll have burnt your bridges for good.'

'I don't know what you want me to say.'

'And what about the child maintenance? You haven't sent me any cash for months. I'm going to make it official if you don't sort yourself out.'

'Oh, give me a break! You earn a lot more money than I do. I've seen your books for sale in the shops. I can hardly cover my own bills, let alone fund your flash lifestyle. I haven't had a holiday for years.'

'That is no excuse.'

'I didn't ask you to have her. I didn't have any choice in the matter.'

Mia sighed, frustrated by his argument. 'Well, she's here now. She has been for four years.'

'Yeah, more's the pity!'

Mia's anger gushed to the surface. 'I cannot believe you actually said that! She's your daughter. You don't bother visiting her. You need to contribute to her care. That's what you agreed to do, remember? If you're incapable of honouring a voluntary agreement I'll see a solicitor.'

'Yeah, so you keep saying, blah-de-fucking-blah.'

Mia had never wanted her medication more in her life. Just to feel normal. Just to feel okay again. Every second seemed like minutes. She'd never felt lower. She checked the clock to her right and wondered why the second hand was moving so very slowly. 'If it is you sending the abusive messages, the police are going to be knocking on your door sometime soon. Let's see how that makes you feel.'

'You're totally mad, woman. Round the bleeding twist. If you bother me again, I'll change my number. Got it? It's easily done. Now piss off and leave me alone.'

Mia ended the call, screamed at full volume then hurled her smartphone at the wall. As she walked towards it, she smiled, despite or perhaps due to the emotive nature of the conversation. The screen was smashed, the case badly dented. Now she was going to have to replace it, as Grav had so passionately insisted. Bin it, buy a pay-as-you-go and pass on the number to the detective. Time for a tablet. Wash it down with a glass of vino. She'd cut down. She'd done the right thing. She could stop taking the damned things when her tormentor was caught and punished. That was sensible.

Grav had the experience. He had the knowledge. How long could it possibly take?

15

Grav stood in his general practitioner's office doorway, allowing the frame to support his weight, forcing an improbable grin that looked strangely out of place, more a grimace than a smile. 'All right, Doc, you're looking a bit grey around the gills today, if you don't mind me saying so. I hope you haven't been overdoing it again. Look where it got me.'

Dr Jenny Rees looked up at her patient of over twenty years and sighed theatrically. 'Sit yourself down before you fall down, Grav, there's a good lad. You're not fooling anyone.'

Grav sat as instructed, glad to take the weight off as his overburdened chest wheezed, tightened and protested. 'Bloody charming, I'm sure. There are other doctors I could see, you know. Maybe it's time for a change.'

The GP stifled a grin, amused as intended, but not wanting to encourage him any more than necessary. 'You can drop the avoidance tactics. You've had three heart attacks. You very nearly died. You need to start looking after yourself. The self-destructive behaviour needs to stop.'

He looked away and, for a moment, she thought he may start weeping. 'Oh, come on, I'm taking the tablets you gave me. What more do you want?'

'For goodness' sake man, get a grip, they're not enough in themselves. I shouldn't need to tell you that. You're not an unintelligent man. The medication can help, that's why I prescribed it in the first place, but it can't work miracles. You can't rely on the tablets entirely. Eat more sensibly, lose some weight, do a little light exercise. You need to make some effort. When are you going to accept that and act accordingly?'

He appeared crestfallen, despondent, defeated. 'It's easier said than done.'

'So it seems, but it's what you have to do. Find a way and get on with it.'

Grav shook his head until he spoke again. 'I need to get back to work, Doc. I need the motivation, the purpose, a reason to get myself up in the morning. If I'm not a working copper, what's the point of living? And that doesn't require an answer, by the way. I'm a police officer through and through. Have been since I was eighteen. It's all I know how to do.'

She dropped her head for a second, then raised it slowly, looking at him with tired eyes and a genuine sense of sympathy for a man she considered a friend as well as her patient. 'You drink to excess, you smoke those damned cigars you seem to enjoy so much, you're at least four stone overweight at best, and your blood pressure's through the roof. You need to start taking responsibility for your own health if you want to live for very much longer. It's time for action on your part. I can't do it for you.'

'Yeah, yeah, I know.'

'And you're not getting any younger, Grav. You need to accept your limitations. None of us can go on forever, not even you. Getting back to work is a long shot, and that's if it happens at all.'

He jerked his head back. 'Oh, come on, you're still here. You are even older than I am. You were in the class above me at school.'

She cleared her throat, adopting a challenging tone. 'Don't go changing the subject. We're here to talk about you, not me. Have you considered a holiday? It's not as if you can't afford it.'

'I don't like holidays.'

'Do you always need to be so negative?'

He chose not to reply.

'Is your son still working in the Caribbean?'

'Dewi? Yeah, he's a golf pro at one of those posh west coast hotels in Barbados.'

'Nice way to make a living.'

Grav nodded. 'Yeah, I guess so. He seems to like it well enough.'

'Why not pay him a visit? It sounds like a good opportunity to me. There are worse places I can think of to spend some quality time. Go and lie on a beach for a week or two, catch up on some reading, swim in a warm sea. It would do you a world of good.'

His eyes widened. 'What, after the last time? You have got to be kidding me. The entire trip was an unmitigated disaster. I must have been frigging mad to go there in the first place. I think Dewi felt the same way by the time I left. I couldn't wait to get home again. The police station was calling to me across the sea.'

She bit her bottom lip hard, trying not to laugh. 'Ah, yes, I recall you telling me all about it.'

Grav screwed up his face, his chest tightening again as his blood pressure soared. 'Look, Jenny, cards on the table. We've known each other a long time, yes? I like to think we understand each other.'

'Where's this going?'

'I need the job to survive, that's the truth of it. It's all there is since Heather's passing. We had plans for retirement, places we intended to go together, she fancied a cruise or two. But that's never going to happen now. Work's what I live for. It's all that's left. Can you see me gardening or playing bowls with the other old fogeys in God's waiting room? The quiet life isn't for me. I've only been home ill for a few weeks and it's driving me around the frigging bend already. I don't know what the hell to do with my time.'

'You've got to find other interests, Grav. There's more to life than work. It comes to us all in the end.'

Grav's expression darkened. 'Maybe I'll be joining Heather even sooner than you think. A bit of me believes it wouldn't be such a bad thing if the grim reaper came calling sometime soon. I still love her. We were together for a very long time.'

Dr Rees leaned forwards in her seat, pushing some medical files aside and resting her arms on the cluttered desk. 'What exactly is that supposed to mean? If you're having suicidal thoughts, you need to tell me. There are things I can do to help.'

He opened his mouth as if to speak but closed it again when he couldn't find the words.

'Come on now, Grav. I need an answer. I can't help you unless I know what's going on in that head of yours. I know you're still affected by the PTSD to some extent: the flashbacks, the mood swings, the poor sleep. Drop the silent tough-guy routine, there's a good lad. You need to be honest with me.'

His eyes filled with tears. 'I can beg if you want me to. I've got to get back to the job. There's something I need to deal with. I need to work, my life's worth nothing without it. I don't know what more I can say.'

The doctor reached out with a paper tissue taken from her handbag but withdrew her hand quickly when he didn't accept it. 'You're not the only police officer in the world. You're going to have to accept that. If there's something that needs attention, leave it to somebody else for a change. You've done your bit.'

'It's something personal, family, something I've got to do myself. If I've got to pack it all in, I've got to do this first.'

She stretched her scrawny neck and leaned towards him with her reading glasses perched on the very tip of her nose. 'Is it serious?'

He nodded. 'Yeah, I think it probably is.'

'And you don't want to tell me about it?'

'Not really.'

She blew the air from her mouth with an audible hiss. 'Lose a stone, cut down on the booze, and give up the cigars. Do that for me, and I'll give you the go-ahead. That's the best I can offer. Have we got a deal?'

Grav's mouth fell open. 'Oh, come on, Doc, a whole stone? It'll take me months! I haven't got that sort of time.'

'For goodness' sake, man, it doesn't have to take that long if you act on my advice for once in your life. I've given you the diet sheets. You can lose the weight in days if you actually use them. I'm going to say it again. Eat healthily, do some light exercise and burn more calories than you consume. It's not rocket science. Cut out the beer, and it will work wonders in itself. Think of that stuff as liquid chips. I think that's the best way of putting it. Not that I think you're averse to stuffing far too many French fries down your throat at every conceivable opportunity.'

'Yeah, yeah, I know.'

'How much are you drinking these days? Have you cut down at all since we last discussed it?'

'Eight, maybe ten pints a day. It's no big deal, I've been doing it for years.'

'That is exactly the problem, right there. You're still drinking too much. You are *way* above the recommended daily maximum. Surely you can understand that? All your alcoholic excess has taken its toll. Your body can't take much more. It's time to stop.'

'Oh, come on, Doc, do you really need to give me the same lecture every time I see you?' And then a line he'd used before. 'If I wanted to be nagged half to death by a woman, I'd have got married again.'

'Here we go again, back to the comic side. Your usual avoidance tactic when you don't much like the direction of the conversation. Do you think I enjoy giving you a hard time? This isn't my idea of fun, in case you were wondering. If you listened in the first place, I wouldn't need to repeat myself.'

'Can't I get back to work and lose a few pounds while I'm on the job? I'll really do it this time. Everything you've told me. We could shake on it. I'll give you my word.'

She gave a little wry smile. 'I've heard it all before. I've told you my conditions. Take it or leave it. I'll ask you again. Have we got a deal?'

Grav lifted himself stiffly to his feet with the aid of the armrests. 'It doesn't look as if I've got much choice. When did you become such a hard woman?'

'Right, shoes off... on the scales, let's get you weighed.'

He pushed up his sleeve and looked at his watch, making it obvious. 'I'm a bit pushed for time.'

'Shoes off, on the scales, if we're going to do this, we're going to do it properly. No half measures. We'll weigh you now and then again in a week's time. If you've lost the weight, I'll honour my side of the bargain. If not, you can continue coming back on a weekly basis until you do. And count yourself lucky. I must be insane for considering your return to work at all.'

Grav sat himself down, bent stiffly at the waist and began undoing his laces one at a time. It was time to raise the white flag. He knew when he was beaten. Maybe he'd get back to work and perhaps he wouldn't. There was no way of telling. If Emily was in danger, he had to deal with it, on sick leave or not. He was her father, her protector. It was down to him. Just like Heather had said.

Just like she'd whispered in his ear. He just had to man up and get on with it.

16

Mattia knew he'd drunk too much as he staggered out of the Purple Parrot Wine Bar hand in hand with a pretty black-haired university student who was even more intoxicated than him. They were both entirely oblivious to the heavily disguised man watching from his car as they searched for an available taxi.

The nineteen-year-old girl bent down, removed her high-heeled shoes and walked on her bare feet, skipping from time to time for the sheer joy of it as the alcohol lowered her inhibitions. 'So how far's your place from here?'

Mattia placed an arm around one of her slender shoulders, holding her tightly as she stumbled and almost fell off the kerb. 'It's only about half a mile or so, no big deal. It doesn't look as if there are any cabs around, but we can walk it in ten minutes if you can stay on your feet long enough.'

'And you definitely haven't got a girlfriend? Be honest now, I'll know if you're lying.'

He kissed her face, checking his pocket for condoms with his free hand. 'No, I told you. I'm a free agent.'

She suddenly stopped, resisting the impulse to vomit as the acidic taste of bile rose in her throat.

'Are you okay?'

She swallowed hard, gagged and swallowed again. 'Give me a second. I was close to puking. It must have been that sandwich I ate in the pub. I thought it tasted a bit odd. Maybe it was off.'

He moved quickly, taking her arm in his to steady her balance. 'Oh, yeah, that's it, something you ate. It's got nothing to do with all that vodka you hurled down your throat for hours on end. I think we finished most of the bottle between us.'

She sniggered despite her continued nausea. 'Well, I guess that may have had something to do with it.'

He squeezed her hand. 'Are you ready to make a move?'

She dropped a shoe, bent down and picked it up again. 'Yeah, I think so. My legs seem to be working even if the rest of me isn't.'

'We need to cross here.' He stopped, reached out and pointed. 'My place is at the top of that long hill. You can't see the building from here, but it's not too far.'

The two young people stepped out onto the road hand in hand, as Adam watched and waited until he thought the time was exactly right. He slammed his foot down hard on the accelerator. The car screeched forward, engine revving, then smashed into Mattia just as he reached the road's midpoint. The front bumper hit Mattia full on and at speed, snapping both his legs and causing severe internal injuries before he somersaulted high in the air, bouncing off the bonnet then landing on the tarmac with a heavy thud that his student companion thought was the worst sound she'd ever heard.

As the girl crawled towards Mattia's prone body, battered, bruised but not seriously hurt, he was already losing the fight for life. Blood poured from his wounds like a dark flood in full flow, and a ruptured abdominal organ meant that the end was fast approaching despite his youth. By the time one of several interested onlookers gathering at the scene contacted the emergency services, it was already too late. As Adam sped off, watching events gleefully in the rear-view mirror, Mattia closed his eyes for the very last time. The girl he hardly knew reached his side and shook him, as if attempting to wake him from sleep. She slumped alongside his corpse when he didn't respond, closed her eyes and joined him in oblivion as her world began to spin. Life, she silently observed, was so very transient, a dream, an illusion of energy and awareness. She'd read it somewhere along the way. Or maybe it was on the telly. She reached out and kissed him on his bloodied head moments after his heart stopped beating. 'Goodnight Mattia, I need to sleep now. Let's not go to your place. See you in the morning.'

Adam sped away, heading out of town and avoiding the main streets so as not to get caught on any roadside camera. He drove faster than was sensible down country lanes, even for a man of his advanced skills. He tensed when he heard a siren whine in the far-off distance, picturing a speeding police car in his mind's eye, but he relaxed with a self-congratulatory smirk as the sound faded away to nothing. The universe, he concluded, was conspiring to protect him. Everything was as it should be.

Within fifteen minutes, Adam was driving down a long, sweeping, beautifully eerie tree-lined hill, leading into the remote estuary fishing village of Ferryside, with a touching western country music song playing on the car's radio. The night was dark now, thanks to the low hanging clouds which had swept in off the sea to mask the stars. He was pleased to note that the relatively narrow road leading through the pleasant West Wales village was quiet, with the majority of residents asleep in their beds, oblivious to his very existence.

Adam turned right, past the red-and-white safety barriers, over the railway tracks, past the signal box on his right and onto the uneven, stone-strewn ground that bordered the sweeping muddy sand beach, just as it began to rain. He manoeuvred slowly past the yacht club, followed by a gradually curving walled enclosure containing sailing boats, speedboats and other pleasure craft, and finally the recently built, two-storey lifeboat station. He stopped very briefly, surveying the scene before steering onto a concrete slipway which led directly from the parking area to the beach and the rising water beyond. Adam switched off the engine and looked out at the fast-flowing, swirling mix of river and salt water as it moved forward at a relentless pace, enveloping the muddy sand at an impressive rate that both surprised and pleased him. He turned up the radio, reclined his black leather driver's seat an inch or two and waited for a little over half an hour as the tide continued to rise, right up to the time he considered its inevitable progression precisely right. He exited the car as a barn owl hooted in a distant woodland thicket, retrieved his belongings from the rear, reached back into the front cabin and released the handbrake before closing the door with the flick of his left foot and jumping aside. Adam watched, spellbound, as the car began to roll down the steep slipway towards the dark water. He performed a little dance of delight, repeatedly hopping from one foot to the other and turning in a circle as the vehicle gradually increased its speed, then rolled in a downward trajectory until its front wheels were enveloped and the miry brown mixture rose to the approximate midpoint of the front doors. Adam stood, hidden by the blackness, and watched, occasionally clapping his hands together when the mood took him. Within ten minutes, the estate car was completely submerged and drifting slowly out to sea at the behest of both the incoming tide and a strengthening offshore wind sweeping in off the Irish Sea.

Adam looked up at the sky as the rain stopped and a yellow moon broke through the dispersing clouds to bathe the world in a mellow light that gave the entire estuary a mysterious, unworldly appearance, as if nature were painting a masterpiece for only him to behold. He stared at the exalted scene with indifference but interpreted its beauty as a great sign. A positive signal amongst many that, he believed, were sent by the creator to confirm his position as unique amongst humanity. He was, he told himself, a prince amongst men, a chosen being sent to earth for a specific purpose. A purpose that, one day, others would recognise and appreciate as he did. One fine day, a judgemental world of fools would celebrate his genius and fear his name. They'd kneel and tremble at his feet like all the ineffectual girls who went before them, with their begging and their pleading and their streams of salty tears pouring from their bodies like an open tap. Begging didn't save them, and it wouldn't protect the victims to follow their lead. Not Mia, not Ella, not Emily, and not whoever came next. He was the angel of death, Beelzebub, and soon everyone would shout his name.

Adam picked up his bag, took one last look out across Carmarthen Bay towards the historic Norman castle of Llansteffan, majestic on a dark hilltop on the opposite side of the fast-flowing water, and began to stroll away with a broad grin that dominated his features. Mattia had been punished. Just as he deserved, as was written in the stars. He'd brought it on himself and had provided some entertainment in the process. The car was gone, but he had another, so it hardly mattered. Ella had lost her lover. Any remaining evidence secreted in the vehicle would be utterly destroyed, and so justice was served. His work for the night was done. It was a triumph of his intelligence and ingenuity, a cause for celebration, for congratulation, for a figurative pat on the back. Things really couldn't have gone any better. Maybe he should kill the pig too, before he had the opportunity to stick his stupid snout into his business. But hold on, he shouldn't get ahead of himself. Why not have some fun along the way? Let him live awhile. Make the swine suffer as he'd never experienced before. Put the big fat pig on a metaphorical spit and roast him until begging for relief only death could bring. It was certainly worth thinking about.

Adam clutched his tool bag tightly in one hand and hurried back over the railway tracks and in the direction of Carmarthen, with plenty of time to think. It was best to stay in the shadows to avoid prying eyes. His night's work was complete and executed exactly as he'd planned. It was time to get going. To pick up the pace. At least it had stopped raining. Maybe that was for him too, to ease his burden, to lighten his load. It was going to be a long walk home.

17

Mia sat at the breakfast table with her young daughter immediately next to her and looked towards the fridge as the family cat slumped to the floor with its head resting in its food bowl, acidic white froth foaming from its mouth.

Isabella, three weeks past her fourth birthday, looked up at her mother with a concerned expression as Mia rose slowly to her feet and crossed the room.

'Is Jess ill, Mummy?'

The cat twitched violently as its muscles twisted and convulsed from head to tail. 'Yes, yes, I think so. Please get down and get mummy's phone from the hall. It's on the small shelf to the side of the door.'

'For the doctor?'

The cat's body stiffened and then slowly relaxed, bowel and bladder evacuating their contents as it stared into the far-off distance with unseeing eyes that were slowly fading. 'Yes, that's right, I'm going to ring the vet. That's what we call a doctor for animals. Do you remember? We read a book about it.'

The little girl lowered herself to the floor and approached her mother with tears rolling down her pretty face. 'What's wrong with her, Mummy?'

Mia stroked the cat's head, acutely aware that it had stopped breathing, as she pondered what to tell her child. 'Jess has gone, Izzy, she's died. Her spirit has gone to heaven to play with her friends. It's a nice place. She'll like it there. God will look after her now.'

The little girl looked bemused as she stared down at the cat's twitching body. 'Can't we make her better? What about a plaster? You put a plaster on my knee when I fell over.' She pointed to her right leg, full of hope. 'It's better now, look.'

Mia shook her head, choking back her sadness as she reached out and gently caressed Isabella's head. 'No, Izzy, we can't make Jess better. A plaster's not going to help this time.'

'Shall I get the phone?'

'No, it's too late.'

Isabella's shoulders curled over her chest. 'Is it my fault?'

Mia pulled her daughter close, hugging her and not letting go. 'No, it is *not* your fault. It isn't anybody's fault. Sometimes sad things just happen. It's the way of the world.' The words stuck in her throat, unconvincing even to her ears. Maybe the cat had eaten something on her travels, something toxic, something fatal. Poison, perhaps, carelessly discarded by a thoughtless neighbour or a pest control company operative not doing his or her job as carefully as they should. That made sense, didn't it?

Mia's breathing suddenly quickened, short, sharp breaths causing her chest to rise and fall as unwelcome thoughts tumbled in her mind, making her flinch. Or maybe *he'd* done it, as a warning... a punishment.

Isabella buried her head in the warm navy wool of her mother's jumper before suddenly pulling away. 'Am I going to school today? It's Amy's birthday.'

Mia focussed on the brown plastic medicine bottle sitting on a worktop at the opposite side of the kitchen, as if calling out to her, seducing her, enticing her in. She shook herself, returned her attention to Isabella and nodded her head. 'Yes, once we're ready. Your uniform's at the bottom of your bed. Go up and get dressed and I'll join you once I've looked after Jess. Is that okay?'

Isabella didn't move, unsure of her mother's intentions.

'Go on, up you go. I'll ring the school and say we're on the way. There's no time for dawdling. What will the teacher say if we're late again?'

Mia fetched a shoe box from a blue plastic recycling bag located outside the back door, as Isabella hurried towards the stairs, the cat no longer at the forefront of her mind.

'Shall I brush my teeth?'

Mia called after her, resisting the almost overwhelming temptation to take her medication. 'Yes, there's a good girl, we always brush our teeth. Wash your face and brush your teeth *really* well. Do that *before* getting dressed. You don't want to get toothpaste on your clothes.'

'Okay, Mummy.'

Mia listened for the bathroom tap before bending at the waist, averting her eyes and lifting the cat by its leather collar, dropping the still warm corpse into the open box and quickly placing the lid on top. She hurriedly put the box outside the back door for later burial in the small walled garden and began washing the kitchen floor, using absorbent paper initially, followed by a wet cloth that had once been a T-shirt. She then threw that into a black bin bag to join the soiled tissues. By the time Isabella shouted out from the top of the stairs only minutes later, the kitchen was pristine once more.

'Can I take dolly to school with me?'

'Yes, yes, of course, you can. But be quick. I'll ring the school, and we'll be on our way. Your doll is on your pillow.'

Mia glanced towards her laptop as Isabella headed to her bedroom. No more emails, thank God. Maybe *he* didn't kill the cat. Perhaps it wasn't him after all. Maybe she was becoming paranoid, as he probably intended. She wanted to believe it. She was desperate to believe it. Then why was she shaking? Why the knots in her gut? Don't let him win, Mia. Don't let the bastard get to you.

Mia picked up the phone, dialled then held it to her face. Keep things as normal as possible for Isabella's sake, that was best. Hold it together, girl. Don't let his sick games cloud your thinking.

Mia didn't see Adam watching from behind a conveniently located high hedge on the opposite side of the street as she left the house hand in hand with Isabella fifteen minutes later. She was trying to stay positive. Attempting to put on a brave face, precariously clinging to a semblance of her former life for Isabella's benefit as much as her own. He focussed on Mia more closely and smiled. She looked brittle, easily broken, psychologically fragile. Caught in a swirling downward spiral from which she couldn't hope to escape, however hard she tried. It was his creation, his achievement, and that felt so very good. His methods were working. He was in control. A puppet master pulling her strings at will. What an incredible sight to behold.

As Mia started the engine and manoeuvred her hatchback out into the street and towards school, Adam stepped out, gaining confidence, watching and waiting until she negotiated the first bend and disappeared from sight. He walked towards the house, feeling infallible now, paying scant attention to the chance of potential passing witnesses or housebound nosy curtain-twitchers as he approached the front door. It was easily opened, in seconds. He had the skills, the experience. Gaining entry posed no problem at all. It was, he'd decided, time to increase the pressure. Time to turn the screw. If the bitch author thought things were bad, they were about to get worse. Worse than she could possibly imagine with that creative intellect of hers. Infinitely worse than any bad dream constructed by her subconscious mind. It was time to blow her brittle world apart. Time to make her squirm.

18

Mia was relieved to find that the morning traffic was somewhat quieter than she'd anticipated as she drove through the picturesque West Wales market town she thought of as home. She put on one of Isabella's favourite music CDs, a compilation of cheery child-friendly hits, and they sang along to one song after another until they arrived at the school gates only ten minutes late.

Mia walked her daughter as far as her open-plan classroom, waved her hand above her head to draw the teacher's attention, apologised profusely for the interruption and then went in search of the headteacher, keen to reinforce her concern that Isabella may face a degree of danger that shouldn't be ignored. The head was sympathetic, supportive – so unlike his secretary – and by the time Mia left the school and drove away about twenty minutes later, she was in slightly better spirits despite the cat's death. The sun was shining, Grav was on her side, her books were still selling well, and she'd finally reduced her medication slightly. It seemed things were looking up at last. There were good times ahead. She'd hang on in there and prevail. Keep saying it, Mia. Drown out your doubts. She wouldn't be beaten – no way, no how. Perhaps life wasn't so bad after all.

Mia found a convenient parking space about five minutes' stroll from her spacious semi-detached home, and she chose to see it as another positive amongst many. Shit happened but good things did too. The small things that made a difference. Why not focus on them and stay positive?

She locked the car, glanced to right and left, then walked along the uneven pavement, avoiding stepping on the cracks as she approached the house. As she reached the front door with its dark-blue paint and the shiny brass furniture that had once meant so much to her, she stopped for a second or two before eventually placing her key in the lock and turning it reticently. She couldn't identify the reason for her reserve, over and above recent events and the symptoms of drug withdrawal she was still so obviously experiencing. There was nothing to see per se, nothing that stood out and grabbed her attention. It was a gut feeling more than reasoned thought. But a feeling that wouldn't let up. An emotional instinct causing her stomach to ache and sending cold shudders up and down her backbone despite the summer warmth.

Mia pushed the door open an inch or two and peered into the hall. Still nothing to see. Nothing out of the ordinary. Maybe she was being silly again. The bastard was getting to her. She was being oversensitive, worrying about nothing at all.

Mia stood and listened on stepping into the hallway, but there was nothing of significance to hear, just the passing traffic in the road behind her and the occasional screech of a soaring gull overhead. She took a big breath, sucking the air deep into her lungs, then lifted one leaden leg after another, as if wading through dark syrup, as she slowly approached the lounge, still unable to shake off her nagging apprehension. Mia didn't notice the cat when she first entered the room. The room's familiarity was reassuring, calming in a day-to-day way. But then there was the feline's corpse in sharp and unrelenting focus, and she asked herself how she could possibly have missed it even for a single second. As if she'd chosen not to see it, as if she'd blanked it from her mind to hold on to her sanity in a menacing world. But now there it was, just feet from where she stood, undeniable, indisputable and seemingly filling the room. Mia tried to turn her head but she couldn't look away. The creature was suspended from the light fitting at the centre point of the lounge, lifeless and dangling from a length of fishing line, its abdomen sliced open and its guts hanging close to the floor.

Mia froze, statue-like, gagged once, then twice, and was about to run from the room and towards the street when her attention was suddenly drawn to a single sheet of paper propped up on the dark wooden mantelpiece, a glowing black candle to either side of it casting flickering shadows on the wall. She realised that she'd been standing there, staring open-mouthed for almost five minutes without moving. She wanted to escape, she was keen to escape and never to enter that room again, but she forced herself to cross the floor, one step, two steps and onwards, until she could clutch that sheet of paper tightly in one hand and retreat, not looking back, never looking back, down the hall and out onto the fragmented concrete pathway that led from the front door to the street. It felt good to be back in the fresh air with the door slammed shut behind her. But she knew she'd never forget that cat. She could still see the poor mutilated creature hanging there in her mind's eye, like some grotesque Halloween installation intended to scare and horrify in equal measure. Like a scene from a fright movie that was all too real. It was seared on her mind forever, never to be erased.

Mia hurried towards her car and checked the rear seat for any potential intruder before jumping in. She locked the doors with a snap movement of her finger the second she landed in the driver's seat, glad of the relative safety the metal shell provided. She was panting hard, her hands trembling, her knees shaking as she reached for her glasses and began reading his typed message with tear-filled eyes, haunted by an image she couldn't hope to delete however hard she tried. She stopped reading, thinking she may pass out at any moment, and then started again, telling herself insistently she had no choice but to continue to the end, that she had to know what it said, however depraved, however profoundly immoral and wicked. She read his communication from the first word to the last, refusing to avert her gaze:

Consider this a warning

Well, hello again, Mia. I'm sorry it's been a few days since I last got in touch. I hope you haven't missed me too much. I've certainly missed you, although I've watched you from time to time as you've struggled through your day. But enough of small talk. There will be plenty of time for that when I consider the time right. Let's get down to business. I think that's best, as I feel sure you'll agree if you can still think clearly enough with that muddled brain that used to serve you so well. I received the photographs you sent me. And, oh, dear, they were such a terrible disappointment. Do you really think I'm that stupid? Did you truly believe you'd get away with it? The images were pleasant enough in themselves. They show everything they need to show in high-definition colour, which was a nice touch that I appreciated. But, the pictures aren't of you, Mia, that's the crucial factor, they're not of you. I'm trying to be forgiving, I'm trying to make allowances for your obvious failings and frailties, but there are limits to my goodwill. I'm only human, after all. Perhaps try again before I lose my patience altogether. Think of the cat's death as a warning. This time it was your pet's turn to suffer, a creature of little, if any, worth. But next time it may be your turn to die. Or I could choose that little girl of yours. The child so blissfully oblivious to the danger she faces due to her mother's many inadequacies. Killing animals has lost its allure. I moved on to humans long ago. It's more rewarding and much more fun. Picture Isabella frothing at the mouth. Picture her on the kitchen floor lying stiff and cold. And picture her hanging by her scrawny neck with her innards spilling out in a bloody tangle, and you'll begin to understand the potential cost of letting me down again. Poison is such a convenient weapon to use in the right hands. Easily available, potentially lethal and surprisingly hard to trace if the right choice is made. Maybe I'll go shopping this afternoon. It's a nice day for it. Or I could abandon the poison and opt for a knife, a hammer or my bare hands next time. The options are virtually endless when you consider it with sufficient enthusiasm. And so don't give me too long to think. That wouldn't be a wise move. I'm sure I could come up with something utterly odious and black-hearted. You've only got twenty four hours this time, and the clock's ticking. I think that's quite generous in the circumstances. It's your last chance to get it right. Your final opportunity to impress with that ageing body of yours. So it's legs open wide and click, click, click. Don't hold anything back, that's my advice. Try to overcome your repressed reticence and throw yourself in. I've almost certainly seen worse. And ensure that your face is clearly visible. Hot, sexy and unambiguous, that's what's required. Send the photos before the time's up or suffer the consequences. It really is as simple as that. I suggest you make the correct decisions this time. Don't ever underestimate me again. That, my dear girl, would be a deadly mistake.

Oh, and one last thing before I let you go. Don't go thinking that the fat detective is going to help you. He's a washed-up drunk. Not an obvious choice when looking for a knight in shining armour to save you. Why approach him of all people?

That's what I asked myself. It baffled me for a time, but then I guess the two of you have a great deal in common. All that pill-popping and the strong wine you're so very fond of. Oh, dear, how very sad! You're spiralling out of control, Mia, unworthy of being a mother. A shadow of the woman you once were. You're an addict, much the same as he is. A pathetic, pitiful junkie clamouring for your next hit. Maybe that's what brought the two of you together in adversity. You're two rotten peas in the same pod, two of a kind. That would explain it well enough, wouldn't you agree? Did you come to the same conclusion as you lie awake at night and think of me, or has your substance misuse addled what's left of your enfeebled mind to such an extent that you don't think at all? You were a successful young woman once upon a time, but not so much any more. I could put you out of your misery, if you like? How does that sound? Maybe you'd be better off dead. Perhaps Isabella would be better off without you. Let's see how well you do with the photos. I'll take a look and we'll decide from there. Bye for now, we'll speak soon.

Love and kisses,

Your number one fan x

Mia's hand trembled as she placed the sheet of paper on the passenger seat for safekeeping. She wanted to tear it to pieces. To fling it out of the window and into the quiet street like confetti at a marriage service, as if it didn't matter, as if it wasn't real. But she knew she couldn't do that. That it may be important. That there could be potential evidence to find. Fingerprints or DNA that gave him away. Maybe he'd made an error this time. Hopefully, he'd become careless, overconfident, complacent. It was time to talk to Grav again. Time to seek his help. The hanging cat was a game-changer. A wake-up call that couldn't be ignored.

19

Mia brought her car to a screeching halt on the two bright-yellow lines bordering Isabella's school gates and left the driver's door hanging open as she raced towards the entrance with a look of unbridled panic etched on her face. She entered the reception at full tilt and came to a skidding halt as the headteacher's PA strode out of her office, arms folded, blocking her path like an obstructive bouncer at a backstreet nightclub.

'Can I help you, *Ms* Hamilton?'

Mia pushed past the secretary, knocking her off balance, and hurried into Isabella's classroom where her daughter was painting a watercolour.

Isabella looked at her mother, then at her teacher, and then at Mia again. 'Is something wrong, Mummy? It's not home time yet. The bell hasn't rung.'

Mia took short, shallow breaths, electing to ignore Miss Fury's confused glare. 'We're going to visit Uncle Grav again. Come on, quickly, we need to be on our way.'

Some children cried, others giggled, as Isabella picked up her school bag and walked towards her mother, taking small, tentative steps. Miss Fury looked on, open-mouthed, lost for words.

Mia took Isabella's hand and spoke out loudly, clearly enunciating each word, as if presenting a lecture to an auditorium full of fools. 'Isabella's not going to be in school for a while. The headteacher knows what's happening. It could be weeks or even months. I don't know when she'll be back.'

'Miss Fury wants to speak to you, Mummy.'

Mia chose to ignore the teacher as she strode after them. She swept her daughter up in her arms and increased her pace, trotting back to the car.

* * *

Mia hammered on Grav's front door, pounding it with the side of each fist in turn, oblivious to the pain and risk of injury, and listened with an overwhelming sense of relief as his heavy footsteps sounded on the hall floor only seconds later. She kept knocking right up the moment he turned the handle and stood to face her, a strained expression on his heavily lined face.

'He killed my cat.'

Grav leaned against the frame, glad of the support. 'Slow down, love, I need to catch my breath.'

She grabbed the front of his shirt with both hands and shook him. 'Didn't you hear me? The maniac killed our cat!'

'Right, I'll tell you what I'm going to do. There's a lovely old lady living next door – Elsie – she used to look after Dewi and Emily sometimes when they were kids. I'm going to ask her to come in and keep an eye on this little princess for us while we talk. What do you think of that? We can have a good chinwag and decide what's for the best.'

Mia relaxed her grip, glanced to the right and left, seeing danger everywhere, and began moving her head up and down like a nodding dog as her need for opioids started to spike. 'He killed our cat.' Quieter this time, almost whispered, as if she couldn't quite believe it herself.

'Take Isabella into the lounge and take a seat, love. I'll be back with you before you know it. You know where the kitchen is if you fancy some refreshments. Treat the place as your own.'

'Is it all right if I lock the door?'

Grav stepped out onto the pavement, squinting as the sun caught his face. 'Yes, you lock it and put the chain on if it makes you feel better. Go on, in you go. Elsie's almost certainly in. I'll be five minutes at most.'

Mia had washed down two tablets with a slurp of French brandy by the time Grav returned to the house in the company of a chubby woman in her late seventies, who reminded Mia of her deceased maternal grandmother.

Grav noted the glass clutched tightly in Mia's hand and hoped it may help her unwind. He made his introductions, attempting to make the process as relaxed and unremarkable as possible, then turned to Isabella with his best smile. 'Elsie here told me she'd *love* to see your school books. Will you show them to her in the kitchen while I talk to your Mum about some boring adult stuff?'

Isabella looked towards Mia, a quizzical expression on her face.

'Yes, go on Izzy, that sounds like a lovely idea.'

The old lady beamed and took Isabella's hand. 'And we can go to buy some sweets after that. There's a shop on the corner.'

Mia tensed, the fine hairs on her nape and arms standing to attention. 'No, not outside, I'd rather you stay in the house.'

Elsie looked back at her, sensing her angst. 'Okay, dear, whatever you say. Now, where are those books?'

Grav waited until he and Mia were alone before closing the lounge door and returning to his seat. 'Right, what's this about, love? Tell me what's happened.'

Mia wiped a tear from her face as unwanted images played behind her eyes, taking her back in time. 'He killed our cat.'

Grav splayed his hands out wide and spoke through his teeth, trying not to show his frustration. 'Yes, you've told me that, love, but I need to know the details. Take your time and tell me exactly what's happened, from the beginning. Do you think you can do that for me?'

Mia spent the next ten minutes telling her story, outlining events from the moment she'd arrived back at her home to the time she'd rushed out to collect Isabella from school.

Grav felt a heavy feeling deep in the pit of his stomach, a sudden coldness hitting his core. 'Okay, I need you to understand that this changes things. The bastard has been in your house. You're in danger, your little girl's in danger. I've encountered men like him before. We can't take any risks.'

'So, what happens now?'

Grav leaned towards her. 'It's time to call in the cavalry. This isn't something I can deal with on my own.'

'I don't want to go to the police station.'

The detective felt inclined to tell her she was being ridiculous, but he glanced up at Heather's disapproving face and swallowed his words. 'Right, I'll tell you what I'm going to do. I'm going to talk to Laura Kesey; she's acting up in my absence. She's a great girl, you're going to like her. She's an excellent detective. I'm going to speak to her, put her fully in the picture and bring her to you. She can interview you here while I keep an eye on the little princess. I'll ring Laura now and tell Elsie she can go home. We're not going to need her any more. Is that a plan you can agree to?'

Mia looked back at him with a blank look of resignation, her shoulders slumped. 'I guess there's no other choice.'

'You're spot on, love. Let's get it done.'

20

Detective Constable Peter Best knocked on Acting Detective Inspector Laura Kesey's office door and opened it without waiting to be invited in. Kesey looked up from her seemingly endless piles of paperwork and spoke with a distinct Brummie twang that some found challenging to decipher, despite its increasing familiarity. 'Morning, George, what can I do for you?'

'Do you have to use my nickname?'

Kesey smiled. 'Sorry, Peter, it's stuck in my head. My partner's a Man United fan.'

He squinted as shards of bright sunshine broke through the marble clouds and illuminated the room. 'The car involved in the fatal hit-and-run I'm looking into has been found in the estuary in Ferryside. It's on the coast about eight miles from here, do you know it?'

Kesey swivelled slowly in her seat, approached a large picture window with a partial view of the town and adjusted the blinds. 'The Turner case was my first murder investigation in this part of the world after I left the West Midlands force. It was the middle of winter, with snow everywhere. Kieran ran me to Ferryside in the

four-wheel drive, poor sod, after body parts were found on the
beach by a local GP. It's not a place I'm likely to forget in a hurry.
It'll be ingrained in my psyche until my dying day.'

'Ah, yes, of *course*, I should have realised. Kieran was one of the
good guys.'

'One of the best!'

'It's hard to accept he's dead.'

Kesey nodded, the past all too vivid right up to the moment she
drove it from her mind. 'Was the car actually in the water?'

'Yeah, I'm afraid so, completely submerged until the tide
changed and left it stranded in the muddy area close to the water
line. The windows and one door had been left open, so it just
poured in. Whoever dumped it where they did knew exactly what
they were doing. They couldn't have chosen a better spot.'

'So, there's not much chance of finding anything useful.'

'Is there any hope at all?'

Kesey approached the kettle, silently wishing she was still on
maternity leave as opposed to in the office talking business. 'Probably not, but that doesn't mean we shouldn't try. If a job's worth
doing, it's worth doing well. That's what my old mum used to say.
Where's the car now?'

'A local tractor dragged it off the beach and into the car park
when the tide receded. I've arranged for it to be brought back to the
station as soon as possible. It should be here in an hour or two, all
being well. A local garage is taking care of it for me.'

'Have you told them the do's and don'ts?'

'Yeah, I spoke to the mechanic in charge. He'll see it's all done
properly.'

'Thinking about it, maybe pop down there yourself and super-
vise. We don't want any cock-ups.'

'Will do.'

Kesey allowed the wall to support her weight. 'Good lad, keep me in the loop, and I'll get the scenes of crime people to give it a good going over as soon as it arrives. You never know your luck, there may be a chassis number to find if nothing else.'

'Whoever drove the car had the sense to clone it. And false plates aren't easy to get hold of. I can't see it happening.'

She shook her head slowly and deliberately. 'No, you're probably right, that would be too much to ask for. My bet is any identification marks have either been obliterated or changed... any progress with your wider enquiries?'

'The genuine vehicle registered to the index number was parked at Luton Airport at the relevant time. Same make of car, same model, same colour – clever really. Anyone running a check on our local car would have come up with the details of that one. I talked with the airport police. They've checked the security cameras. There's no doubt the car was there the entire time.'

'So, it looks as if the hit-and-run could have been planned.'

The DC nodded. 'It's a possibility we've got to consider.'

'Any joy with a description of the driver?'

'I've interviewed all the known eyewitnesses for what it's worth.'

Kesey's brow furrowed. 'For what it's worth? What's that supposed to mean?'

'It was the end of the night, they'd all been drinking heavily, and no one got a clear view of the driver. Or at least not that they were telling me about. A local man in his mid-thirties thought the driver may have had blond hair, but couldn't be sure, and a second onlooker, a student nurse in her early twenties, thought the driver may have been a man wearing glasses. I asked her how certain she was, and she said fifty-fifty. It's next to useless. Any half-decent defence barrister would tear it apart without breaking a sweat.'

'Oh, for fuck's sake!'

Best grinned, tickled by her candour. 'I haven't heard you swear before.'

'It's been a long week... have you got time for a coffee? I'm making one anyway.'

He pushed up his shirtsleeve and checked his watch. 'I was hoping to finish early, ma'am. It's the wife's birthday.'

She poured herself a cup, adding powdered milk, unusual for her, but no sugar. 'Is that a no?'

'Not for me, thanks.'

Kesey sipped her coffee and winced as the boiling water burnt her lip. 'Are there any cameras between the location of the incident and the dumping ground?'

'Not unless he went through town. It seems unlikely to me. It wouldn't be hard to avoid the main streets if you know the area.'

'Yeah, that's what I thought. I'll ask one of the probationers to spend a few hours checking anyway. There's no point in wasting the time of a more experienced officer.'

'Thanks, ma'am, it makes sense.'

Kesey returned to her seat, placing her cup on her desk. 'Okay, get yourself down to Ferryside, sort the car out and ask some questions. Knock on a few doors. Talk to the locals. Someone may have seen the driver. It's our best shot unless something unforeseen happens. Once that's done, your time is your own. You've got some owing. And say happy birthday to Sonia for me. If she's married to you, she's got a lot to put up with.'

He gave her a knowing look. 'Thanks a bunch, she tells me much the same thing with surprising regularity.'

Kesey smiled, glad to have raised the mood but keen to get back to business. 'If you get a decent description, let me know straight away, yeah? You can get me on my mobile and leave a message if I'm otherwise engaged. I'm planning to discuss a potential press release with the chief super first thing tomorrow morning. To ask for the public's help. Has anyone seen anything? That sort of thing. The more information we've got to share, the better. You never know, someone may give us a name.'

The DC pulled his tie loose at the collar, approached the door and stopped. 'Any news on the DI, ma'am?'

'Not a great deal. It's been some time since I've seen him.'

'Is he coming back, or will you be taking over full time? That's what I meant to ask. The place just isn't the same without him. Not that you're not doing a good job, or anything like that. I wasn't suggesting...'

Kesey picked up a blue cardboard file from the top of the pile. 'I'd stop digging if I were you, George, the hole's big enough already. You don't want to be back in uniform and directing traffic for the rest of your career.'

He looked back at her sheepishly, unsure if she was joking but very much hoping she was. 'So, is there any news?'

'I'm getting together with the boss later this afternoon, as it happens. It seems he's got something important to discuss. He's had me making a few phone calls in preparation for the meeting.'

'It sounds as if he may be onto something.'

'It wouldn't surprise me.'

'Can I ask what it's about?'

Kesey shook her head. 'I'm going to keep it to myself for now. Need to know, you understand what I'm saying.'

'Do you think he'll be back?'

'Let's hope so. As soon as he tells me anything, I'll let the team know. I'm as in the dark as you are.'

21

Grav was standing at the bar engaged in animated conversation with Liz, the regular, long-suffering, busty bottle-blonde barmaid, when Kesey entered the room. He winked at Liz, enjoying one last appreciative glance at her impressive cleavage as he turned to greet his fellow officer. 'Well, hello, Laura, long time no see. What are you going to have, love?'

Kesey smiled warmly and threw her arms around the big detective, hugging him tightly with genuine affection. 'It's terrific to see you again, boss. You're looking wonderful.'

Grav laughed, head back, Adam's apple protruding only slightly in his fleshy throat. 'Oh, come on, don't go overdoing things. I've never looked wonderful in my life, passable possibly, but nothing more. I've never been a looker. Heather used to tell me that all the time. "Lived in." I think that's how she used to put it. "Like an old comfortable slipper."'

Kesey released her grip and grinned back at him. 'Well, you look pretty good to me. How are you doing? Are you feeling any better? You look as if you've lost a bit of weight.'

He patted his overhanging beer belly. 'Oh, could be worse, I suppose. Things can always be worse. Look on the bright side, isn't that how the song goes?'

Kesey laughed, comfortable with his familiar banter. 'What are you going to have to drink, love?'

'Just a coffee for me, thanks.'

Grav shook his head forlornly. 'Some things never change. Drinking coffee in a rugby club: that's sacrilege. I don't know if Liz will ever get over the shock.'

He raised a hand and waved to the barmaid, attracting her attention as she rearranged some bottled beers on a low shelf to little effect.

'One pint of bitter and a coffee, please Liz, my lovely. Black without sugar if I recall correctly.'

Kesey nodded her confirmation as Grav handed Liz a crumpled ten-pound note.

Liz held the note up to the light. 'Take a seat, Grav, I'll bring them over. Do you want anything to eat?'

'Yeah, I'll have one of your gourmet pasties. What about you Laura, are you eating?'

'Nothing for me, thanks. I had a sandwich in the canteen.'

'Just the pasty, please, Liz. Nice and greasy mind, just like you usually make them.'

'Yeah, hilarious as always, the old ones are always the best. Do you want it heated up?'

'Warmed by your fair hands with a bit of brown sauce will be perfect.'

Liz sighed dramatically, blowing the air from her mouth. 'Do you want the change, or shall I put it in the charity box?'

'Stick it in the box as usual. What do I want with a bunch of coins?'

Grav led Kesey to his favourite table in a far corner of the room behind a worn-out pool table. 'So, how's life for an acting DI?'

'Busy.'

'Tell me about it.'

'I appreciated you recommending me.'

He looked up as Liz delivered their order to the table and winked once before she turned and walked away. 'Yeah, I must have been pissed, either that or delirious with anaesthetic.'

Kesey gave him a playful nudge. '"The best person for the job by far!" That's what you told the chief super. She told me that herself. I made a note of it in my diary.'

'Yeah, okay, you've got me. You're a good detective, Laura, who else was I going to recommend?'

She sipped her coffee as he sank his teeth into his pasty, leaving pastry crumbs all over his shirtfront.

'I want you to know I'm grateful. I don't think it would have happened without your input. Some more experienced officers missed out.'

'I'm glad the move to Wales worked out.'

'It was the best decision I've ever made. That and asking Janet to marry me. My life's changed so much in a relatively short time.'

Grav seemed more upbeat all of a sudden, his melancholy dissipating. 'Emily mentioned that you're a mum now. Was she right?'

Kesey beamed. 'Yeah, Edward, he's two months old. An old university friend acted as a sperm donor. Not exactly the most conventional way of going about things, but it worked for us.'

'Is he going to be involved with the child?'

'The three of us are talking. We'll work something out.'

Grav decided not to pursue the matter. 'I'm sure you'll do what's best.'

'I've never felt more fulfilled or more tired. I wish my mum wasn't quite so far away, that's the one downside of leaving the Midlands.'

'Yeah, I get that. Extended family matters when you've got young ones.'

'We want you to be a Godfather.'

'You're asking *me*, really?' Grav's voice rose in pitch.

'Of course, you.'

'Are you sure Janet's up for it?'

'She's my partner, do you really think I'd have asked you without her agreement?'

He cleared his throat, feeling emotional, and looking away for fear of blubbering. 'In that case, I'd be honoured.'

'We were hoping you'd say that.'

'I'm pleased for you both, love. Really I am. He's a lucky boy.'

'It was a long time coming. We were beginning to think it was never going to happen. We'd even considered adoption. We'd had a social worker to the house to start the application process.'

He took a swig of beer. 'That's the way it works sometimes. A similar thing happened to a mate of mine.'

Kesey nodded and picked up her coffee cup as Grav's expression became more serious. He raised a hand to his face in mock salute, his palm facing forwards and open. 'How has her majesty been since my illness?'

'The chief super?'

'Who else?'

'Oh, she's missing you terribly.'

Grav grinned. 'Oh, yeah, I'm sure she is. I bet she's praying I don't come back at all.'

'Well, screw her. I'm hoping that you do. We all are.'

'But not so much the top brass.'

Kesey gripped her chin. 'No, maybe not!'

'I suppose you're wondering why I've asked to see you?'

'Well, yeah, I am curious.'

Grav's eyes lit up as he focussed on the job. 'Did you make the enquiries we discussed?'

'Yeah, I came up with three recent cases fitting the bill.'

'Around here?'

'Two in the South Wales force area and one in Gwent.'

'So what happened?'

'All three women went missing after receiving threatening emails. They still haven't been found.'

Grav sighed, forcing the air from his lungs through his nostrils. 'How much time passed between them receiving the final messages and disappearing?'

Kesey opened her black plastic-covered pocketbook and consulted her notes, confirming what she already knew. 'It varied from days to several weeks. The first woman, a teacher in her mid-twenties, disappeared after just four days when she ignored the emails altogether. The other two were both in their mid-thirties. One went missing after twenty-two days and the other after forty-one. All the emails were written in a similar language, containing threats, manipulative statements and criticisms that appear to be intended to undermine the recipients' confidence and self-esteem. He's playing with their psychological wellbeing until he's ready to attack, that's my assessment. Breaking them down before snatching them when he thinks the time's right. Whether they're dead or not is a matter of conjecture. But what we can say with certainty is that there's no trace of any of the three, despite extensive enquiries. We could be talking about a serial killer. I think that's a logical conclusion. Someone who's hunting and killing within a defined geographical area he's likely to know well. What you always used to refer to as a *zone of comfort*.'

Grav nodded. 'Yeah, I can't say I'm surprised. He sounds like a right psycho. Something told me it was more than a stalking case.

Have the respective forces had any luck tracking down the source of the emails?'

'No, not as yet, although it seems blatantly obvious they're dealing with the one perpetrator. Everyone seems to agree on that. There's a coordinated effort attempting to identify him as we speak. It's proving a lot more difficult than anyone anticipated. He's one slippery sod, I'll give him that much.'

'I had a horrible feeling you were going to say that.'

'What's this about, boss? Is there something I need to know?' Grav spent the next fifteen minutes succinctly outlining events, starting with the recent email he'd received and then moving on to Mia's two visits to his home. Kesey sat and listened, asking pertinent questions when she thought it appropriate and jotting down the occasional note in blue ink for later reference. 'So both sisters claim they kept Mia's visit to themselves?'

'That's what they say.'

'It seems unlikely to me.'

'It's a small town. Any number of people would have known we were family friends. He could have threatened me on the off chance she'd turn up at some point.'

Kesey's eyes narrowed. 'Maybe.'

'It's a possibility, that's all I'm saying.'

'And this Mia's at your house now?'

'Yeah, they both are, the mother and the daughter.'

'And, she's dead against making it formal?'

'She's crapping herself, that's the bottom line. The scrote's got her believing he's some sort of superhuman who watches her every move. I'm hoping that talking to you persuades her to make a statement, woman to woman, know what I'm saying? You're good at that sort of stuff. Play to our strengths. Work as a team. That's what I taught you. Let's use that to our advantage.'

Kesey met his eyes. 'Okay, I get that, but why didn't you bring them here with you? It's quiet enough. Liz could have opened up the snug if needed. Why leave them at the house?'

'Mia's a nervous wreck. If you're going to talk to her, I thought it was best done somewhere familiar. Her parents used to bring her to visit when she was a kid. I think she feels safe in my place. Or at least as safe as she feels anywhere in the current circumstances. Leaving her where she was seemed like the most sensible option if we're going to gain her cooperation.'

'Right, I get your point, small steps. It must have seriously freaked the poor woman out when she walked in to find the cat hanging in her lounge like that. I wouldn't fancy it.'

Grav's face took on a sullen expression which seemed to age him. 'Yeah, and knowing the bastard has been in her house can't be easy to come to terms with. The situation has escalated from threatening messages to a home invasion in a surprisingly short time. She's got to be asking herself what's coming next. Anyone would be. He's got under her skin. We've got to find a way of convincing her we can keep them both safe until he's arrested and convicted. Once that's achieved, we're winning.'

'You won't hear me arguing.'

Grav drained his glass. 'Okay, it sounds as if we're on the same page. Are you ready to make a move?'

'You lead the way. I'll follow in my car.'

'I can drop you back here if that's easier?'

'No, you're all right, thanks, boss. I'll speak to Mia for as long as it takes and get straight off. There's somewhere I need to be. Hopefully, we can get a statement down on paper and progress matters from there. The quicker we catch the vicious bastard, the happier I'll be.'

22

Mia sat in a sunny window alcove and stared at her phone as it continued to ring.

'Are you going to answer it, Mummy?'

Mia forced a brittle smile. 'Um... yes, yes, it may be Aunty Ella or the nice policeman we came to visit.'

Mia lifted the mobile to her face and said, 'Hello,' in a tentative voice that reverberated raw emotion.

Adam didn't speak at first, sensing her discomfort and making her wait. Because he liked it. Because he could. 'Well, hello there, Mia. I hope you enjoyed the small gift I left you. And you received my letter, I presume. I'm certain you'll have read it by now. I like to think the contents are self-explanatory. Do you still love me as much as I admire you? I hope so for your sake.'

Mia let out a loud guttural groan which Isabella appeared to find strangely amusing and disconcerting in equal proportions.

Mia searched for the correct words, the right phrases, something that may shatter his hard shell. She wanted him to understand the distress he'd caused, not yet realising it gave him nothing but pleasure. She opened her mouth as if to speak but all was silent.

He could hear her breathing and pictured the rise and fall of her chest. 'Are you still there, Mia?'

'Yes, I'm still here.'

'Are you in pain, my girl? You sound as if you're suffering to me.'

Mia parted her lips and blurted out the words, 'How did you get this number?'

He chuckled to himself, honing in on the vibrating worry in her voice, aroused by it. 'Oh, dear, you sound as if you're in a dreadful state. Confused, perplexed, as if your situation has become infinitely more burdensome than you can possibly tolerate. I don't think you're nearly as capable as you like to think you are. Is that the problem?'

Mia tensed her pelvic floor muscles, fighting to control her bladder as it threatened to soak the carpet. 'How did you get the number?'

He laughed again, genuinely amused. 'Well, you are a surprisingly determined creature. How did I get it? How did I get it? Now, let me think... ah, yes, that's it. You gave your number to the fat detective, and now I've got it. Think about that and consider the implications for a moment or two if you will. Don't ever go thinking you've escaped me, Mia. That could be a fatal error. I know exactly where you are every second of every day. Maybe I'm watching you now. Look behind you. Perhaps I'm ready to pounce.'

She placed a protective arm around Isabella's shoulder and pulled her close. 'Please leave us alone.'

He snorted disdainfully. 'What, after everything you've done to hurt my feelings? I told you exactly what would happen if you failed to follow my instructions. I warned you time and again! Did you think I'm not a man of my word? Are you questioning my integrity? It wouldn't go well for you if you are. There are some extremely unpleasant ways to die. Some of my previous victims discovered that to their cost. I can still hear them screaming in my dreams. It's music to my ears. A joyous sound I've come to love above all else. You may join them soon enough. Now, wouldn't that be nice? Or perhaps you don't share my interests.'

There was something about his voice that seemed familiar, just occasionally, a word here, a word there, the hint of an accent that resonated in her mind. A familiarity which raised her confidence momentarily, as if he were just an ordinary man and not the dark-clad monster she'd built up in her mind. 'What the hell is wrong with you? You're sick, mentally ill. You need help!'

'Oh, dear, now you're becoming rather unpleasant in that way you sometimes do. Naughty, naughty! That won't do you any good at all. Look out of the window, Mia. Can you see me peering in? I could be hiding behind a hedge or high wall, or passing from time to time in the van, lorry or car. Scan the street. Watch and listen. I'm coming after you. I'm coming after Isabella too, and you can't hope to protect her. Are all the doors locked? And the windows, have you checked the windows? I'd only need the slightest opportunity to get in. Or maybe I'm already in the house – a shadow on the wall, an apparition, a grey spectre come to haunt you. Have you considered that very real possibility? Listen Mia, can you hear me moving? One step, two steps, coming towards you, nearer, nearer, or motionless and silent, waiting to swoop. I could be hidden in a wardrobe or the attic, secret, invisible. I could be almost anywhere, clutching a knife or a length of rope or a hammer with which to shatter your splintery skull. I could be observing you now, feasting on your lack of confidence and fear, drinking it in.'

'*Please* leave us alone.'

He spoke in a mocking voice now, mimicking her efforts to appease him. '*Please, please*, Mr Nasty Man. *Please* won't help you! I've heard the word before, more times than you could ever imagine. Tell me you love me, Mia. That's your best hope. It may persuade me to let your brat live awhile. You could beg. You could fall to your knees and plead your case. I *may* be merciful, but probably not. Killing is *so* much fun, you see. I enjoy it too much. Tell me you love me, Mia. I'm your number one fan.'

'Okay, I'm begging you, if that's what you want to hear. I'm pleading with you. I'll tell you anything you want. Please back off.'

He counted to five in his head before responding. 'No, I don't think so. Where would be the fun in that?'

Mia dropped the phone to the floor, swept Isabella up in her arms and ran for the stairs, her white socks flashing as she ascended to the top.

'What's wrong, Mummy? Why are you crying?'

'It's a game, just a game, like hide and seek. We're going to hide in the bathroom and lock the door until the nice policeman gets back to the house.'

'Will he look for us?'

Mia was panting hard as she reached the landing, white in the face, half expecting her tormentor to appear and grab one or both of them at any moment. 'Yes, Izzy, he'll look for us.'

Mia opened one door, peering into an unkempt bedroom, and then another door, finding the bathroom on the second attempt. 'Come on, in we go. I'll lock the door, and we'll be very quiet. Like a little mouse not making a sound.'

Mia held Isabella's hand tightly in hers and stared at the closed door. The lock seemed so inadequate, the protection it provided so horribly insufficient.

'Are we still hiding, Mummy?'

She spoke in a whisper. 'Yes, Izzy, we are.'

Mia lowered herself to the floor and huddled in a corner to the side of the bath with her daughter immediately next to her. She attempted to stand with the sudden intention of retrieving her phone, but her legs failed her, numb, lacking the necessary strength to lift her upright, as if injected with some form of anaesthetic. It was no good. A lost cause. She just couldn't bring herself to do it however hard she tried. 'Lie flat down in the bath, Isabella, and I'll cover you with towels. That will be a good place to hide. Try to make yourself smaller. He'll never find you then.'

The little girl followed her mother's instructions with unbridled enthusiasm, but Mia feared it was hopeless. If the monster man came, she'd almost certainly lose. If he appeared as threatened, she'd likely fail to protect the one person who mattered most. How could she hope to fight him? How could she possibly stand her ground? All she could do was wait for Grav to return and pray that he arrived before the hunter found them. Their lives were in the ageing detective's hands. It was that simple.

Mia raised herself to her knees, placed the palms of her hands together and began praying to an almighty creator whose existence she often doubted. She spoke out the words, ever so quietly, so that even Isabella couldn't hear her clearly. 'Please, God, please let us live. I'll be a better mother and a better person. I'll even start going to church if you really want me to. I went to Sunday school as a child. Do you remember? *Please* don't let Isabella die. Not here, not now, she's got her whole life to live. She's far too young for that.'

23

Grav entered his lounge with Kesey in close attendance, surprised and concerned not to find Mia ready and waiting as she'd promised. He poked his head through the kitchen door without success and then hurried back towards the hall where he called out in a hoarse smoker's rattle, 'Mia, it's Grav, I've got DI Kesey with me, where are you, love?'

Mia didn't reply, temporarily lost for words and doubting everything and everyone.

Grav turned towards Kesey, meeting her eyes. 'Her car's still outside, she's got to be here somewhere.'

Kesey nodded. 'Maybe in the garden?'

He called out again, louder this time, making himself heard. 'Hello, Mia, it's Grav, love. Where the hell are you?'

Mia looked at Isabella as she sat upright in the bath, but she still didn't reply.

'Are we still hiding, Mummy? Is the policeman going to find us?'

Mia rose to her feet, suddenly stronger. 'Yes, that's right. Do you think it's him calling to us?'

Isabella nodded enthusiastically, glad the game was over.

'Are you sure? Did you recognise his voice?'

Isabella nodded again, more assuredly this time, then smiled before climbing out of the bath and onto the linoleum-covered floor.

Mia unlocked the door, pulling the bolt back tentatively, as Grav began climbing the stairs, each step creaking under his weight.

She opened the door an inch or two and peered out, her relief almost tangible when she saw his familiar face. 'Oh, thank goodness you're here. I'd almost given up on you. I thought it might be *him.*'

Grav smiled, keen to put her at her ease. 'You're safe now, love. Come on down and talk to DI Kesey. I'll put the kettle on. A nice cup of tea will do us all some good.'

Mia began descending the staircase with Isabella close behind, as Kesey joined Grav in the hallway. She reached out and shook Mia's hand with a surprisingly firm grip. 'It's good to meet you, Mia. The boss has put me in the picture. And this must be Isabella. What a pretty girl you are.'

The little girl looked up and relaxed, taking her mother's lead, as Mia took reassurance from the officers' presence. 'He's been on the phone!'

Grav headed towards the kitchen, allowing Kesey to take the lead. 'What, here?'

'On my new mobile, it's a pay-as-you-go. I can't understand how he got the number.'

'Who've you given it to?'

'Just Grav, nobody else at all.'

'What, not even your sister?'

'No!'

'You're certain?'

'One hundred per cent.'

Kesey looked far from convinced. 'Where's the mobile now?'

'I dropped it on the floor in the sitting room.'

Kesey led the way. 'Let's all take a seat, and we'll progress matters from there, one step at a time.' She spotted the purple mobile on the floor, half-hidden by an old oak table leg, and bent down easily to pick it up. 'Do you mind if I keep this? We can get you another to replace it easily enough.'

Mia sat herself down on a worn but comfortable armchair with Isabella perched on her knees, the girl still thinking that the game of hide and seek wasn't nearly as much fun as she'd expected. 'Yes, no problem, I'll be glad to be rid of the damned thing.'

Kesey looked up as Grav suddenly reappeared, carrying an old tin tray laden with three non-matching mugs of tea, a tall glass of blackcurrant squash and a plate of chocolate biscuits that were well past their sell-by date. He placed the tray on the coffee table, picked up his mug, took a slurp of hot tea and gave Isabella his best smile. 'Why don't we go upstairs and have our drinks in Emily's old bedroom? There are still some of her dolls in a cupboard there somewhere. We can have a good look for them while your Mum talks to Laura. What do you think? You can choose a doll to keep if you like.'

Kesey spoke up and said, 'We'll need to talk about what's happened, *in detail*,' when Mia stalled.

'Oh, that sounds like fun, Izzy, up you go with Uncle Grav, and I'll come and see what you've found in a few minutes' time. Think of a nice name for the dolly when you choose one.'

Isabella stood reticently with her mum's continued encouragement as Grav picked up the tray. Interviewer and interviewee waited for them to leave the room, both women giving a little wave of their hands when Isabella stopped and stared back upon reaching the door.

Kesey opened her pocketbook, rested it on her lap, took a pen from her handbag and met Mia's hesitant gaze. 'Right, Mia, you know who I am. DI Gravel has explained exactly what's been happening. It can't have been easy. You've been going through a tough time. That seems pretty obvious. But I want you to know that I'm here to help. I will do *whatever* it takes to keep you safe and to catch the man who's done these things.'

Mia scratched her head. 'He said he'd kill Isabella if I talked to the police. He said he'd hurt my little girl.'

Kesey nodded, feeling genuine sympathy, parent to parent. 'As the mother of a young child myself, I can understand how truly awful those threats must have been. And then having him break into your house must have been ghastly. Especially with finding the cat as you did. But we *can* protect you. We can keep you safe. Whoever he is. I can't stress that sufficiently. Whoever sent you those messages pressured you into not contacting us because he knows we can catch him. He knew that avoiding a police investigation was his best chance of staying free. We can lock him up with your help. Are you ready to make a statement?' Mia shut her eyes for a few seconds, struggling to come to terms with her new reality. She pictured the cat, that poor mutilated creature, ruminated on the monster man's many threatening remarks and then opened her eyes with a newfound resolve she hadn't known existed. It was time to fight, for herself, for Isabella. There was no way she was going to let the bastard win. 'What do you need from me?'

Kesey broke into a smile, relieved more than anything else, and opened her pocketbook at an appropriate page, marked by an oversized paperclip. 'I know that you've told the boss all the pertinent facts, but I want to hear them from you myself. I want you to start at the very beginning, when you received that first email, and then move on to tell me everything that's happened since. If you've had any suspicions, any hypotheses as to whom may be behind all this, don't hesitate to tell me about it. Even if it now seems ridiculous to you. We can rule people out easily enough. If you suspect or have suspected anyone, give me the names. Gut instincts can sometimes prove to be surprisingly reliable. Grav taught me that.'

'Um... there really isn't anyone who springs to mind. I did think it may be my ex for a short while, but I'm certain it's not him. It's got to the point where I'm not thinking straight. I'm chasing shadows.'

'Was there anything specific that brought him to mind?'

'I don't want to waste your time. I wasn't thinking logically.'

Kesey poised her pen above the first blank page. 'Give me his full name, address and date of birth. It won't do any harm to run a few checks.'

Mia provided the information as requested. 'Do you know if he's got a record?'

'Not that I'm aware of. He used to smoke a bit of weed when he was younger from what he told me, but I don't think he was ever caught.'

'I'm only interested in violence or threats of violence.'

'No, nothing like that. He's never been physically aggressive.' Kesey finished writing her notes and looked up. 'Okay, that's helpful. Now, unless there's anyone else we need to talk about, we'll focus back on the emails.'

Mia shook her head slowly, to the right, to the left, and then back again.

'I want you to start with the first message you received. Tell me everything that happened, everything you did, everything you said, everyone you talked to. I need to hear it all. And we'll need to look at your computer, of course. That's going to be crucial.'

'Grav told me to hold on to it.'

'Yeah, I get where he was coming from before the whole cat business, but things have changed. It now looks as if we're dealing with a perpetrator who has done this sort of thing before. I need to be honest with you. We know of three other women who have been sent very similar emails. All three recipients are now missing.'

Mia's eyes popped. 'Oh, my God, are you saying he killed them?'

'We can't say that with any certainty, but we have to accept that it's a distinct possibility. Extensive efforts to find the women have failed.'

The colour drained from Mia's already pasty features as she rose to her feet. 'I need to take a tablet. I'm going to fetch a glass of water from the kitchen, if that's okay?'

Kesey hid her frustration well. 'Yes, yes, of *course*, no problem at all. Getting things right is far more important than rushing things. Take as long as you need.'

Mia returned to her seat a couple of minutes later, feeling slightly less tense but still anxious for the effects of the medication to fully kick in. Not so much a high, but to feel ordinary, as she had in the long gone past before illness changed the rules. 'I can't go home, not with Isabella, not until he's caught.'

Kesey reached out and squeezed her hand. 'No, I wouldn't want you to do that, not for a second. Your safety has to come first.'

'So what happens now?'

'Right, to reiterate, we're going to go through everything that's happened very carefully and then get something down on paper. We'll do that as soon as you're ready. I just need to check where your computer is as of now?'

Mia looked towards the hall and smiled as Isabella laughed upstairs, as if everything was okay. As if she faced no danger at all.

'You were about to tell me about your computer.'

'It's in the house, on the kitchen counter.'

'And the letter he left you?'

'On the front seat of my car.'

'Okay, we can attend to those things later. Are you ready to make a start?'

Mia nodded, looking a lot more ready than she felt. 'Then off you go.'

Mia spent the next forty minutes telling her story with emotion and passion, leaving nothing out and expanding on any fact, feeling or opinion Kesey chose to clarify. Grav and Isabella appeared at one point, Isabella holding a dark-haired doll dressed in a brightly coloured flamenco dress brought back from a holiday on the Costa Del Sol decades earlier, but they returned back upstairs on the pretext of finding a doll's house in the cluttered attic, when Kesey stated she needed more time.

When the statement was finally finished, Kesey told Mia to read it through carefully and then asked, 'Is there anything you want to change or add, or are you ready to sign?'

Mia froze momentarily, the monster man's threats still playing on her mind, but things had moved on, he'd been in her home, sullied it forever and killed the cat too, that innocent pet that became part of his game. Mia poised her pen above the paper and signed with a flourish. It was time to make a stand. Time to fight back. She was, she told herself, going to do whatever was required to assist the police in their quest. She wasn't safe, Isabella wasn't safe, and they weren't going to be until the bastard was caught and imprisoned. Here was hoping he wouldn't prove as hard to find as he liked to make out.

Kesey smiled, folded the statement forms and placed them in her handbag for safekeeping. 'Just to be clear, Mia, you're ready and willing to give evidence in court if and when the perpetrator is arrested and prosecuted, yes?'

Mia's facial contours changed as the muscles tensed. 'What do you mean if?'

'Three police forces are looking for him as of now, that's a lot of resources. We're looking for a killer. It's going to be a no-expense-spared investigation. There are no guarantees in my line of work, but I'm confident in saying that it's just a matter of time. I will not rest until he's arrested, prosecuted and put away for a very long time.'

Mia relaxed slightly, reassured by the intensity of Kesey's declaration but still wanting more. 'Do I have your word?'

Kesey moved to the edge of her seat, leaned towards Mia and placed a hand on her shoulder. 'You have my word. I want him caught as much as you do.'

'So, what happens next?'

'Well, the first priority is keeping you safe while the investigation progresses.'

'We can't go back to the house, not after he's been there. I'm not sure I can ever go through the front door again.'

Kesey nodded her agreement. 'No, I think we've established that well enough. Is there anyone you could stay with for however long it takes?'

'There are only my sister and her fiancé here in town, but their place is small. It just wouldn't be practical, even if they were in agreement. And maybe staying in Carmarthen isn't such a good idea at the moment anyway. I'm not sure we'd be any safer.'

'I could talk to the chief superintendent regarding the use of a safe house, somewhere away from town. I can't see her objecting in the circumstances. What do you think?'

Mia thought for a moment, quickly rejecting the possibility. 'I could stay at my mum and dad's place in Sorrento. They've got a lovely Roman villa overlooking the sea.'

'Do they know what's happening?'

Mia shook her head. 'No, I haven't told them as yet. Mum's not too well, given her arthritis, and they've had enough worry in their lives, what with my cancer diagnosis. I'll tell them when I get there. It's better they hear it from me than somebody else. It's going to be all over the media soon enough, and Dad still buys the British papers.'

'Is that something you can do quickly?'

'Yes, I don't see why not. I just need to ring them, book the flights, and we can be on our way. They'll be over the moon to see Isabella again. Mum says she misses her terribly.'

'Are you going to do all that today?'

'Yes, straight away, the quicker we're on the plane, the better.'

'Where are your passports?'

'In a drawer at my house.'

'Which room?'

'The master bedroom.'

'I'm going to arrange for scenes of crime officers to go over every inch of the place as soon as we're done here. They can collect the passports, your computer and anything else you need at the same time. It would be helpful if you could make a list of everything you're going to need for the trip.'

Mia's expression became darker, her anxiety betrayed by her face. 'I'm running short on tablets. I'm going to have to see my doctor at some point before we go. It's usually a few days before I can get an appointment. That's going to screw things right up.'

'It doesn't have to. I can sort that out with the principal police surgeon without any problem. She's always ready to help when called on. Just tell me exactly what you need and why, and I'll ensure you get it. How does that suit?'

Mia's relief was evident. 'That would be wonderful, thank you.' She wrote her requirements on a single sheet of paper, ensuring it was legible, and handed it to Kesey.

'I'll ask her to arrange for a prescription to be delivered.'

'Here?'

'We'll have to talk to Grav first, but yes, I can't see that being a problem. I want you to make the necessary arrangements for your trip from here, maybe even stay the night if you can't get any flights until tomorrow. Only tell those who really have to know. And when you do, stress how essential it is that they keep it to themselves. I'll contact Isabella's school to inform them that she's going to be absent for an indefinite time by necessity, but – and this is crucial – I will not be telling them where she's going to be. The fewer people who know, the better. I'll speak directly to the head. We're on a local child protection committee together. I feel certain he'll be entirely cooperative.'

'You're taking my laptop, right?'

'I'm afraid so. There's no avoiding it. There could be crucial evidence to find.'

'I'm going to need a new one. I've got a writing deadline looming. I need to continue working.'

Kesey nodded. 'Yes, I can see that.'

'I could pick one up at the airport.'

'No, let's do that here in town. We need to avoid leaving any clues as to your location. If you tell me what you need and give me a bank card, I'll arrange for one of my officers to sort it out for you. And let's purchase a new pay-as-you-go phone while we're at it. We need to take every precaution from here on in. I'll take your existing phone and see what we can find out. He may well ring again.'

Mia reached into her handbag and retrieved a gold credit card from her purse.

'What kind of computer have you got in mind?'

Mia provided the information as requested, writing it down in bold capitals for no particular reason she could think of.

'Right, I'll sort that out straightaway. And when you get it, do *not* connect to the internet. As I said, let's not leave him any clues where you both are. The less technology you use, the safer you're going to be. Just use it for writing.'

Mia looked up on hearing footsteps descending the stairs. 'I really appreciate your help, Laura. You've been brilliant.'

'It's no problem at all. It's what I'm paid for.'

Mia smiled warmly as Grav carried Isabella into the room, the little girl now holding one of Emily's old dolls in each hand. Grav met Kesey's eyes and asked, 'Are you ladies nearly done? Isabella wants to show you the doll's house we found. We've been having a great time.'

He lowered Isabella to the floor, allowing her to run to her mother.

Kesey met Grav's insistent gaze. 'Yes, we're done for now. Isabella's going to visit her gran and gramps in Italy with her mummy, lucky girl. I'm just going to need the keys to the car to collect the letter before I head off.'

Mia confirmed the keys' location, as Grav indicated his reluctant approval. The baton had been passed, his apprentice had blossomed. He'd never felt older or more obsolete in his life. A new breed of officer had superseded the dinosaur he'd become. It was staring him in the face, undeniable. 'That sounds fantastic! I wish I could come too. With all that swimming in the warm sea and spaghetti and ice creams to eat.'

Isabella's eyes sparkled as she climbed onto her mother's lap.

Kesey collected the keys and returned to the lounge en route to the front door. 'I was hoping Mia and Isabella could stay here until they leave for Italy, if that's all right with you, boss? There are a few things to sort out today, but hopefully, they can fly out tomorrow. If Mia could use your landline to buy the tickets, rather than go online, that would be to our advantage.'

'Of course, no problem at all.' He looked towards Mia stiffly, turning his entire body rather than just his head. 'The phone is there whenever you need it, love. Just help yourself. There's no need to ask. Treat the place as your own for as long as you're here.'

24

Ella's festering post-coital guilt had become full-blown remorse by the time she finally sat down to share a meal with Adam a few days after the event. She was keen to please him. Motivated to make up. Eager to let him know she still loved and respected him, despite occasional feelings to the contrary. Ella looked at her fiancé across the table, with its pristine white cotton tablecloth and flickering romantic red candle, and smiled warmly. 'The food looks lovely, thank you. You've clearly gone to a lot of effort. I want you to know I appreciate it. You're a wonderful partner, the best. I don't tell you that often enough.'

Adam grinned. 'Oh, it's nothing really. You've just got to make certain you've got the correct ingredients, follow the recipe step by step, set the temperature correctly, put the timer on the cooker, wait for it to buzz and it's done.'

'Well, I'm grateful. Not all men are nearly so caring.'

He moved the boiled rice around his plate and stared at her. 'I saw something about a fatal hit-and-run on the Welsh evening news. A Mattia, a Mattia Bianchi I think they said. Didn't you use to go out with him? I'm sure I've heard you mention the name.'

Ella lowered her eyes, keen not to reveal her distress. 'Um... yeah, we did go out once or twice a few years back.'

He stiffened, angered by her dishonesty and desperate to hit out. 'Oh, really, I thought it was more serious than that?'

Ella felt her face flush. 'No, he was keen, but I knew he wasn't my type. He was a bit flashy for my tastes, too much of a superficial charmer. I was looking for a more reliable man. I finished it almost before it started.'

'Really?'

'Yes, absolutely!'

'How's your vindaloo?'

Ella gulped her mineral water, her mouth burning. 'It's lovely, the nicest I've ever tasted.'

'It's not too hot for you?'

'Not at all, but it tastes a little different to how you usually make it. I'm not saying that's a bad thing. It's different, that's all.'

Adam pictured Ella collapsed to the floor, clutching her midriff, her face twisting, and felt his spirits soar. 'I added a special ingredient just for you. I thought you'd appreciate it.'

'What is it?'

'Oh, I can't divulge my culinary secrets.'

'Well, whatever it is, it's delicious.'

Adam's eyes narrowed as he turned up the pressure a little further. 'I was just thinking about our earlier conversation. I'm sure someone mentioned that you were close to Mattia for a time. I thought you were a couple. Am I mistaken?'

Ella searched for the right words, something to shut him up, a sentence to appease him as the conversation took another unwelcome turn. 'I stayed at his place once or twice, but that was about it. It was nothing serious. It's all in the past. If I could turn back the clock and change what happened, I would.'

'Just sex, is that what you're saying?'

She put down her knife and fork. 'I hadn't even met you then, what's your point? I'm not the only one with a history.'

'Another glass of vino?'

Her jaw tensed. 'No, I've had enough.'

'Perhaps I should have bought champagne. Would that have suited you better?'

Ella avoided his accusing gaze, beginning to wonder if he knew more than he was letting on. 'The wine is fine, thank you. I've got an early start in the morning, that's all. Please don't read anything into it.'

He rested his elbows on the table and leaned towards her, so that she could feel his warm breath on her face. 'Mattia was run down in the street as if he were nothing. The driver didn't even bother stopping. No effort to break, no skid-marks on the tarmac, nothing. Whoever it was, just drove off into the night and escaped justice. Mattia's life was snuffed out in seconds. Who would do such a horrible thing? To use a car as a weapon like that. Maybe we'll never find out the truth. It seems the police haven't got a clue.'

Ella clenched her teeth, fighting back her tears. 'I didn't know the details.'

'Oh, really, didn't you see the report? It was all on the Welsh news.'

They sat without speaking for almost two minutes before Adam finally spoke again, shattering the pervasive silence. 'How's Mia doing? I meant to ask earlier. Have there been any significant developments in her situation?'

Ella relaxed her jaw, relieved he'd changed the subject. Glad to focus on her sister's issues rather than her own. 'She rang earlier. The police were talking about a safe house, but Mia's decided to go to stay with Mum and Dad in Italy. It seemed like the logical thing to do, apparently.'

'It doesn't seem like such a bad idea.'

Ella was keen to agree. Eager to keep him onside. 'No, I guess not. They're going to be a lot safer there than here.'

'What do the police think?'

'They didn't raise any objections, or at least not according to Mia. Although, I don't think she'd have told me if they had. Once she's got an idea in her head, it's hard to dislodge.'

He wrinkled his nose. 'I don't understand why you didn't ask me to help your sister when all this began. She's being threatened. I'm in security. I could have given her some advice at the very least.'

'It was all computer stuff until this business with the cat, manipulative emails, threats, that sort of thing. You're useless with technology. You've told me that yourself.'

'Well, yes, I'm not going to argue with that. But I could have checked out her house, fitted some better locks to the doors and windows at the very least. It's amazing how easy it is to break into most properties. People aren't nearly careful enough.'

'I didn't think.'

His expression softened. 'Are you going to finish your meal?'

She lifted her fork to her mouth. 'Of course, it's lovely.'

'So, have the police got any idea who they're after?'

'Not that I know of.'

He laughed. 'No surprises there, they're next to useless in my experience.'

'Mia said she's not the first victim.'

'Really?'

'It's all more serious than it first appeared.'

'When are they travelling? Has she booked the flights?'

'They're staying at the detective's place tonight, and then they'll be going up to Gatwick by train. Their flight leaves at just after four tomorrow afternoon.'

He adopted a concerned expression, screwing up his face. 'Is a police officer going with them? For protection, you know what I'm saying. If the guy's as murderous as they seem to think he is, we need to know that they're both safe.'

Ella began massaging her stomach as it churned and twisted. 'Um... I'm not sure. You can ask her yourself. She said she'd be calling early tomorrow morning to say goodbye on her way to the station.'

'Are you okay, Ella? You're looking a bit peaky all of a sudden.'

Ella put on a brave face, wiping sweat from her brow with the back of one hand. 'It's nothing, just a bit of gut ache.'

He looked back at her on approaching the fridge. 'Mia and Isabella are very welcome to stay here tonight if that helps. We could make room. I'd be happy to sleep on the sofa if necessary.'

'I offered, but she's staying put.'

Adam filled a glass with water and took a sip. 'Do you want some antacids or something? I can see you're struggling.'

'Please.'

He left the room, returned a minute later and handed her two tablets with a sham look of concern. 'I hope it wasn't the curry.'

'I think my period may be starting.'

'Why don't I pick Mia up from this detective's place in the morning? She doesn't want to be lugging a load of heavy luggage about if she doesn't have to. Especially not when she's looking after Isabella.'

'Oh, thanks, Adam, that's a great idea. I'll give her a ring as soon as I'm feeling a little better.'

'You're welcome. What are friends for?'

Ella pushed her plate aside as her cramps became more severe.

'Are you planning to go to the funeral?'

'The funeral?'

'Mattia's, who else's? I don't know anyone else who's died, do you?'

She lowered her eyes, focussing on the table. 'Um... I hadn't really thought about it.'

Adam sat back down and faced her, leaning back in his chair and spreading his legs wide. 'Oh, come on, I doubt that very much. You were close once. I really think you ought to go.'

'Do you?'

'Yes, I do. You've got to do the right thing. There's no need to worry about my sensibilities. It was all over long before we met. You said that yourself.'

Ella blew the air slowly from her mouth to ease the pain. 'You surprise me sometimes.'

'I'll even come with you to hold your hand if I'm still here. Funerals are never easy.'

Her brow furrowed. 'If you're still here? What's that supposed to mean?'

Adam drained his glass and placed it back on the table. 'I may fly out to Italy with Mia and Isabella to make sure they get to your parents' place safely. But I'll be back in plenty of time for the wedding. There's nothing to worry about.'

'You'd do that?'

'Yes, absolutely! They're family, it's the least I can do.'

'And you really don't mind me going to the funeral?'

'I suggested it, didn't I?'

'Thanks, Adam, that's wonderful. I don't know what I've done to deserve you.'

He visualised her severed head on a spike and smiled. 'I'm the lucky one and don't you forget it. You're the girl of my dreams. I'm going to make it my task in life to make you the happiest woman in the world. You see if I don't.'

Ella reached across the table and kissed him on his stubbled cheek. 'That's lovely to hear you say, Adam.'

'You deserve everything you get.'

She struggled to her feet with the aid of the tabletop, stumbling and almost falling as she approached the door to the hall. 'I'm really not feeling too well all of a sudden. Can you give me a hand to lie down?'

He skipped around the table and took her arm. 'How about an early night? It's been a while. I can help you up the stairs.'

Her face fell. 'I really need to rest.'

He guffawed, head back, chest heaving, bordering on the manic. 'I wasn't thinking of *that* kind of early night, not with the state you're in. I was planning to finish my book. It's one of your sister's. I'd never read one before. It's not at all bad. I may read another when I finish it.'

Ella began climbing the stairs, each step seemingly higher and more demanding than the last. 'I think you may have to call me a doctor.'

He recalled the muffled thud as his car smashed into Mattia's drunken body and smirked. 'It's the story of a female serial killer in America. Not my usual genre of choice, but I'm enjoying it.'

She was panting now, her gut twisting as the anticoagulant irritated her stomach lining. 'Didn't you hear me? I need a doctor.'

His reply was mumbled, barely audible. 'It can take up to two weeks to take full effect.'

'What?'

He assisted her in the direction of the bed. 'Sorry, I was thinking about your sister's book... come on, let's get you lying down and comfortable. If I call you a doctor, it's going to be hours before they come out. You know what the on-call service is like.'

'What about taking me to casualty?'

'Are you in pain, Ella?'

She slumped on the edge of the bed and hugged her knees to her chest. 'Yes, it's getting worse.'

He adjusted his trousers as his penis began to swell. 'Come on, into bed with you. I'll bring you one of my sleeping tablets. That'll do the trick.'

'But what about the hospital? I really think—'

He placed his hand on her right shoulder and pushed her down, not allowing her to finish her sentence. 'There's no need for that. I'm going to look after you. I passed a first-aid course in the army. I've told you all this before. You've got to learn to trust me. You really couldn't be in better hands.'

She resisted the impulse to vomit. 'Are you certain, Adam? It feels a lot worse than the last time. It may be something serious. It's scaring me. I'm really ill.'

'Oh, come on, you're making a fuss about nothing. Calm yourself down, take some deep breaths and try to relax. I'll get the sleeping tablets from the bathroom cabinet.'

'If you're sure?'

'I'm assuming you've got the detective's contact details?'

She clutched her gut, struggling to reply. 'Mia rang from his house. I wrote the number in the book.'

'I'll give her a ring when I go downstairs.'

Ella groaned loudly as the pain spiked. 'The sleeping tablets, I need the tablets.'

He wanted to laugh. He so wanted to laugh. But he didn't let it show. 'You'll be feeling much better by the morning, Dr Adam's on the case. Just wait and see.'

25

Emily Gravel entered her hallway at 7:10 a.m., just in time to see a brown package drop through her letterbox, accompanied by three white envelopes of various sizes. She yawned, casting off the residual elements of sleep as she slowly approached the door. The package was different to the previous padded envelope and its maggot-ridden contents. It didn't set off any alarm bells, not initially. There were no glaring causes for concern, nothing that stood out. But as she bent down and picked it up, along with her other mail, she recognised the style of writing. The bold capitals in black marker pen were all too familiar. Just like the last time. Exactly like the last time. She held the parcel in one hand and examined it closely, positioning it only inches from her face. The smell was self-evident and revolting. She felt angry, nauseous. Another dead rodent, maybe, or something even worse, if such a thing were possible. She dropped the parcel to the floor, placed the white envelopes on the hallstand for later reference and hurried towards the kitchen to fetch a pair of rubber gloves and collect a sharp knife. Emily sat cross-legged on the hall tiles with her cotton nightdress pulled up above her knees, gripping the package in one hand and the knife in the other. She used the tip of the blade to prize loose one corner of the cardboard before peeling the plastic tape from its edges.

Emily stopped, questioning the wisdom of opening the parcel right up to the second her inquisitiveness overcame her hesitation. She had to know what was in it. Horrible or not, she just had to know. She lifted the lid slightly and peered in. Surely it wasn't real. She swallowed hard and swivelled her body, opening the lid a little further and taking full advantage of the soft morning light shining through the door's glass panes. Emily stared at the mottled blue-white human hand with its long and delicate fingers, one of which was severed at the knuckle, with the remains of a jagged bone poking through the flesh. She glared at it, sickened, horrified by the implications, but unable to look away. All the nails were missing, torn from the fingers to leave shreds of ripped and bloodied skin. And there was a note. A short typed note.

Tell the fat detective to back off or it may be you next.

Emily dropped the folded paper back in the box and pushed it aside. She jumped to her feet and ran up the stairs to the bathroom, ascending two steps at a time. She knelt, hanging her head over the toilet bowl for almost five minutes, but somehow resisted the urge to throw up her breakfast. It was time to contact her father. Time to seek his urgent help.

Emily sat on the bottom step of the stairs with the offending parcel just a few feet away screaming for her attention, as she dialled her father's home number. She listened to the ringtone and waited, counting slowly in her head to occupy her thoughts and calm her nerves. Come on, Dad, get a move on old man. Where the hell are you?

When Grav finally picked up, Emily's release from anxiety

was almost touchable. She looked down at the hand, pale and milky-white in the daylight, the skin semi-transparent, and blurted out her words. 'He's sent me a woman's hand in the post.'

'He's done what?'

Emily was weeping now, streams of tears running down her face as her chest heaved. 'He's sent me a severed hand. I'm looking at it now. And a threatening note. It could be me next! That's what it says. What do I do, Dad? What the hell do I do? He wants you to back off. He doesn't want you involved with the case.'

Grav looked up and turned away as Mia appeared, dragging her suitcase towards the front door.

He refocussed on his call. 'Is it in some sort of packaging?'

Emily blew her nose. 'It arrived in a cardboard box wrapped in parcel tape.'

'Where's it now?'

'It's on the hall floor. I'm looking at the damned thing as we speak.'

'Right, I want you to pick it up, take it to the kitchen and put it in the fridge. That hand is our best potential source of evidence. We need to look after it. Can you do that for me?'

She stood on unsteady legs, the phone's lead stretched to the maximum. 'Are you coming over?'

Grav nodded in automatic response. 'I'm waiting for Mia to be collected from the house any minute now. As soon as her lift arrives, I'll be on my way. Just hold on until I get there.'

'Do you want me to ring Laura?'

'No, you're all right, love, I'll do that from here. I've got her home number. She'll want to get the damned thing down to the morgue as soon as practically possible. You never know, this may be the breakthrough we need. Hopefully he's become careless. That happens sometimes. Killers start thinking they're infallible.'

'Hurry up, Dad. I don't want to be on my own.'

'Hang on in there, love, I'll be with you before you know it.'

Emily looked away and winced. 'This is all strangely reminiscent of Turner... déjà vu. If I didn't know what happened to him, I'd think he'd come back to haunt us.'

'We beat that bastard, and we'll beat this one too.'

'Yes, we will. I wish Mum were still with us. What I wouldn't give for one last hug.'

Grav smiled warmly, his pride almost overwhelming. 'Me too, love, me too... oh, hang on, someone's knocking on the door.' He lowered the phone and called out, his voice rattling. 'I think your lift's here, Mia. Are you both ready?'

Mia called back. 'Yeah, I think we've got everything.'

'Tickets, passports? And leave me your car keys. I'll sort it out later on. Perhaps park it outside your house ready for your return.'

She patted her handbag. 'Yes, all ready.'

'What about the keys?'

'On the dining room table.'

There was another bang on the front door, louder this time, more insistent, causing Mia to flinch and cower. As if *he* may be there. As if *he* was coming to get her.

Grav shouted out, making himself heard. 'Hang on, mate, she'll be with you in a second.'

He spoke to Emily again as Adam stood and waited on the doorstep. 'I've got to go, love. I'll be on my way in five minutes.'

26

Mia sat alongside Adam – Isabella ensconced in the rear seat – as he drove slowly away from Grav's Carmarthen home.

'Thank you so much for collecting us, it's really appreciated.'

Adam met Mia's eyes and smiled before refocussing on the morning traffic. 'You seem surprised I came at all. Am I correct, or am I missing something?'

Mia looked at Isabella in the vanity mirror as she played with her Spanish doll, removing its dress. 'Well, we've never been that close, if we're honest. We've hardly spoken for months. You're the last person I was expecting to step up. I was genuinely surprised when you rang last night.'

He switched on the radio, turning down the volume as the DJ announced the next song with a dour Scottish drone. 'You're Ella's sister, you're obviously in grave danger, you need help, and I'm going to be your brother-in-law soon enough. Why wouldn't I help you?'

Mia raised a hand to her left eye and rubbed it as it began to twitch. 'I'm grateful, Adam, really I am. I hope we can be good friends in the future.'

He signalled and turned to his left, sounding his horn and raising a clenched fist as a white van swerved into his lane no more than ten metres in front of the car. 'Oh, we'll get to know each other *really* well. I can promise you that much.'

Mia wasn't sure how to take his comment but gave him the benefit of the doubt. 'I'm glad to hear it.'

Adam accelerated hard, sounding the horn for a second time and giving the driver the finger as he sped past the van.

'You seem a little tense, Adam. Are you feeling okay?'

He imagined himself slicing her throat from one ear to the other. '*I'm* a little tense? That's rich coming from you! I'm not the one with a raving maniac hunting him down. You're a quivering mess, paralysed by indecision. That's why I'm here.'

Mia sank into her seat, making herself smaller. 'For goodness' sake, I don't want Isabella hearing this stuff. She's far too young to understand what's going on.'

He gripped the steering wheel with one hand while gesticulating with the other. 'Relax, she's asleep.'

Mia glanced back, confirming his assertion.

'You're looking skinny, Mia. Your eyes are sunken. They're surrounded by dark shadows. I can see the situation's really getting to you. It's hardly surprising, you're dealing with an extremely dangerous man.'

Mia looked down and realised that her hands were shaking. 'I just can't believe what's happening to me. It has been horrendous. I keep seeing him everywhere I look. Every man becomes a killer in my mind's eye. I never feel entirely safe, not for a single second, not in the house with Grav, not even here with you now. How ridiculous is that? I'm on constant hyperalert, even in bed at night. Especially in bed at night. It all seems never-ending. I don't know how much more I can take.'

He reached across and patted her knee, proud of what he'd

just heard. 'You're right to be scared. Your lives are at risk. There'd be something wrong if you weren't shitting yourself.'

Mia held her head in her hands.

'Look, I've been thinking about it. You know I've got an army background, right? I provide protection for people at risk, for a fee. Celebrities, rich business people, it's what I do. And it's something I'm good at. That's why people pay me as much as they do.'

'Yes, Ella did mention something. I never really understood what it involved until now.'

'I'd like to fly to Italy with you. To ensure your safety. And Isabella's too, of course. I've checked the flights. They're cheap enough, and the plane's only half-full. I'd be happy to do it. What do you think?'

Mia had never felt more relieved in her life. 'I'd be happy to pay you the going rate.'

Adam grinned and knew he was winning. 'No, don't be silly, there's no need for that. We're family now, and I've got no other commitments for a week or two. I'll sort out a ticket as soon as we're back at the house.'

'Well, at least let me pay for your flights. That's the least I can do.'

'No need.'

'Are you sure?'

'I'm certain.'

He pulled up in a convenient spot a couple of minutes' walk from the house. 'Right, let me get out and check the street before you exit the vehicle. You disembark on the passenger side and don't step onto the road at any point. You can take Isabella from the back from the pavement side. We need to eliminate as many dangers as possible.'

Mia followed Adam's instructions, reassured by his self-confidence, and walked closely behind him, Isabella asleep on her shoulder. 'I'm looking forward to seeing Ella.'

'She mentioned that you're taking too many tablets.'

Mia bristled. 'Well, she should keep her nose out. I take as many as I need and no more.'

He unlocked the front door and stood aside to allow them to pass. 'Yes, that's what I told her.'

'Then why didn't she listen to you?'

Adam followed Mia into the hallway. 'I should probably warn you that Ella's not feeling too well at the moment. She was still in bed when I left.'

'Really, what's wrong? She seemed fine when we last spoke.'

He laughed. 'She got seriously hammered last night at a girl-friend's leaving party. I'd never seen her so drunk. She may still be a bit woozy after a sleeping remedy she insisted on taking when she woke up.'

Mia rested Isabella on the leather sofa, placing a satin cushion under her head as Adam switched on his laptop.

'Really, that bad?'

'Oh, yeah, I've tried to persuade her to cut down on the booze, but you know what she's like. She can be one stubborn woman when she wants to be.'

Mia smiled. 'She was the same when we were teenagers.'

Adam stared at his computer screen with a bank card in hand, making a show of purchasing the plane ticket he'd actually bought the previous evening. 'You pop up and see how Ella's doing, and I'll pack a few things as soon as I've booked the plane. Have you got the flight number? I want to make certain I book the correct one. The last thing we want is to be on different flights.'

Mia delved into her handbag and handed him her tickets, silently acknowledging that she was developing a soft spot for a man she'd previously ignored. 'I really do appreciate your help,

Adam. You've been wonderfully supportive. I hope Ella realises just how lucky she is.'

He resisted the temptation to laugh. 'Go on, up you go, I'll keep an eye on Isabella for you. It's no problem at all.'

Ella was close to unconsciousness when Mia reached her bedside. Mia reached out and shook her sister, but she barely moved. She shook her again, a little more robustly this time, and said, 'Hello,' close to her ear, but Ella's response was limited to incoherent mumbled sounds. Mia looked at Ella and grinned as a thin line of drool ran from the side of her open mouth. 'Look at the state you're in. It's going to be me lecturing you from now on. Let's see how you like it.'

Ella tried to turn her head to face her sister, to tell her how ill she felt, that she needed a doctor, but she was lost in a chemical haze that she wouldn't escape for hours.

Mia bent forwards and kissed her sister on the forehead. 'Look after yourself, Ella, sleep it off. I'll ring you when we get to Italy. Thanks for letting Adam come with us. He's too good for you. But then, I think you already know that. You'd be crazy mad not to marry him.' Mia turned back and gave a little wave on reaching the bedroom door. 'I'm going to remind you of this one-sided conversation when you're in a fit state to hear me and remember it. You could do one hell of a lot worse than Adam. He's reliable, kind, thoughtful. And he's good-looking too, in an unconventional way, if you choose to look closely enough. If you don't want him, why not give him to me? He couldn't do a worse job than Rhys has. Nobody could. You've landed a keeper with that one.'

Adam beamed when Mia returned downstairs, Isabella still asleep on the sofa. 'I've bought a one-way ticket. I guess it's impossible to know how long we'll need to be there.'

'I did the same thing. It seemed sensible.'

'I'll just pack a few things, and we can be on our way. There's no

point in delaying things unnecessarily. All it would take is a punc-
ture or something along those lines, and we'd be pressured for
time. We need to minimise every potential risk. Consider every
possibility.'

Mia cleared her throat. 'I'm a bit worried about leaving Ella in
that state. I couldn't get any sense out of her at all, not a word. I've
never seen her like that before.'

Adam held her gaze. 'Do you trust me?'

'Yes, yes, of course I do.'

'Then listen to what I'm telling you. Ella drank too much, that's
all. And it's not the first time she's taken a sleeping tablet to sleep off
a heavy night. A few hours from now she'll be up and about and
feeling fine again. That I can guarantee you. If we delay our trip
we'll be putting Izzy's life at risk for no good reason at all.'

Mia looked at Isabella with a sideways glance and nodded
reluctantly. 'Okay, if you're sure. It's just that she looked so ill.'

Adam imagined Ella vomiting, dark blood seeping from her
nose, eyes and mouth as the poison ravaged her system. 'It's a hang-
over, nothing more. Give me ten minutes, and I'll be good to go. Ella
wouldn't want us to hang about. If we're still here when she wakes
up she'll be absolutely gutted. The quicker we're on the road, the
safer you're going to be.'

Mia took a single step towards Adam and pecked him on his
right cheek, reassured. 'Thank you, Adam, you're an absolute star.
You've stepped up when I needed help the most. Not everyone
would have done that, and it's appreciated. I don't know what I'd do
without you.'

He looked back at her, asking himself if all women were as
gullible. Prospective victims awaiting a slayer, as she was. 'Did you
mention that you'd bought a new mobile phone?'

'Yes, I did. One of the police officers got it for me on Detective

Inspector Kesey's insistence. She seems to know what she's doing. I'm only supposed to use it in emergencies.'

'So, does that mean she's in charge of the investigation now? This Kesey woman?'

'Yes, I think so.'

'The fat detective's not involved any more?'

'Well, he never was, not formally. He's still on sick leave.'

'Then, why talk to him?'

'He's a family friend. He seemed like the obvious person to seek advice from.'

His lip curled. 'He seemed like a bit of a fool to me.'

'Oh, come on, be fair. He's one of the good guys. You only met him very briefly.'

Adam reached out his hand. 'Best give the phone to me to look after, don't you think? That way, if the murdering psycho tries to contact you again, and I can guarantee he will, I'll be there to answer. I'll know what to say. Maybe I can frighten him off.'

'I was planning to ring Ella when we got to Italy. You know, just to tell her we're okay and ask how she is.'

'That's *not* a good idea! No contact with anyone unless we agree it first. We've got to do everything we can to stay safe. That's got to be the number one priority.'

She handed the phone over a little reticently.

'And best give me the passports and tickets too while we're at it. I'll keep everything together in the one place. It'll be safer that way. There'll be less for you to worry about.'

Mia reached into her handbag. 'If you're really certain it's necessary?'

Adam slotted everything into the inside pocket of his jacket. 'If I'm going to protect you both, you've got to learn to trust me completely. I can keep you alive, but only if you do everything I say.'

27

The two-hour-forty-minute flight from London Gatwick to Naples International Airport passed relatively quickly. Mia spent the first half an hour or so colouring a picture book with Isabella until the little girl finally closed her tired eyes and drifted off to sleep with her head vibrating against the passenger cabin window. Adam, who had insisted on sitting in the aisle seat, removed his seatbelt and stood up five minutes later, as if on full alert, pacing up and down the aisle three times and glancing surreptitiously at the various male passengers before finally returning to his seat with a sullen expression.

Mia turned to face him. 'Is everything all right? You seem a little concerned.'

He waited before responding, upping the tension. 'I need to make sure he's not on the plane.'

Mia's jaw dropped. 'You need to make sure *who's* not on the plane?'

He turned his head and looked behind him, first to one side and then the other. 'The killer, we need to ensure he hasn't followed us.'

Mia took a sharp intake of breath. 'What? Surely not! Do you really think he may have?'

'Well, it's a possibility we can't afford to ignore, that's all I'm saying. I'm sure there's nothing to worry about. I'm just ticking all the boxes. It's what I'm trained to do.'

Mia reached for her tablets and waved to the nearest stewardess. 'But how could he possibly find out where we're going? Only the police know.'

Adam waited while Mia spoke to the stewardess in her immaculate livery, ordering a glass of water to wash down her medication. He craned his head, watching the young woman walk away, before speaking again in hushed, breathy tones he thought best conveyed a sense of urgency. 'Ella knows where we're... you're going. She can be a bit of a blabbermouth after a few glasses of wine. You know that as well as I do. It wouldn't surprise me if she said something to the wrong person when a bit worse for wear. That's all it would take.'

'No, I really don't think that would happen, not for a minute. I trust Ella completely.'

He raised an eyebrow. 'Really?'

'Yes, *really*! She'd never do anything that placed Izzy or me at risk. It's a ludicrous idea.'

'I'm not saying she'd do it on purpose.'

'She wouldn't do it at all.'

'I'm not so sure.'

Mia accepted her water on the stewardess's return and swallowed two tablets, taking a second gulp when one stuck in her throat. 'Well, I couldn't be more certain. If he has found out where we are, he didn't hear it from Ella. No way, no how... she's loyal, she's caring. I won't contemplate it even for a single second.'

'Okay, if you say so.'

'I do!'

Adam was silent for a few seconds, considering his next move. 'I'm right in thinking that the killer spoke to you at the fat detective's house, yes?'

She avoided his eyes. 'Yes, what's your point?'

'Well, if he knew you were there, he could have followed us when we left. I kept an eye out in the rear-view mirror, but this guy seems to know what he's doing. It wouldn't surprise me if he's ex-military, like me. He could have sat two or three cars back. There are ways of avoiding being spotted.'

Mia adjusted her blouse. 'Do you really think he may have?'

'It's a definite possibility. He could have followed us all the way to the airport. It's a chance, that's all I'm saying. There were seats available on the flight. We know that. There's plenty of spare seats. He could have bought one easily enough. All he'd need is a passport and a credit card.'

Mia cupped her face in her hands and began weeping silent tears.

He gripped her arm, squeezed it and then released it slowly when she tensed. 'Oh, come on, it's not that bad. I'm here to protect you. At least you're not on your own any more. I'll do everything I can to keep you alive. The killer may be good at what he does, but then so am I. I'm on your side now, every step of the way. Be glad of that.'

Mia lowered her hands, opening her reddened eyes as he continued to stare at her. 'I'm grateful, really I am. I appreciate everything you're doing on our behalf.'

'How about a glass of brandy before Izzy wakes up? We won't be landing for another forty minutes. We've got time for one.'

'I shouldn't really, what with the codeine.'

'Oh, go on, one's not going to do you any harm. If not now, when? You haven't exactly had a pleasant time recently. It will do you some good. Take the edge off.'

Mia clasped her hands to her chest. 'Oh, go on then, it may help me relax.'

'I'll order one if and when they bring the trolley round again.'

'Okay, thanks. I shouldn't really, but in the circumstances... you know what I'm saying.'

'That's the spirit, keep your chin up. I've had a good look at everyone on the plane. If I see any of the same men anywhere near your parents' villa or following us around the town, I'll know to check them out. There's only so much I can do, of course. I haven't got any powers of arrest. But I can keep a close eye on them. If it happens, and I conclude he's our man, I'll talk to the local police and try to convince them it's genuine. Hopefully, they'd take it seriously enough to interview him. There are no guarantees, but it would be worth a try.' He pictured Mia imprisoned and helpless in his garage lair, bruised and bleeding in his killing ground of choice, and stifled a grin as the image gradually faded. 'The Italian police may react with more urgency if told the danger pertains to someone as famous as you. You could come with me and tell them everything that's happened, the threats, the cat, the lot. Either that, or we could fly straight back to the UK and talk to DI Kesey. That might be the best bet. We'll talk about it again and make a decision if and when it happens. You never know, we may be lucky and stay safe.'

Mia leaned across and ran her hand through Isabella's hair as she began to stir. 'I really do hope so, more for Izzy's sake than my own. I hate to think of her being at risk. She's just a little girl, for goodness' sake. She shouldn't have a care in the world.'

Adam envisaged Mia's body sliced open from sternum to pelvis, much like the cat, her intestines spilling out, pink and wet with bodily fluids. 'I hate to admit it, but your world has become a very desperate place. I hope we've done the right thing by flying to Italy at all.'

28

By the time the plane landed in Naples, three miles north of the city, Mia had downed a double brandy and had taken more tablets than prescribed, spurred on by Adam, who was keen to encourage her. She almost lost her footing twice as she negotiated the metal steps leading from the aircraft, and she was glad when Adam took control of Isabella, holding her hand and leading her towards the waiting bus. Adam was sorely tempted to give Mia a little shove and watch her tumble to the hard tarmac as she'd struggled down each step, but he thought better of it at the last second. There were too many witnesses, however subtle his actions. The potential rewards, he decided, were outweighed by the risks.

The Italian summer heat met them like a raging furnace as they crossed the ground towards the bus, seemingly rising from the earth and getting hotter with each step they took. All three were left standing and sweating as they journeyed towards the terminal in close proximity to the multitude of other passengers, and it was a relief to each of them when they entered the spacious air-conditioned terminal building, Isabella now riding high on Adam's shoulders, pretending he was a unicorn. By the time they'd collected their luggage from the carousel about thirty minutes later, Mia was feeling slightly better, the effects of the alcohol wearing off, despite Adam's encouragement to call at an airport café to enjoy a glass of chilled white wine. 'Go on, Mia, one glass isn't going to do you any harm. You're under a great deal of pressure. Why not take the edge off?'

Mia sat herself down and glanced at the menu. 'No, I don't think it's a good idea. We'll be meeting Mum and Dad soon.'

Adam quietly seethed as Mia ordered a bottle of sparkling water for herself and two scoops of fruity gelato for Isabella, who ate it with gusto, excited to be visiting her grandparents and their swimming pool with a view of the sea. 'Anything for you Adam, my treat?'

He held his hands wide, chest thrust out like a fighting cockerel, and hated her more than he'd ever thought possible. 'No, we haven't got time to hang about. It's not a good idea to stay in one place for too long. You have to consider these things if you're both to stay safe. What the hell were you thinking?'

'Not now, Adam, please, not in front of Izzy.'

'What is it, Mummy?'

Mia forced a brittle smile. 'It's nothing. Uncle Adam's being silly.'

His nostrils flared, his chin high as his thoughts turned to murder. 'We'll see how silly I am if he turns up and gets you. I won't be too silly then.'

'Please, Adam, leave it for now.'

He could almost feel the knife in his hand as he glared at her. 'Okay, but we need to talk about this later. You're not taking the situation nearly seriously enough for my liking. If I'm going to protect you, you have to play your part.'

'All right, Adam, I hear you. We'll discuss it later when we're alone, but not now. You've said enough.'

'Okay, have it your way, but tonight we talk, no more excuses. It's too important.'

Adam made a show of scanning the terminal building with keen eyes as they stood in a long queue waiting to negotiate customs, passports in hand, increasing Mia's insecurity when she'd begun to unwind.

'I'm checking, Mia, that's all. He could be here now. He could be watching us. If I don't do my job properly, what's the point of me being here at all?' He pointed towards a tall bearded young man waiting to collect his suitcase about fifteen metres away. 'What about him? Do you think he looks suspicious?'

Mia shook her head, becoming increasingly frustrated with Adam's approach. 'No, not really, he just looks like an ordinary traveller. A businessman, maybe, someone like that. He's just standing there waiting for his case like everyone else.'

'Yeah, that's the problem! He looks *so* typical, so unthreatening. But he could easily hide a weapon under that jacket. Why's it too big for him? Have you asked yourself that? He could come over here right now and kill you without blinking.'

Mia sighed dramatically as Isabella began rocking back and forth where she stood, her eyes glazing over. 'Not now, Adam! You're frightening Izzy, can't you see that? Please don't say anything else.'

Please, please, fucking well, please! That word again. The word he loathed above all others. They all relied on it in their pleading, every single one of them. It was utterly pathetic. Couldn't they come up with something more original even in their darkest moments?

He turned his back on his charges as Mia lowered herself to the floor and hugged Isabella tightly, quietly singing a favourite lullaby before saying, 'It's all right Izzy, we'll see Granny and Grampy soon. That will be nice, won't it?'

* * *

Within twenty minutes, they were standing outside the airport building, sheltering from the diamond-bright sun under a wave-like overhanging metal roof as other travellers boarded busy tourist buses and queued for white taxis. Adam had said nothing more, biding his time and planning for the evening, as they waited for Mia's parents to collect them.

Mia jumped up and waved exuberantly on seeing her mum walking towards them with a beaming smile on her girlish face. She looked tanned, slim and happy, as if Italy suited her. Mia ran forwards, hand in hand with Isabella who was laughing long before her grandmother picked her up and kissed her.

'It is so good to see you both. You look tired, Mia. All that writing's taken its toll. You need to look after yourself. I'm sure the break will do you good.'

Mia threw her arms around her mother as she gave Isabella one final kiss and lowered her to the floor. 'Let me introduce you to Adam, Ella's fiancé. I'll explain everything later when Izzy's safely tucked up in bed.'

Myra Hamilton studied her daughter with a puzzled look but chose not to ask questions. There would be plenty of time for talking in the hours ahead. She took Mia's hand in hers on one side and Isabella's on the other, holding them both tight. 'Come on you two, Grampy's waiting in the car. He's dying to see you.'

29

Conversation was limited to small talk during the one-hour journey from the airport to Sorrento. Adam sat in the car's front passenger seat alongside Roy Hamilton, totally oblivious to the glorious vista of the Gulf of Naples as they snaked along the twisting coastal road to the sound of soaring operatic arias playing on the radio. The dark majestic cliffs, shimmering azure-blue sea topped by galloping white horses, the Isle of Capri and even Mount Vesuvius, standing proud across the water, were lost on Adam. It wasn't that he chose not to see beauty. It was simpler than that. Nature's majesty just didn't register in his mind. His focus was on the suffering of others, as opposed to joy. A world red in tooth and claw. Each and every thought in his head was directed towards Mia's gradual destruction and the pleasure it gave him. Such things defined him, and in his opinion, there was a logic to that. Travelling to Italy had been a regrettable inconvenience. But such things were necessary in achieving his ultimate goal. That's what mattered. He repeated the notion, shouting it in his mind. Whatever sacrifices life imposed were a price worth paying. Mia would suffer for the trouble she'd caused him, and his experience would be all the better for it. He was a man who liked to work through his frustrations with a punch, a kick or worse, much worse. The self-righteous bitch would discover that soon enough. He'd tear her fucking face off! He just had to look forward to that.

* * *

Roy drove up to the two-storey villa he and his wife considered home, as a single cotton wool cloud crossed the sky and masked the sun. Adam exited the vehicle first, fetching the luggage from the boot and making a show of perusing the impressive lawned grounds and terracotta-tiled pool area with repeated furtive glances as he carried the heavy cases into the building. He chose a bedroom immediately next to Mia's on the whispered pretext of maintaining her security, examining her room for a full five minutes before finally returning to his own.

The five of them sat in the large, high-ceilinged family kitchen, once the visitors were settled in, to share a delicious pre-prepared meal of fresh local organic salad and white fish bought that morning in the nearby harbour. Both Roy and Myra Hamilton were more than keen to establish why Adam had accompanied their daughter and granddaughter on the trip, but they somehow resisted the overwhelming temptation to ask. Mia had said very little in arranging the last-minute stay, other than stressing its importance. Both her parents knew that something wasn't quite right, Adam's presence apart. There was a tension in the air. And more than that, Adam seemed on edge, tight and impatient as he gulped down his food and walked back and forth to the window, peering out without explanation as the sun began to set and cast its shadows.

Mia took Isabella up to bed once it was dark, leaving the landing light on, reading her a bedtime story and lying down alongside her until she finally drifted off.

Mia crept out of the room, ever so quietly, and made a brief but necessary bathroom visit before heading back downstairs to provide her explanations. She sat down with her mum and dad in their cavernous sitting room while Adam paced the grounds, shining a light into dark corners with a powerful torch he'd brought with him.

Mia talked for almost half an hour, pouring out her angst as her parents listened open-mouthed and wide-eyed.

'I'm sorry to put this on you. There was nowhere else to go.' Both parents moved forwards and hugged their daughter, tears in their eyes and a thousand unasked questions occupying their unsettled minds. Roy was the first of the three to release his embrace, sitting back on his haunches and searching for words of comfort. 'You're always welcome, Mia, of course you are. Where else would you go in times of trouble? You're a grown-up now, an adult with her own life to live, but you'll always be our little girl. Don't ever forget that.'

'Thanks, Dad, I love you.'

He raised a hand to his chin. 'We love you too, unconditionally. We always will. You'll be safe here. Stay for as long as you need. You could both move in permanently, if you wanted to. There's plenty of room.'

'They'll catch him soon enough, the Welsh police. He'll be arrested and locked up for a very long time.'

Roy nodded, hoping beyond hope that her assumptions proved to be true. 'Of course they will, and you've got Adam here to protect you until that happy day dawns.'

'Yes, he's been brilliant. Just having him around makes me feel better. If anyone can keep us safe, it's him.'

30

Grav sat opposite Gail Jones, the Detective Chief Superintendent's overly officious secretary, and marvelled at the degree of dedication she devoted to her role. She was a gatekeeper. A barrier between her boss and the rest of the world, and it was a role in which she excelled. Grav checked the clock dominating the wall behind her desk for the umpteenth time in less than ten minutes and noted that the hands were moving a lot slower than he'd like in a perfect world.

'Is her majesty going to be much longer?'

Jones looked up from her paperwork, her metal-framed glasses perched on the very tip of her nose. 'Your appointment isn't for another five minutes. I'm sure the DCS won't keep you waiting for too long.'

Grav crossed and uncrossed his legs, pondering if he should have bothered polishing his shoes for the first time in months. And why the hell had he put on his best bib and tucker? The tweed jacket, the checked shirt and the rugby club tie. Why bother? It probably wouldn't make even the slightest difference. The DCS didn't like him. It really was as simple as that. 'Just give her a quick call for me, love. I'm sick of waiting. What harm can it do?'

She fixed Grav with a look that said a thousand words and picked up the phone. 'Detective Inspector Gravel is here to see you, ma'am.' She listened to the response and then added. 'Yes, of course, ma'am, I'll tell him now.'

Grav tapped his foot on the floor. 'So, what's the news?'

Jones had a faint but discernible hint of a smirk on her face. 'She's going to be another twenty minutes or so. She asked me to convey her sincere apologies. It's unavoidable, regrettably.'

'Oh, yeah, I'm sure it is. She's probably got another form to sign. All that paperwork is far more important than me getting back to work and catching criminals.'

She chose to ignore his sarcasm. 'Can I get you a hot drink, Inspector? There's no milk, I'm afraid, but I've got a reasonably pleasant powdered substitute, if that will suffice?'

'Not for me, ta, I'm going to have a quick cigar.'

She glared at him, fixing him with an expression that withered lesser men. 'You can't smoke in the building. If you really need to light up, you'll have to go outside.'

He struggled to his feet, acutely aware of his declining powers. 'Yes, I do know that, love, I've been working here for over thirty years.'

Grav sat in a toilet cubicle and took a long appreciative drag, sucking the poisonous smoke deep into his lungs before sending clouds of grey fumes billowing around his head. It was just like her majesty to keep him waiting for as long as possible. She took every conceivable opportunity to drive home her seniority and make him feel small. She didn't miss a trick despite her comparative youth and inexperience, and, he silently acknowledged, he begrudgingly respected her for that. She'd crashed through the glass ceiling, shattering it without the advantage of his years on the job. Moving on from one rank to the next at breakneck speed. A new breed of copper he found increasingly difficult to comprehend or accept. Such was life. It seemed he just had to get used to it.

Grav checked his watch, took one last puff then stubbed out his cigar on the floor at his feet before throwing the butt into the white porcelain toilet bowl and flushing it away. He'd been defiant of authority for years, disrespectful and dismissive at times when he thought it justified, but the days of storming into her office were over. The DCS held all the cards. She had all the power, and she'd know it full well. It was time to beg her mercy. To show her the respect her position demanded. It was that or surrender. There was no other option. And surrender was no choice at all.

Grav sat facing his boss in her excessively large office with its panoramic view of the town, encircled by undulating green hills that travelled into the distance on every side. He glanced around the room, noting that little, if anything, had changed since his last visit. Her seat was still higher than his. She again appeared perched on a pedestal by comparison. It was more a throne than a chair. And she was looking down on him in the self-satisfactory way she always did. Snooty: that was the word for it. It was one part of the job he hadn't missed at all.

'It's good to see you again, Inspector. I was planning to get in touch at some future date when my commitments allowed. I'm assuming this isn't a social call. I'm a little pushed for time. What can I do for you?'

Grav glanced at the numerous framed academic certificates

hanging on the office walls and experienced a sinking feeling deep in the pit of his overstretched stomach. 'I'm ready to come back to work.'

The DCS frowned hard. 'Oh, really? I assumed we'd be talking about your retirement, rather than a resumption of your career. I'd be happy to support an application for an enhanced pension on the grounds of ill health. You'd have to go through the usual red tape, of course. There'd be some inevitable form-filling, but I think that you can safely assume that your application would be approved as quickly as possible. It's in everyone's interests to avoid any unnecessary delays, wouldn't you agree?'

He tensed, sputtering at full volume, 'I've got almost three years to go before retirement, and I plan to serve every single day of it.'

She shook her head. 'Oh, I don't think so, detective, none of us can go on forever. You're not a well man, that's blatantly obvious. I can see the sweat on your brow.'

'I've seen my doctor; she's given me the go-ahead. I'm as fit as any man twenty years younger. She told me that herself.'

The DCS looked far from persuaded. 'I appreciate your enthusiasm, but this is an increasingly demanding job. Why not go now, with my support, and be grateful for a long and industrious career? You'd be well rewarded. A generous monthly pension and a lump sum. It would be something to enjoy in your advancing years.'

He raised himself in his seat, breathing hard, bristling with exasperation. 'Maybe I don't want to leave. Perhaps I like it here. Have you thought about that?'

'I have to consider what's best for the service as a whole, not just my individual officers. It's one of the burdens of rank, as I'm sure you'll understand. I'm far from convinced that it's in your or the force's interests for you to return to the fold.'

Grav's eyes flashed red. 'Just say what you really think, love.

Spit it out, there's a good girl! Why hide behind all your usual bullshit? It suits you to kick me into touch. I bet you're creaming your knickers as we speak. It's a dream come true.'

'I do not appreciate your—'

'Oh, give me a break, love. I was locking up criminals when you were still in your school uniform. My GP has told me I'm fit to return. She's put it in writing. I'm going to be coming back. Just get used to it. It'll be easier that way.'

She shuffled some papers on the desk in front of her, steadying herself and buying time before she was ready to speak again. 'Now, you listen to me and listen good. I'm going to insist on an independent medical report, and then *if*, and I stress *if*, the expert supports your general practitioner's absurd conclusions, I'll welcome you back with open arms. *But* – and this is not negotiable – you will *not* return to an operational role. You'd retain your rank, of course – there's little I can do about that given the generally misguided affection with which you're held – but it would be a desk-bound position. Something in the training department, possibly, or administration, where we could take full advantage of your many years of experience and keep you out of trouble. Your days as a detective are over.'

Grav quietly seethed. She had him by the balls, and she was squeezing just as hard as she could. 'You're loving this, aren't you, love. It's made your day.'

'I'm doing my job, nothing more.'

'Maybe I'll take you up on your offer. Have you considered that? Just to spite you for as long as possible. I'll drag myself here and sit at whatever desk you allocate. That would wipe the smile off your smug, stuck-up face.'

She glared back at him with unblinking eyes and grinned. 'What, with no investigations to lead and no rules of evidence to bend in that oh-so-distinctive way of yours? I can't see it happening, somehow. You couldn't stand being desk-bound for a week, let alone three long years. Best accept you're beaten, Grav. I think that's best, don't you? I'll ask the Personnel Department to put the relevant forms in the post. The quicker you're gone and forgotten, the better for the both of us. The police service has changed beyond recognition. There's no room for your type any more. You're no longer relevant. You're obsolete, a throwback. It's time to accept that reality.'

Grav pushed himself to his feet. 'This isn't over.'

She remained seated, speaking as casually as possible, driving home her advantage. 'I think we're done for today, detective. I've got work to get on with. We can't all live a life of leisure.'

'What, more pen-pushing? That's going to make all the difference. I can hear the local criminals quivering from here.'

'Close the door on your way out.'

Grav opened her office door and slammed it shut behind him, kicking the secretary's metal wastepaper bin hard and sending it crashing into the nearest wall as he went.

Jones' eyes widened as she retreated in her seat. 'What on earth do you think you're doing, man?'

'Go fuck yourself, Gail. You're not all that. You're the monkey, not the organ grinder. It might be an idea to remember that. Take the broomstick out of your arse occasionally and lighten up. You might be a bit more popular that way.'

* * *

Grav sat in his car for twenty minutes, listening to classical music turned up loud and smoking one cigar after another, before finally building up sufficient resolve to return to the familiar building he loved. He said a cheery, 'Hello,' to Sandra on the front desk, ignoring her enquiries after his health, and took the lift rather than use the stairs to reach the serious incident room on the top floor.

Grav stopped briefly on exiting the elevator, catching his breath before finally pushing through the double doors and entering the room to loud cheers of welcome from the various officers in attendance. He held a Churchillian hand in the air to both acknowledge and silence them and approached Kesey's desk with a solemn expression on his face. 'Hello, love, I thought it might be useful to have a quick catch-up while I'm here.'

Kesey stood and smiled. 'I was just about to grab a sandwich in the canteen. Are you going to join me?'

'You know me, love. I'm never one to turn down a bit of stodge.'

* * *

The two officers sat at the back of the room engaged in small talk for a few minutes, before Grav asked the inevitable question, 'Any developments with the case?'

Kesey nibbled her cheese and tomato sandwich. 'Nothing dramatic, but we're making progress.'

'Receiving that hand in the mail shook Emily right up.'

'Well, yes, it would.'

'Did it help us at all?'

Kesey sipped her hot drink and nodded. 'There was a group of tiny stars tattooed above the knuckles and signs of torture.'

Grav winced. 'Oh for fuck's sake!'

'Yes, exactly, the bastard tore her fingernails out.'

'That must have been painful.'

'Horrendous!'

'Do we know who the hand belonged to in life?'

'Yeah, the teacher – the girl in her twenties. She had the tattoo done on holiday in Crete in her teens. The pathologist believes the hand was frozen for an extended period before being posted.'

'Who did the examination?'

'Sheila Carter.'

Grav slurped his tea. 'Okay, that's good. She's sound, you can trust her judgement. Any luck finding the rest of the body?'

Kesey shook her head. 'Not as yet.'

'All you can do is keep looking.'

She took a bite of sandwich, waiting for Grav to continue. 'Did the scenes of crime people find anything useful at Mia's place?'

Kesey nodded once and swallowed. 'Now, this is where it gets interesting.'

'I'm listening.'

'There were covert, night-vision wireless cameras and microphones hidden in every room of the house. And I do mean *every* room. Even the bathroom. Whoever fitted them knew everything she was doing. He wasn't a mind reader. Neither sister said too much to the wrong person. He was watching and he was listening. How the hell he managed to convince her that all was necessary is a mystery to me.'

'Manipulative people can be very persuasive, particularly when the target's vulnerable.'

'Yeah, I guess so.'

Grav scratched his nose. 'Any fingerprints?'

'No, afraid not, whoever installed them was forensically aware.'

'Have you talked to Mia about all this? She must be able to tell you something.'

Kesey took a final bite, washing the crust down with a gulp of warm liquid. 'Yeah, at the airport before they flew out to Italy. At least she's safely out of the way. It's one less thing to worry about.'

'What did she tell you?'

'She's had two men to the house in recent weeks, claiming to be from the fire service. The first man fitted several alarms, and the second two more. I've talked to the fire people... they had no record of it. Neither man was working for them. We can say that with certainty.'

'That would have been too much to ask for.'

Kesey laughed. 'Yeah, that's what I thought.'

'Did Mia give you decent descriptions of the suspects?'

'They were both overweight, both of average height, five foot eight to ten, and in their mid-to late thirties. One, the first to visit, had black hair and a well-established beard. The other, blond hair, a beard, tinted glasses and buck teeth. It's something to go on.'

'No one comes to mind?'

'No, I thought Gary Williams may fit the bill for man number two. He's put on a lot of weight in recent years and has a history of violence towards women, but he was banged up in Cardiff nick for eight of the last nine months after an indecent assault conviction in the Newport area.'

'Have you circulated the descriptions?'

Her eyes blazed bright. 'Well... yeah, I do know what I'm doing. I'm not a complete muppet, despite the rumours.'

'I know that, love, no offence intended. It's just my way, that's all. It's no reflection on your ability. You know what I'm like by now.'

Kesey focussed back on her investigation, swallowing her irritation as she had many times before. 'Both men's appearances are distinctive enough. That's got to be to our advantage. I was just surprised that we appear to be talking about two men working together. I've heard of it, of course, but it's not something I've ever encountered myself.'

Grav drained his cup and stood to buy another. 'Unless we're dealing with one man who changes his appearance. It seems likely to me. People almost always believe what they see. Put a tart in a business suit and people will see a businesswoman, simple as.' He walked towards the serving counter, leaving her hanging with a self-satisfied smile on his face. He turned stiffly and called out across the room, 'Anything else for you, love? I'm having a bag of crisps.'

Kesey shook her head while considering Grav's revelation and awaiting his return.

He sat himself down. 'So, what do you think?'

'Yeah, it makes sense. Our man's a bit on the fat side – he couldn't hide that. But the rest of him... now, that's something he could change easily enough. A wig, a false beard, glasses. It has got to be worth considering.'

Grav began munching his crisps, speaking as he ate. 'I'd say so.'

'I've been looking into the availability of the relevant technology.'

'Anything that helps us?'

'No, not a great deal. Everything is surprisingly easy to obtain online. I've got a couple of people making pertinent enquiries, but I'm not holding my breath. You can buy that stuff from all over the world. Bottom line, we've got very little to go on.'

Grav threw his empty packet aside and licked the salt from his fingers. 'Well, anything's a lot better than nothing.'

'I guess so.'

'Didn't you tell me one of the hit-and-run witnesses said the driver had blond hair?'

'"May have had blond hair," were the exact words.'

'Okay, it's next to useless as potential evidence, but it may point you in the right direction. Maybe you're looking for a blond guy, or maybe you're not.'

Kesey nodded. 'Have you received any more emails?'

'No, just the one I told you about.'

'What about Emily?'

'Not that she's mentioned. I've tried to talk her into staying at my place for the foreseeable future, but she's not having any of it. She's an independent girl.'

Kesey swirled her remaining coffee around her mug. 'I'm expecting an email or two myself now that I'm heading up the investigation.'

'It wouldn't surprise me. It's what he does.'

She picked at her fingernail. 'How are things with you, boss? Have you got a date for your return? I could do with all the help I can get.'

Grav dropped his head. 'I think your acting inspector role is going to be made permanent a lot sooner than you thought. You don't need me holding your hand any more. But then, I think you know that, don't you?'

She pulled her head back. 'You're not going to tell me you've decided to pack it all in, are you? I thought they'd have to drag you out of here kicking and screaming.'

He gave a thumbs-up as a long-serving colleague waved and shouted his best wishes from the other side of the room. 'I've just had a meeting with her majesty, doff my cap, curtsey and all that. She wants me gone.'

'What does your doctor say?'

'That I'm ready to come back.'

'So, what's the problem?'

'Can you see me in a non-operational role? Sitting at a desk all day pushing bits of paper about, or training a load of probationers still wet around the ears?'

'Is that what she offered you?'

'Yeah, she's got me exactly where she wants me.'

Kesey's brow furrowed. 'Do you want me to have a word with her? I'd be more than happy to. I can't promise it will make any difference, but I'd give it a good go.'

Grav pointed at her, jabbing a digit. 'You do *not* do that under any circumstances. And that's an order, in case you were wondering. You've got a new baby, and you're in line for a promotion. The last thing I want is for you to cock it all up on my account. If the chief super thinks you're in my corner, it'll be the kiss of death for you. She'll promote Trevor Simpson or some other numpty who's not fit to lace your shoes. Have I made myself perfectly clear?'

Kesey pressed her lips together, touched by his generosity of spirit. 'Are you certain?'

'I couldn't be surer. And it wouldn't do me any good anyway, even if you did go down on bended knee. Her majesty's been waiting for an opportunity like this for a very long time. We never did get on. I'm old-school, and she's the opposite. She's got all the qualifications in the world but toss all real-life experience.' He grinned. 'You were considered an academic if you had five O levels when I joined the force. We were bound to clash sooner or later. It was as inevitable as night and day.'

Kesey wiped a tear from her face. 'It's the end of an era. I'm going to miss you terribly.'

A flush crept across Grav's cheeks as he glanced to the right and left. 'Pull yourself together, girl, or you'll have me blabbing. That's not going to do my tough-guy image any good at all.'

Her frown became a smile. 'The christening's booked for a week Saturday at St Mary's Church in the high street, if you're feeling up for it?'

'Just try and stop me.'

'And we're going to have a bit of a celebration at the house afterwards. You know the sort of thing, a few drinks and something to eat. Emily's very welcome if she feels like coming.'

Grav stood up slowly, a shooting pain firing in his right knee and making him flinch. 'I'll let her know. She can do the driving.'

'It's been good to talk, boss.'

He looked her in the eye. 'If somebody's got to take my place, I'm glad it's you.'

'Thank you, that means a lot.'

'If you receive any information that suggests Emily's in immediate danger, you'll let me know, yeah?'

'I'll be straight on the phone, guaranteed.'

'And I'd like you to fit a panic alarm in her place, linked directly to the station. Maybe then I could sleep nights.'

Kesey nodded her ready agreement. 'Consider it done. I was thinking along the same lines myself. And I've asked uniform to drive past whenever they're in the area. It can't do any harm.'

'Thanks, love, it's appreciated. I'll see you at the christening, if not before. And send me a reminder of the time and date. My memory's not what it was.'

'There's an invitation in the post.'

Grav turned and sauntered away, knowing without doubt that he was leaving Police Headquarters for the very last time. Life really had gone full circle. He wasn't a working copper any more. Just a lonely old man who was of no use to anyone. He saw his beloved Heather appear alongside him as he strolled out into the car park without looking back. 'Oh hello, love, that's it then, all done and dusted. Time to send back the warrant card. I think I'll put it in the post. It'll be easier that way. Why drag things out unnecessarily? It wouldn't achieve anything at all.'

Heather held his hand in hers as he approached his car with a morose expression etched on his face. *'They'll want to arrange a leaving do, Grav. And there'll be a presentation. Something nice for you to put on the mantelpiece. Laura could arrange things. She'd like that.'*

'Oh, I don't know if I fancy all that, love.'

'You could do something at the club. Ask all your old friends to come. You know, be selective. You don't have to ask everyone.'

'Yeah, maybe, I'll give it some thought.'

'You do that, Grav. You know it makes sense.'

He unlocked the doors, always a stickler for security, and

climbed into the driver's seat. 'You're going to resent me having a few pints at the club tonight, are you, love?'

She smiled again, even more warmly this time, eyes shining, lips touching his. *'No, not tonight, my lovely boy, drink your fill and try to enjoy yourself. It's not every day one gets to retire.'*

He started the tired engine on the second turn of the key and drove towards the open road, swallowing his sadness, longing for the past, his veined eyes reddening as his dead wife's image faded. 'Right, love, the rugby club it is. I may even leave the car overnight and get a taxi home. What do you say? A few whisky chasers would go down very nicely.'

'I love you, Grav.'

'Fucking cancer!'

She folded her arms below her generous bosom. *'I was the one living the healthy lifestyle: yoga, swimming, low-fat this, low-calorie that. Imagine how I felt. Bowel cancer wasn't exactly the best way to go.'*

'I miss you, Heather.'

'I know. Trust me, I know.'

He closed his eyes tight shut, then opened them quickly as a single tear ran down his face and found a home on his collar.

'Go and get drunk, my lovely boy. There will be plenty of time for tears when you're done.'

31

Newly promoted DI Laura Kesey pushed a local arson file aside and answered the phone on the fifth ring. 'CID. How can I help you?'

'Hello, Laura, it's Sandra on the front desk. Or should I call you *ma'am* now that your promotion is permanent?'

'Either *boss* or *ma'am* will be fine when we're on the job. *Laura* if we're not. Let's start as we mean to go on.'

'Are you serious?'

'What can I do for you?'

Sandra raised a clenched hand to her mouth and coughed, clearing her throat. 'I've got a Mr Jackson Lewis here with me who wants to speak to a detective about the car found in the estuary.'

Kesey delved into a desk drawer for a statement form. 'Put him in whichever interview room's free and tell him I'll be with him in two minutes.'

'That will be room three.'

'Thanks, Sandra, I'm on my way.'

* * *

Kesey entered the interview room to be met by a somewhat underweight middle-aged man with a balding head and pebble glasses, which made his eyes appear disproportionally large, almost to the point of hilarity. She reached out and shook his hand in greeting before introducing herself, adopting her formal rank, and inviting him to take a seat. Kesey pulled up a chair, sat opposite him on the other side of the small Formica-topped table and handed him a pen and paper. 'If you could write your name, address and full contact details on there for me that would be extremely helpful.' It was a simple technique she's learned from Grav, one of several she continued to use.

Lewis completed his details as requested and handed Kesey the sheet of paper.

She glanced at it, confirming it was legible. 'Right, thanks for coming in. What have you got to tell me?'

'It's about the vehicle found in the Ferryside estuary, the one on the news.'

'What about it?'

'I saw a man pushing the car down the slipway in the early hours.'

Kesey tapped the tip of her pen on the tabletop three times, trying to figure him out, to read his thoughts. 'Okay, that's good to know, but why haven't you come in before now? The news report you referred to made it perfectly clear that we were looking for witnesses. Why not contact us immediately?'

He adjusted his glasses, taking them off, cleaning them and then returning them to their original position, as if they'd never left his face. 'I didn't see it. My missus told me about it a couple of days after it was on.'

'Do you live in the village?'

'Yes, on the bungalow estate near the bridge, as you come into the village from the Carmarthen side.'

'One of my officers made house-to-house enquiries. Ferryside's a small place. I'd be amazed if you didn't hear about it.'

He lifted an open hand to his face, covering his mouth.

Kesey silently admonished herself. Why risk alienating the man? Pursuing the matter served little, if any, purpose. 'What is it, Mr Lewis? This is a murder enquiry. Now isn't the time to hold anything back. I'd appreciate any assistance you can offer.'

He blurted out his response, the words spilling from his mouth almost as one. 'I'm sorry, I was netting salmon, I haven't got a licence. I lost my job last year. I can't afford the fine if I'm prosecuted. I was in two minds about talking to you at all.'

All of a sudden she understood his reticence. 'Why even mention it?'

'It wouldn't take you long to find out if you asked about. Like you said, it's a small place.'

'Okay, fair point, but I need you to understand that it's my job to catch a killer, not to worry about a bit of poaching. You help me, and I'll help you. That's how it works. Just tell me what you saw.'

'Do I have your word?'

'You're here as a witness, not a suspect. You haven't been arrested or cautioned. You're assisting us of your own volition, and you can leave whenever you choose to. I need to know what you saw that night, and nothing more. I'm going to assume that you won't be doing any more illegal fishing. We don't need to discuss why you were on the beach that night. It's not relevant to my investigation.'

His relief was plain to see, the tension dissipating. 'I was walking back along the path bordering the dunes when I saw a car's headlights coming towards me. I dived off the path and watched from behind a clump of gorse bushes, fearing it may be the bailiffs. The way my luck's been recently, it wouldn't have surprised me at all. It's been one disaster after another since my employer went bust. Shit happens, but it always seems to happen to me.'

'Tell me everything you remember, paint a picture, every little detail.'

'I watched, and I waited until the bloke finally drove onto the slipway and got out of the car. I thought he may be thieving – people steal outboards from the boats sometimes – but then he reached into the car, took off the handbrake and let it roll down into the sea. I was thinking, what the hell is that about? Was he some kind of nutter, or perhaps an insurance job? Well, you would, wouldn't you? It's not every day you see someone dumping a nice car like that.'

'How far away were you at the time?'

'Oh, I'd say about fifty metres or so, no more.'

Kesey raised a hand and pointed at his spectacles. 'Did you get a good look at him?'

'Yeah, my eyesight's pretty good as long as I'm wearing the glasses.'

Kesey visibly relaxed. 'Right, that's good to know. Can you give me a description?'

Lewis bobbed his head. 'Yes, once I realised he wasn't a bailiff I moved a bit nearer, staying in the shadows, walking slowly and stepping on the sand... avoiding the gravel. He didn't have the slightest idea I was there.'

'How close did you manage to get?'

'Maybe twenty metres away at most.'

'What, and he didn't see or hear you?'

'He was prancing around like a lunatic Cuban dancer after giving the car a shove with his foot.'

She massaged the back of her neck. 'Dancing?'

'Yeah, he was leaping about and spinning in a circle.'

'Really?'

'That's what I saw.'

'And you're certain you had a clear view of him?'

Lewis played with his glasses, jiggling them up and down. 'Yeah, it's like I said. I'm blind as a bat without these, everything's blurred, but they work pretty well all considered. My eyesight's up to driving standard when I'm wearing them, even in poor light.'

She nodded, satisfied with his explanation. 'Okay, I'm going to ask you a series of questions regarding his appearance. I want you to give me as specific answers as you possibly can, but please don't guess. If you don't know the answer, or if you're unsure, just say so. Are we clear?'

He nodded enthusiastically, glad to be talking about anything other than fishing.

'How tall was the man you saw?'

'Five foot ten, maybe six foot.'

Kesey noted his response in blue ink. 'And his build?'

'A bit on the fat side. Obese would be a fair way to put it. Fifteen, maybe sixteen stone with a beer belly.'

She continued writing. 'Thanks, that's helpful... what about his hair?'

'Blond and collar length with a fringe.'

'You seem very certain.'

'I started training as a barber in my teens, before jacking it in. I fell out with the boss. Leaving was the worst decision I ever made. Hairstyles still interest me; the building game's not my bag.'

'Let's focus on the description. Did you see his face?'

'Briefly. I don't know how much I can tell you.'

'Do your best, anything you can say may help.'

Lewis gazed into the distance, recalling that night, travelling back in time. 'There was nothing very remarkable. He was white, clean-shaven, that's about it. Just an average bloke who wouldn't stand out in a crowd.'

'Yeah, maybe that's the point.'

'What was that?'

Kesey shook herself, thinking her sleepless nights weren't conducive to concentration. 'Sorry, I was just thinking out loud.'

He smiled. 'I do the same thing sometimes. It drives my wife mad.'

'You said *clean-shaven*. Are you certain he didn't have a beard?'

'No beard.'

'Definitely?'

'Definitely!'

'Was he wearing glasses?'

'Yes, plastic frames.'

'You're sure?'

'Yeah, I'm certain. Spectacles tend to stick in my mind, for obvious reasons.'

She tried not to laugh, finding herself liking Lewis and his self-deprecating banter. 'What about his teeth?'

He screwed up his features. 'His teeth?'

'You didn't think they were particularly prominent?'

'Not that I noticed.'

'Okay, let's move on. What about his clothes?'

'I'd be guessing.'

'A suit, a jacket, casual clothes, can you tell me anything at all?'

'He may have been wearing jeans, a shirt and a jumper, or maybe not. They were dark clothes. That's as much as I can say with any confidence.'

'You can't be more specific?'

Lewis shook his head. 'Um... no, not really, I didn't give it any thought.'

Kesey decided not to push it, stifling a yawn as her eyes threatened to close. 'Do you think you'd recognise the man if you saw him again? In an identity parade, for example, at some future date?'

'Yeah, I don't see why not.'

'And you'd be prepared to do that for me if the opportunity arose?'

'Yes, I would. Just say the word.'

Kesey placed a form on the table between them. 'Okay, thank you for your cooperation, Mr Lewis. I'm glad of your assistance. I'll take a short statement, and you can be on your way.'

'Do you think I've helped at all?'

She nodded. 'Don't quote me on this, but yes, I think you probably have. I'll be circulating a description later today. Hopefully, you've given us the break we needed.'

32

Kesey stared at the text, attempting to hold it together as Janet fed Edward his bottle in the adjoining room. Threatening a baby! Referring to the hanging cat, with its abdomen sliced open. And drawing connections between the two! It was pure evil, the lowest of the low. What kind of maniac were they looking for?

'Are you going to join us, Laura? I was thinking of watching a film. This new telly you've bought is about as big as a cinema screen. We may as well make use of it.'

Kesey dragged her eyes away from her phone, unwelcome mental images assaulting her mind as she tried to blink them away. 'Yeah, very funny. I'll be with you in a minute. I've just got a bit of work to finish first.'

'What do you fancy watching?'

'You choose, you're fussier than me.'

Janet lifted the baby to her shoulder and patted his back gently, winding him as he began to whimper. 'I'll put the kettle on as soon as I get Ed settled, unless you fancy doing it?'

Kesey screenshot the message. 'You haven't seen anyone

hanging around outside the house, have you? An overweight blond guy, maybe? Or a guy with black hair and a beard?'

Janet lowered Edward into his wicker Moses basket, stroking his head tenderly until he closed his eyes and settled. She looked up, troubled, as Kesey entered the room. 'Why do you ask?'

'Oh, it's something and nothing.'

'Tea or coffee?'

'Tea, please, you know how I like it.'

Janet hurried towards the kitchen, returning a few minutes later with a matching porcelain mug in each hand. 'Right, come on, what's this about? Something and nothing doesn't cut it. You should know that by now.'

Kesey sat herself down and blew the air from her mouth with an audible whistle. 'It's this case I'm working on, the missing women.'

'What about it?'

'He's threatened me.'

Janet moved to the edge of her seat. 'Who, the man you're looking for?'

'Yes, I think so. It's just an anonymous text, nothing to worry about. I really shouldn't have said anything at all.'

Janet placed her fingers together as if in prayer. 'Oh, so I'm not supposed to worry. It's a bit late for that, don't you think?'

'So, have you seen anyone?'

'No, no, but then I haven't been looking. Why would I?'

Kesey glanced away, averting her eyes to the wall. 'It might be an idea to take Ed to visit your brother for a few days. You know, better safe than sorry.'

'I thought you said there was nothing to worry about?'

Kesey began pacing the floor, her mind rushing with ideas, opinions and questions and tumbling from one to the other. 'I don't know what to think. There could be, I just don't know.'

'Maybe you're overreacting.'

Kesey reread his text with haunted eyes before handing her mobile to Janet, who stared at the cracked screen in shaken silence as the colour drained from her face.

'Why would he say those horrible things?'

'He's a deviant. I suspect he likes to shock.'

Janet's lip began to tremble. 'Well, he's certainly done that.'

Kesey clutched her arms to her chest and nodded.

'Are you any nearer to catching him?'

'No, I really don't think we are.'

'He's threatened Edward, our baby.'

'Yes, he has.'

'Does he mean it?'

Kesey's words were whispered, barely decipherable, her face contorting. 'I think he probably does.'

'He's a killer, this man, a killer. I'm right, aren't I?'

'Yes, Jan, he is. Three times over.'

Janet rushed towards the hallway. 'Ring Andy for me. Tell him to expect us. And get Edward's things together. I'm going upstairs to pack.'

33

Adam set his phone to vibrate at 3:00 a.m. on his second night in Italy, though he lay awake for hours waiting for precisely the right time to implement the next stage of his plan. The alarm call had been an additional safety net, a sensible precaution. That's what he told himself. He was a military man, a professional. Meticulous planning was everything.

Adam threw back his single sheet, rose from the bed, switched off the air-conditioning and pulled on a pair of knee-length, dark-navy shorts and a black cotton T-shirt. He fetched a can of blood-red aerosol spray paint from his suitcase and stood at the bedroom door listening intently for even the slightest sound. All was quiet, except for intermittent soft nasal snoring emanating from Mia's parents' bedroom, which he mistakenly assumed was her father's laboured breathing as he sneaked onto the landing, spray can still clutched tightly in one hand.

Adam's anticipation was virtually overwhelming as he approached the staircase, descending quickly but cautiously until he reached the bottom. He rushed down the hallway, approached the front door and opened it, ensuring not to make even the slightest sound which could potentially disturb the family's slumber. Speedy silence, he assured himself, was the key to success.

The light of the moon was brighter than Adam would have wished in an ideal world as he strode around the building, but he moved even more rapidly now, with sinewy grace, gaining confidence as his plan came to fruition, almost exactly as he'd rehearsed it in his mind. He circled the entire villa twice before finally settling on a wall he considered ideally suited to his purpose, located at the back overlooking the garden. The wall was large, providing an unsullied canvas of the right shape and height, and it had the distinct advantage of not being visible from the road.

Adam removed the can's hard plastic cap, placed it on the ground close to the base of the wall, shook the can vigorously and began spraying, starting with Mia's name in large bold capitals approximately four feet high. He continued spraying, taking his time and ensuring his creation was entirely legible and well-spaced, until it was completed to his satisfaction only minutes later.

Adam stood back and admired the results of his efforts, reading his written words time and again, as his levels of excitement and arousal spiralled almost without limit.

MIA HAMILTON MUST DIE!

He reread it again, jumping up and down on the spot and punching his fist in the air in silent triumph, as was his custom. It was truly excellent, a stroke of inspired genius. She'd be back in Wales, begging and pleading in his garage cell before she knew what hit her.

Adam secured the can's cap back in place and began stroking his expanding genitals with his free hand as he walked back towards the front door, reluctantly dragging himself away from his artwork and brimming with anticipation like a child at Christmas. He couldn't wait for Mia to see it. To witness her reaction. The look of shock on her stupid face. And her parents too, how would they respond? Ha! Not long to wait. Only a few hours and he'd witness the scene.

Adam returned the paint can to his suitcase and opened the room's wooden shutters to let in the night-time air, still on a high from his activities. He lay back down on the bed without taking the trouble to get undressed and watched the seconds tick by on his watch until dawn. Time passed slowly, ever so slowly, and he gave a silent cheer of celebration when the house finally began to stir at just after seven that morning. He waited with growing impatience, relativity at its most extreme, until all the other occupants had gone downstairs for breakfast. He joined them minutes later with a look of feigned concern on his face which the adults noticed as soon as he entered the room.

'I don't want to worry you all, but I thought I heard someone outside on the terrace in the early hours.'

Mia's father was the first to respond. 'What exactly did you hear?'

'Just a loud thud, as if something was dropped. I've got no idea what or by whom. By the time I rushed outside to take a look around, whoever it was, was long gone. Maybe it was the man we're looking for. There's no way of telling with any certainty. Did anyone else hear anything?'

Mia and both parents shook their heads in unison as Adam retained centre stage, directing the orchestra. 'Okay, just me then. I think it comes from the years of training, honing my senses to pick up on the slightest deviation from the norm. There's not much I miss. It saved my life more than once in the Gulf.'

Mia twisted her bracelet around her wrist. 'What happens now? Should we contact the local police?'

Adam shook his head with a contemptuous sneer. 'Let's not jump to any conclusions. I'll have a good look around now it's light and find out if there's anything to see. If there is, we can decide what action's appropriate. Take my lead and you won't go far wrong.'

All but Isabella indicated their willing agreement, as the little girl continued to eat her melon, one nibbled bite at a time, avoiding the peel.

Adam exited the villa and strolled around the building, returning to the kitchen only minutes later and standing at the open door, filling the space. 'There's something I need you to see. Myra, it might be an idea to keep Izzy inside. There's no point in upsetting her unnecessarily.'

Adam led Mia and her father to witness the results of his crime, while Myra took her granddaughter up to her bedroom and closed the door against the world. They stood and stared at the red-painted message, Mia and Roy recoiling in horror and Adam doing a convincing job of conveying similar emotions. Mia hugged herself, clutching each shoulder with the opposite hand, and began emitting faint but discernible intermittent whelps, like a new-born puppy separated from its mother and desperately in need of suste-nance. Roy Hamilton placed a supportive arm around his trembling daughter and led her back over the sun-drenched terrace towards the front door, her unsteady legs wobbling and threatening to give way at any moment as her world became a neo-impressionist blur.

Adam ran a finger over the large painted M and stood back, taking various photographs with his smartphone, as Roy glanced back towards him. Mia and her father were sat huddled in the family kitchen by the time Adam returned to the property, both still eager to protect Isabella from the full realities of the situation. Adam rested both hands on the pine table but remained standing, looking down at them both, keen to maintain control and reinforce his dominance. 'The wall was completely dry when I touched it.' He held up both hands, fingers splayed, demonstrating they were paint-free, before adding, 'I must have missed him by seconds. It's frustrating, to say the least, but I just didn't see the message in the darkness.'

Both adults looked back at him, lost for words as Isabella and her grandmother made their way downstairs.

Adam lifted himself to his full height, puffing out his chest and hurrying his words, speaking in breathy tones intended to convey urgency. 'Roy, if you'll lend me the car, I'll call at the local police station and stress the level of danger faced by Mia. The sooner we report the matter, the better for everyone. I've had some experience in dealing with law enforcement in my role with the military. I seem to be the obvious person to do it.'

Roy rose to his feet, flustered, rushing, fetching the keys. 'I'll come with you.'

Adam was quick to reply. 'No, I really don't think so. It wouldn't be a good idea to leave the women on their own. If the police need to speak to any of you, I'm certain they'll be in touch. Let them come to you rather than the other way around. Believe me, it's better that way.'

Myra entered the kitchen hand in hand with Isabella, but she retreated rapidly on sensing the tension in the air.

Adam reached out a hand and shook the car keys theatrically. 'Right, I'll be on my way. Hopefully, the Italian police will take it as seriously as the British police have. I can't see why they wouldn't. We're talking about murder, not some triviality. Please stay inside until I'm back and keep the doors and all ground-floor windows locked. It's crucial we take every possible precaution. We know the perpetrator's an extremely dangerous man. We need to stay safe if we can.'

Mia raised a hand in the air like a child in a classroom. 'Do you think I should contact DI Kesey?'

'No, absolutely not! Leave all contact with the police to me. Trust me, I can't stress that sufficiently. I understand how to deal with these people. I know what to say and what not to say to get the best results. Don't speak to Kesey again unless we've agreed to it first. If it proves necessary, which seems unlikely, we'll rehearse the conversation in advance. Are we on the same page? I need to hear you say it.'

Mia nodded, her eyes frozen in fear, like a rabbit caught in the headlights. 'Anything you say, Adam. I'm so glad you're here to protect us all. Just tell me what to do, and I'll do it. I'm sure my parents feel the same way. I don't know what we'd do without you.'

'It's no problem, I'm happy to be of service. But I don't want either you or your parents to speak to anyone outside of the villa. And I do mean *anyone*. We don't know who's listening.'

* * *

It only took Adam ten minutes to drive down the long sweeping hill into Sorrento, and another five to find a petrol station that sold plastic fuel cans that he thought served his purpose well. He purchased a receptacle, rejecting two out of hand before finally settling on the one he wanted. He filled the container with fuel almost to the top, squeezing in the last few drops and paying in cash before hurrying to the back of the vehicle. He placed the vessel well out of sight in the boot, wedged upright by a fortuitously located windbreaker and a cool box which hadn't been used for months.

Adam drove out onto the open road, negotiating the busy

morning traffic as he headed along the coast in the direction of Amalfi, white-painted homes and restaurants silhouetted against dark granite cliffs that plunged towards the sea. He pulled up at a roadside café after twenty minutes and sat in the shade of an Umbrella Pine tree drinking freshly squeezed orange juice from a tall glass and eating bread and honey, while he waited for the seconds to tick by. He began tapping his foot up and down beneath the table as the pressures of the day played on his mind. How the hell was he going to get the petrol into the villa without being spotted? It was crucial that it wasn't seen either before or after use. A simple slip-up could potentially ruin everything at the worst possible time. It was too horrible to contemplate. Things couldn't go wrong, not now, not when he was very close to achieving his goal.

Adam's breathing quickened as the dilemma played on his mind, oxygen-rich blood flooding his system. Fight or flight but with nowhere to run. Maybe he should leave the receptacle hidden outside in a bush rather than try to get it into the building before darkness. Or, perhaps do some food shopping and bring the container in concealed in a large carrier bag, taking it to his room while the others unpacked his purchases. That may work.

He rechecked his watch and decided to wait for another five minutes before heading back towards Sorrento to locate a suitable supermarket. The decision was made. He was back on track. On top of his game. He felt his mood rise, wild elation gradually replacing mild contentment as he downed the remainder of his juice, savouring the intense sweetness at the bottom. Tonight was the night. If they thought things were bad, they were about to get worse.

Adam left sufficient cash to meet the bill on the white linen tablecloth, including a generous tip which was unusual for him, then skipped back towards the car with thoughts of death and destruction filling his mind. He jumped into the driver's seat, adjusted the rear-view mirror and laughed. He could see the results of his scheming in his mind's eye. He could hear the soundtrack playing in his head – the flames, the fear, the tears and screams – as if it were all happening in real time. It would be so good, so very good. It was going to be the worst night of their sad lives and one of the best of his. The family wouldn't know what hit them! Buckle up Hamiltons, it's going to be a bumpy ride.

34

Ella was feeling slightly better by the time she contacted the villa shortly before lunchtime. Her gums were still bleeding on brushing, but her stomach was less painful, enabling her to get out of bed and face the day. Ella wasn't ready to go back to work, not quite yet. Her head was still pounding as if something were attempting to break out of her skull. But she thought that whatever virus had laid her up so very suddenly was finally on the wane. And at least she didn't have some maniac trying to ruin her life and kill her like her poor sister. She had to be grateful for that.

Ella dialled and waited until she heard her father's familiar voice at the other end of the line. 'Hi Dad, it's Ella, how are things in Italy?'

'Um... not great, to be honest. How are things with you?'

'Never mind about me. What's happening there? I haven't heard a thing.'

'I don't know how much I can tell you.'

Ella's mouth slackened. 'Oh come on, Dad. I know what's going on with Mia. She's told me all about it. Just tell me what's going on.'

'Maybe it would be better if Adam gave you an update. I wouldn't want to say the wrong thing.'

She sighed, losing patience. 'Then, put him on the phone.'

'He's out.'

'Out where?'

'He's driven into town.'

'What about Mia?'

'She's upstairs.'

'Well, can I speak to her then?'

He raised his shoulders, pulling back his head. 'Okay, I'll call her. But please take it easy. She's a bit fragile at the moment. We all are.'

* * *

Mia held the phone to her face trying to figure out what to share and what to keep to herself. Maybe *he* was listening. Adam was right to be cautious. 'Hello, Ella, I hope you're feeling better.'

'Yes, I'm fine, but what about you?'

Mia couldn't stop herself, the words spilling from her mouth like a torrent she couldn't hope to prevent. 'He's here, the killer, he's here in Italy. He was at the villa last night. I think Adam must have scared him off, but he's definitely here. He must have followed us all the way from Wales.'

'Are you sure?'

'Oh yes, I'm sure. Adam's been fantastic! If it weren't for him, I wouldn't be coping at all.'

'What are you going to do?'

'Adam's talking to the local police as we speak. I'm just going to have to wait and see what he says when he comes back.'

'Do you want me to talk to Grav for you? He may be able to offer more advice.'

Mia ran a hand through her hair. 'No, Ella! We can't talk to anyone. The killer could be listening. Adam stressed that. We've got to take his lead.'

'Are you coming back to Wales?'

'I've probably said too much already. I may send you a text from Mum's or Dad's phone once I know what's happening, but only if Adam thinks that's safe. It may be better if I go old-school and put it in a letter.'

Ella shook her head, asking herself when Adam became such an expert. 'What about Laura Kesey? Do you want me to talk to her? You said she seemed nice enough. What harm could it do? I don't understand your reluctance.'

Mia gripped the phone tightly and began stamping her foot. 'No, not under any circumstances! Don't talk to anyone. That's what Adam advised. If you do, I'll never forgive you.'

35

Mia looked into Adam's eyes and resisted the urge to kiss him. 'What did the police say?'

'They took a statement.'

She stepped towards him, moving closer. 'Are they going to do anything?'

'They're arranging surveillance. We won't see them, but they'll be watching. It's starting immediately.'

'That's good, isn't it?'

'Yes, it's good, but we can't rely on it completely. If the killer's as good as I suspect he is, he may avoid the police altogether.'

Mia's head dropped.

'I'm here to protect you all. I'm not going to let you down.'

She looked up, feeling more positive. 'Ella's been on the phone.'

Adam felt his body tense. 'Where are your Mum and Dad?'

'They're in the pool with Izzy.'

'I told them to stay inside.'

'She wet the bed last night. They're trying to help her relax. It seemed like the right thing to do.'

He decided to let it slide. 'What did Ella want?'

Mia approached the kitchen taps and washed down a tablet, the third of the day. 'She offered to speak to the British police for us, either Grav, Kesey or both. She really wants to help.'

The whites of his eyes flashed. 'And what did you tell her?'

'I told her not to say a word. I said she has to talk to you before doing anything at all.'

He touched her elbow. 'She thinks you're making everything up.'

'What?'

'Look, I've been in two minds about telling you this, but you deserve to know the truth. Ella thinks you're desperate for attention. She says your brain's fried by the codeine. That you're an addict. She doesn't believe anything you say.'

Mia's face blanched as she looked away, covering her mouth. 'Then why talk about the police? It doesn't make a lot of sense.'

He wanted to hit out. He so wanted to hit out. 'She says what she thinks you want to hear. That's all she's doing. I can't believe you haven't figured that out. She says it's easier that way. Ella hates confrontation and doesn't want to upset you. She's got her own issues to deal with. She's opting for an easy life.'

'Well, can't you tell her the truth? I thought I could rely on her. I really thought she was on my side.'

Adam looked past her, considering his next move. 'Ella doesn't trust you. She thinks you're in love with me. That you've pulled the wool over my eyes. I've told her how ridiculous that is, but she doesn't want to hear it. She's even talked of calling off the wedding.'

Mia reached for her tablet bottle. 'I need to talk to her. I need to explain. We used to be so close.'

'Take your medication, sit down and I'll fetch you a glass of wine. You speaking to Ella is the *last* thing we need. She's an unhelpful distraction. We need to concentrate on each other and decide how we're going to keep that little girl of yours safe. Got it?'

Mia swallowed another tablet and nodded. 'Can I hug you?'

He smiled, lips pressed closed. 'Of course, if it makes you feel better.'

She threw her arms around him, Adam fighting the impulse to recoil, repulsed by her feelings of affection. Emotions he'd never experienced towards anyone but himself.

She released her grip. 'What are we going to do, Adam?'

'It may be an idea to go back to Wales.'

'He followed us here, what's stopping him from following us back there too? I'm not sure going back to Wales is going to help. If the Italian police are watching the villa, that may be our best chance.'

His tone changed and became sharper, assertive, with a hint of aggression. 'Are you an expert all of a sudden?'

'I wasn't trying to suggest—'

'Am I an expert, Mia?'

'Yes, yes, of course you are. I didn't mean to question—'

He interrupted her again. 'Then I'll tell you what we're going to do. I'm going to cook everyone a meal this evening, once Isabella's fast asleep in bed. We'll all sit down together and discuss everything that's happened. I'll tell you what I think, and by the end of the evening we'll have agreed on the best way forward. What do you think of that?'

Mia pressed her palms to her eyes and flopped back in the nearest chair. 'Thank you so much, Adam. I knew we could rely on you. You're the best thing that's happened to me in a very long time.'

* * *

Adam cooked his signature spaghetti Bolognese that evening, utilising fresh ingredients, complimented by tinned tomatoes bought on his visit to the Sorrento supermarket earlier in the day. Both Mia and her mother offered to help, but he resisted their overtures, insisting it was something he wanted to do himself. His treat.

'Does everyone like plenty of garlic?'

Everyone replied in the affirmative as Adam continued cooking. 'How about a little music?'

Roy Hamilton rose to his feet, a quarter-full glass of Chianti in hand as he approached the CD player. 'Classical or contemporary? We've got a fairly eclectic collection of both. I think we should let the chef choose. He's doing all the hard work.'

No one objected.

'Oh, okay, how about something modern and mellow to help us relax, something laid back? We could do with it given recent events. I can tell you from hard-won experience. Giving in to fear only helps the enemy.'

All were in agreement.

They discussed events and the best way forward for the next half an hour or so, each family member contributing their thoughts under Adam's direction, as he steered the conversation back in the direction of Wales.

No one argued. No one contradicted him. Adam talked while he cooked until he considered the time right. He dished up Mia's and his own meal first, before taking a small pre-prepared foil package from a pocket, unfolding it quickly, ensuring not to be seen, and dropping six crushed and powdered sleeping tablets into the Bolognese mixture. He stirred in the white granules, vigorously agitating the mixture with a wooden spoon until there was nothing unusual or suspicious to see.

Adam plated and served the food, ensuring each person received the correct meal, double-checking before pouring himself a second glass of red wine and opening a third bottle with a rewarding pop of the cork. Conversation gradually slowed as the evening progressed, the effects of the drug causing both victims to yawn repeatedly as their eyelids became heavier and threatened to close. Myra and Roy finished their meals, more out of politeness than anything else, but the demands of sleep meant that bed was calling with increasing urgency. Roy dragged himself to his feet at shortly before ten and yawned expansively. 'I don't know what the hell's wrong with me tonight. It must be the stress. I can hardly keep my eyes open. I think I'm going to have to say goodnight.'

Myra joined him on her feet, flinching as a car horn sounded in the road. 'Yes, I'm feeling much the same. I can't quite believe it. I was beginning to think I'd never sleep again.' She reached down and hugged Mia before kissing Adam on his cheek. 'Thank you for a lovely meal. It makes a nice change to have someone cook for me.'

Adam said goodnight to them both for what he hoped was the last time. 'You're welcome. Glad to be of service. And try to relax. We've got the police surveillance in situ and I'll check the grounds and ensure everything's locked and secure before finally heading upstairs myself. I'm a light sleeper. If he comes back, I'll hear him.'

Mia nodded, reassured despite the dangers they faced. She told herself there were better times ahead. That it would soon be over. Finished, as if it never started. 'Yes, thanks, Adam. The food was delicious. You're a wonderful cook. And thank you for keeping us all safe. Just having you here makes a massive difference to the way we're all feeling.'

'You're very welcome.'

Mia gave a quick wave of her hand as her drowsy, heavy-eyed parents glanced back on approaching the hall. 'Goodnight, Mum, goodnight, Dad, thanks for all you've done. Everything's going to work out for the best. Just you wait and see. I'll see you in the morning.'

36

Adam rose from bed at just gone 3:00 a.m., already dressed and eager to implement the next stage of his plan. He pulled on a pair of black, size nine, soft-soled trainers he considered ideal for the task, collected the petrol container and a box of Strike Anywhere matches from the carrier bag left at the end of the bed and stood in the room's open doorway, listening, just as he had the night before. This time all was silent, Myra drugged and sleeping on her side as opposed to her back.

Adam crept across the landing but stopped, swearing under his breath as he returned to the bedroom to retrieve the passports and his wallet from the bedside cabinet. He dropped them into a large zipped pocket on the side of his thigh and hurried down the stairs towards the sliding doors that led onto the terrace at the back of the property, rather than utilise the front entrance as he had before. It seemed wiser, more sensible and far less risky. That seemed so obvious now, and he couldn't understand why he hadn't realised it before. Maybe his close attention to detail was slipping. Or was his excitement getting in the way of reasoned thought? He had to concentrate. There was no room for error. The car keys. He had to grab the car keys.

Adam stood outside in the warm, comforting semi-darkness of the night, grateful for the cloud cover that shrouded the entire area in shadow. A self-fulfilling prophecy in his eyes. A manifested reality created by his intellect. Everything was exactly as it should be.

Adam unscrewed the cap of the petrol can and began hurling the contents over the building, ensuring he soaked the bone-dry wooden window frames from top to bottom. When the container was three-quarters empty, he returned to the open doors and poured in the remainder, soaking the kitchen floor before throwing in the plastic receptacle with the intention of destroying the evidence.

Adam stood back with a smile on his face. He struck a match, stared at the yellow flame, watching it dance, and then casually tossed it through the doors, where the waiting fuel exploded into life. The blaze took hold in seconds, engulfing the kitchen's wooden units in a raging inferno, thick black smoke discolouring the ceiling.

Adam sprinted around the villa towards the front door and began hammering it with the side of one fist. He turned and kicked it mule style, causing it to shake in the frame as he yelled, 'Fire!' at the top of his voice. He barged the door with his shoulder, once, then twice, using all his weight and strength to burst it open as Mia jumped from bed and hurried towards Isabella's room with a look of panic etched on her face.

Roy Hamilton woke momentarily as his wife slept next to him, but he closed his eyes again almost immediately, returning to his dreams and oblivious to the developing crisis. Adam shouted again as he stumbled into the hallway, even louder this time as he fell forwards and collided with the wall. Dark smoke seeped in from under the kitchen door and restricted his breathing as he dragged himself upright and approached the stairs. 'Fire! Fire! Get up! The place is on fire!'

Mia appeared on the landing only seconds later, holding Isabella in her arms, looking down the stairs towards safety, but unwilling to move as her parents continued to lie close to unconsciousness as if nothing at all was happening.

The hungry flames had overcome their internal barrier now, the blaze moving relentlessly onwards as the kitchen door blackened, glowed and disintegrated almost to nothing. The temperature was rising relentlessly, the heat on the staircase spiralling alarmingly as the flames leapt and danced, devouring everything in their path.

'Listen to me, Mia, we haven't got much time if you want to survive. I want you to go to the bathroom and soak a large towel with cold water. Wrap it around your heads and come downstairs as quickly as you possibly can.'

Mia tugged at her cuff. 'What about Mum and Dad?'

Adam was shouting above the roar of the flames now, yelling at full volume to make himself heard. 'Just do what I say, Mia. Come on, get on with it! We'll get Izzy to safety first and then worry about your parents.' He glared at her when she didn't react quickly enough, shielding his face with his hands. 'Now, Mia! I'll meet you at the halfway point. Move! Do what I say or you're both going to die.'

Mia moved quickly, shaken from her indecision and running towards the bathroom while uttering words of reassurance in Isabella's ear. 'Everything's going to be okay, Izzy. We're going to be fine. Uncle Adam's going to help us. Just wait and see.'

Mia wrapped a drenched bath towel around them and hurried back across the landing towards the staircase, descending cautiously as Adam stood on the fifth step and reached out a hand, guiding them through the increasingly acrid smoke towards the front door. All three stumbled out into the comparatively fresh air, coughing and spluttering as the fire truly took hold, a ball of flames exploding from the kitchen and engulfing everything in its path.

Mia lowered Isabella to the ground and threw her arms out wide, a look of shock and fear changing the contours of her face. 'My parents! Oh, my God! What about my parents?'

Adam made a show of approaching the open door, his features blackened by the smoke, but he was beaten back by the flames. He turned away and yelled, 'It's too late. We've got to retreat or we're all going to die.'

Mia stared at him with utter hopelessness, despair etched on her face. Then she looked towards Isabella, sat in a tight huddle on the ground, before her eyes focussed on the quickly spreading inferno which was illuminating the entire area in a yellow-orange glow. The burning heat singed Mia's hair as she took two steps towards the villa, and she knew in that instant that Adam was right. Her parents' cause was lost. They were gone, nothing but a memory. There was no room for denial, no time for indecision. Izzy's safety had to come first.

Mia patted her body, searching for her codeine, and feeling a sense of growing panic. She took Isabella's hand in hers and led her towards the road, where Adam was waiting in the car. He switched off the engine, exited the vehicle and looked into Mia's eyes. '*He's* done this, Mia. He tried to murder us all.'

'My mum and dad, my poor mum and dad! If we hadn't come, they'd still be alive.' She was weeping uncontrollably now, streams of tears running down her blackened face.

'Come on, in you get, both in the back.' Adam shook Mia when she stalled, looking back at the inferno with fear and distress as her parents' demise resonated in her mind. 'Get in, woman! He's almost certainly watching. He could strike again at any moment. Do you want us all to die?'

'But where the hell are the police?'

'I can't answer that. Now get in!'

Mia hugged Isabella tightly in the back seat, desperately trying to force unwelcome images from her head as Adam sped towards town.

'Right, I'll tell you what we're going to do. I'm going to drive straight to the airport without stopping. We're going to leave the car there and we're going to wait in the terminal for however long it takes to get a flight back to the UK. You can freshen up while you're there. Maybe buy you both a new outfit too. It's the only way I can keep you both alive.'

'What about the police?'

'Did the police stop him setting fire to the villa?'

Mia shook her head, her face frozen by grief. 'No!'

'Did they stop him killing your parents?'

She pictured their bodies burned to a cinder and yearned for her medication like never before. 'No! My poor mum and dad! I can't stand the thought of them in that fire, helpless, trapped by the flames. He's a monster, whoever he is, he's a monster! What kind of man would do something like that, something so awful, so merciless?'

'And did the police prevent that monster almost killing us in the most horrible way? Just like your parents? Just like them?'

'No, they didn't. No, they didn't!'

Adam dipped his headlights to accommodate the oncoming traffic and smiled a quickly vanishing smile. 'Forget the police, they can't help you. If you trust me implicitly and follow my instructions without question, we may get through this with our lives intact. I'm not giving any guarantees. I don't want to make any promises I can't keep, that's not my style. But what I can tell you with absolute certainty is that I'm your best hope. Trust me, Mia, if you're going to survive this, it will be down to me.'

37

Mia was sweating profusely as she sat on the flight from Naples to Cardiff, large damp patches forming under both arms and small beads of glistening moisture glossing her brow. The symptoms of drug withdrawal were becoming ever more severe now, her resulting misery exacerbated by the crushing grief she felt at the loss of her loving parents. Caring for Isabella had become more onerous as the hours passed, Mia's need for codeine gradually overwhelming her mothering instincts and abilities. Adam again made a show of checking the plane's male passengers, feigning concern and saying he's spotted one man whose face looked dangerously familiar. Mia looked back at Adam with pinpoint pupils when he sat back down. She was shaking and shivering, lost in a sea of despair as her gut churned and her body ached.

'I need you to move, Adam. I need the toilet.'

'What, again?'

'Yes, again!'

'But I've only just sat down.'

Her tone was anguished, her expression urgent. 'If I don't go now I'll have an accident. I don't think either of us wants that.'

'Okay, okay, if I must, I must. Give me a second.'

Adam supervised Isabella while her mother locked herself in the toilet cubicle for the fourth time in less than an hour. Mia looked close to collapse when she finally exited the convenience with black mascara smudged over her tear-stained face.

Adam's childcare responsibilities weren't something that bothered him particularly. He didn't object to giving his time to what he considered a pointless task. It did at least give him the opportunity to think as Isabella played with a plastic cup. He ignored her in the main, nodding or shaking his head when he felt it necessary and planning the next stage of Mia's decline and ultimate demise. It was her time now. He'd become her Machiavellian overlord. A puppet master par excellence. Why not abandon the brat somewhere remote and transport her mother straight to the garage? Or kill Isabella and dump her body in the interests of security? Yes, that made sense. And it would tear Mia's heart out. He laughed as he pictured the scene. Dance to my tune, you supercilious bitch. Swirl and prance as I tug your strings.

Mia struggled along the aisle, a small but discernible part of her wishing she'd breathed her last along with her parents. At least then it would be over.

'Are you all right, madam? Is there anything I can do to help you?'

'A glass of water please, I'm not feeling at all well.'

The dark-haired stewardess nodded twice, smiling uncertainly. 'Do you want me to find out if there's a doctor on the plane? I can make an announcement if you think it's necessary.'

Mia was about to say yes, but what if *he* was on the plane? What if *he* responded to her plight with evil intent? He could pretend to be a doctor, couldn't he? Adam had said he recognised someone. Best decline the offer. Best not see anyone at all.

'Is everything all right, madam? Did you hear what I said?'

'No, no doctor. I just need to sit down. Help me to my seat, and I'll be fine.'

'Okay, if you're sure. But please don't hesitate to call me if you change your mind.'

'Thank you, I will.'

Mia squeezed past Adam and into her seat, floundering for her seatbelt with trembling hands. 'That glass of water would be appreciated. I'm going to try to get some rest.'

'I'll just fetch it. You'll be home soon. We'll be landing in half an hour.'

Mia stared back at her blankly, her residual strength spent. That was good news, wasn't it? Wales was beckoning. Or would *he* follow them? Maybe he'd be there too.

Mia dropped her head. Was there any escape, even with Adam's help? Only time would tell.

38

It took Adam just over an hour to drive from Cardiff Airport to the outskirts of Carmarthen in the early hours, keeping a watching brief for non-existent police cars and breaking the speed limit almost the entire way. He stayed in his vehicle with Isabella asleep in the back during the final toilet stop, Mia running towards the service station's conveniences and only just making it in time. She looked at the floor and spotted a fifty-pence coin as she answered nature's call, instinctively deciding to contact Ella while she had the opportunity. It seemed like the right thing to do, whatever the rift between her and her sister. Ella had the right to know that their parents had passed on, whatever Adam's likely objections. It wasn't something she should keep to herself however ill she felt. Ella loved their mum and dad as much as she did.

Mia washed her hands thoroughly and grimaced on seeing her bedraggled refection in the large illuminated wall mounted mirror, before drying her hands with a paper towel. She failed to find a payphone that accepted coins, but an exhausted-looking woman in her sixties finally agreed to allow Mia use of her mobile for what she understood was a local call.

Mia slid the coin across the café's plastic table before dialling. 'Hello, Ella, it's Mia. We're back in Wales.'

'Have you seen the time? Couldn't this have waited until morning?'

'I've got bad news, Ella.'

Ella stiffened. 'What is it?'

'There's no easy way to tell you this, so I'm just going to say it. Mum and Dad are dead.'

Ella was fully awake in that instant. 'What?'

'I'm so sorry, Ella. It was arson. They died in a fire.'

Ella choked back her tears. 'Oh, God, that's terrible! How... how the hell did it happen? You said arson. Who'd do such a thing?'

'The man who sent the emails. The sender... I wasn't making it up whatever you thought.'

'What on earth are you talking about? I always believed you. I tried to help, didn't I?'

Mia winced as Adam suddenly appeared in the foyer, glancing in every direction with rapid movements of his head. Then his head stopped, his glare fixed on Mia. He paced towards her.

'What the hell are you doing?'

Mia ended her call without another word and handed the phone back to its startled owner. Adam was closer now, almost at touching distance.

'I asked you what you were doing. Who were you talking to?'

'Ella, I told her about Mum and Dad. It was too important to keep to myself. She had to know.'

Adam felt his rage building, a red mist descending, but he somehow managed to suppress it as people began to stare. 'What else did you tell her?'

'Just that we're back in Wales.'

He grabbed her arm and began rushing her towards the car,

parked in a dark corner under an overhanging tree. 'For fuck's sake, woman! Are you trying to get us killed?'

'I used a stranger's phone. What harm could it possibly do?'

He increased the pace, Mia losing her footing and stumbling as he dragged her to her feet. 'What if Ella blabs? Have you considered that? It may be an idea to put your brain into gear before you do anything else to jeopardise our safety. What the fuck's wrong with you?'

'The murdering bastard was in Italy with us. He burned down the villa. He killed my parents. Who do you think Ella's going to tell?'

'Just get in the car and shut up. Maybe then I can keep you alive.'

'You're not making a lot of sense.'

Adam started the engine and sped towards the exit. 'Which part of shut up didn't you understand?'

Mia clung to Isabella's hand. 'Where are you taking us?'

'Home to stay with Ella and me until we can come up with a better alternative. Why do you ask? Have you got a better idea?'

Mia moved up close to Isabella as she started to cry. 'It's all right, Izzy. Uncle Adam's not cross, he's just tired, that's all.'

Adam wasn't ready to let it go. 'I asked you if you've got a better idea.'

'I'm sorry, Adam, I know you're doing your best. It's just that this is all so utterly terrifying. I'm finding it difficult to trust anyone.'

He glanced in the rear-view mirror, enjoying her obvious distress but hiding it well. 'I hope that doesn't include me. Not after everything I've done. I've put my life on the line for you. A bit of appreciation wouldn't go amiss.'

She lowered her eyes. 'Of course it doesn't include you. You're the one person I can rely on. I won't forget that.'

'I'm very glad to hear it.'

Mia's gaze bounced from one place to the next. 'I badly need some codeine, Adam. If you take me to the doctor's surgery first thing in the morning, I may be able to convince the receptionist that it's urgent.'

'I know someone who'll supply it for cash. Forget the doctor. I can get you as much as you need.'

Mia's eyes lit up. 'Tonight?'

He made her wait for a few seconds before replying. 'No, not tonight, we all need to rest. There's only so much I can do without collapsing.'

The hours stretched out in front of Mia like an insurmountable desert she couldn't hope to cross. '*Please* get the tablets as soon as you can. I'd be hugely grateful. I've come to rely on the drug. I can't function without it.'

He waited, for a little longer this time, as Mia wriggled in her seat. 'You can take one of Ella's sleeping tablets when we get back. By the time you've woken up, I'll have bought the tablets. Or at least I will have if I can get hold of the dealer. It shouldn't be a problem.'

Mia felt as if she were on an emotional rollercoaster, battered from hope to disillusion within split seconds. 'Please try your best.'

He chose not to answer, concentrating on his driving.

'You will, won't you, Adam?'

'No more talking, close your eyes and try to sleep. I'm far too exhausted to say any more.'

39

Ella left the house at 8:00 a.m. two days after her family's return from Italy, taking a second bus to West Wales General Hospital, having left the house unannounced. She had never felt more nervous as she sat in the busy casualty department, each and every face morphing into Adam's at first glance and every unseen male's voice becoming his as she sat and waited. She jumped more than once, half expecting him to suddenly appear and admonish her.

Ella visited the toilet after about half an hour and noticed that her gums were bleeding to a greater degree than before as she stared into the mirror, every facial flaw cruelly highlighted by the overly bright fluorescent light above her head. Ella knew at that moment that her suspicions were true. It was serious. She was in danger. Waiting patiently along with the other prospective patients was no longer a viable option.

Ella felt a sharp stabbing pain deep in the pit of her stomach as she struggled back out into the waiting area, and she collapsed to the carpeted floor long before reaching the reception desk. Within five minutes she'd been urgently transported to one of the department's reception beds, but she didn't regain consciousness for another twenty minutes. When she finally came around, she was wearing nothing but an unflattering light-green hospital gown fastened at the rear, a young ginger-haired staff nurse looking down at her with a concerned expression on her face.

'Well, hello, nice to have you back with us. Sorry about your clothes. You had a rather bad bleed from your back passage. They're going to need a wash before wearing.'

'You haven't told anyone I'm here, have you?'

The nurse shook her head. 'No, I don't think so. Or, at least not that I'm aware of. Is there anyone in particular you'd like me to contact?'

Ella raised herself up onto her elbows, her expression stark. 'Nobody at all, you mustn't contact anybody, that's absolutely crucial! I need your assurances.'

'Well, it's a bit unconventional, but if you say so.'

'*Please* ensure nobody else contacts anyone either, particularly my fiancé, that's *really* important. I think he's trying to kill me.'

The nurse pulled her head back. 'Right, give me five minutes. The consultant should be with you very shortly. She's going to want to know what this is all about.'

Ella looked at the clear plastic intravenous infusion line in her arm as the inserted tube pulled against her skin and smarted. 'What's this thing for?'

'You've been haemorrhaging, like I said. It's to replace the fluids you've lost. Try to relax, Dr Thomas will tell you everything you need to know. I'll be back in five minutes. I'll go and make sure no one makes that call.'

* * *

Ella waited patiently while Dr Elena Thomas completed her initial examination. 'Have you experienced bleeds before?'

'Yes, yes, I have.'

'From your gums and anus?'

'Yes, and from my nose too.'

'When did all this begin? Is it something you've discussed with your general practitioner?'

Ella swallowed the residual blood lingering in her mouth, preparing to speak and make herself heard. 'This is probably going to sound ridiculous to you, but I think I may have been poisoned.'

There was something about Ella's countenance that rang true. A credibility of sorts that made her statement difficult to dismiss out of hand. 'What makes you think that?'

'I've experienced severe stomach pains in recent weeks after my fiancé's cooked for me. The pain is followed by bleeding. And he's discouraged me from seeking medical attention. I looked the symptoms up online. Poisoning seems to be the most likely explanation.'

'Ah, yes, Dr Google! Self-diagnosis is rarely a good idea. There are other viable alternative diagnoses we need to consider.'

'The symptoms gradually subsided when he went away for a few days. They started again after he cooked on his return.'

'Has he been ill at all?'

'No, he hasn't, only me.'

'Are you taking any medication, warfarin for example?'

'I only take an antihistamine for hay fever.'

'Nothing else?'

'No.'

'Okay, I've heard enough. We'll run a few blood tests and admit you for observations until we know more. Staff mentioned that you don't want us to contact anyone on your behalf. Let's not jump to any conclusions, but I can understand your reticence given the circumstances. I'll ensure your instruction is respected for as long as you're with us.'

'If my fiancé finds out where I am, I don't want to see him, not under any circumstances.'

'What's his name?'

'Adam, Adam Newman.'

'Have you got a photograph?'

'No, he's always avoided them, but I can describe him well enough.'

'I'll let the sister know once you're on the medical unit. This is a hospital, not a prison, but we'll do what we can.'

Ella didn't see the consultant again until 4:10 p.m. the following afternoon. When she did see her, Dr Thomas had a dark look on her otherwise friendly face that told Ella all she needed to know. The doctor moved a chair up close to Ella's bed and pulled the curtain around it, affording what privacy she could. 'How are you doing?'

'I've been better.'

'I had the results of the tests rushed through.'

'And?'

The doctor spoke quietly now, uttering her words directly into Ella's right ear. 'I'm sorry to tell you that your assumptions may well prove to be correct. A combination of anticoagulants were found in your bloodstream. Unless you can give me some rational explanation as to how they got there, we need to contact the police.'

'So, he has poisoned me? Is that what you're saying?'

'Have you had any rat poison anywhere near your property? Anywhere close to your food or water supply possibly?'

Ella touched her parted lips with a quivering finger. 'No, not that I know of. And even if there was, why would it only affect me? That wouldn't make any sense at all.'

'That's not something I can comment on.'

'There's a particular police officer I'd like to speak to, a Detective Inspector Laura Kesey. She's based at Police Headquarters here in the town. If you give her my name, I'm sure she'll want to help. And please explain the circumstances. She needs to know not to approach Adam.'

The doctor pushed her chair aside. 'I'll make the call personally and report back to you as soon as I know what's happening.'

Ella shook her head slowly. 'I can't believe all this. We're supposed to be getting married. My world's gone mad.'

'Hang on in there, Ella, you're on the mend, that's the good news. Let's take this one step at a time, shall we? You'll need to stay here for two or three more days before you're fit for discharge. Hopefully by then, the police will have clarified matters and you'll know exactly where you stand.'

'He's at home with my sister and niece. Maybe I've been selfish. What if *they're* in danger? Where do my actions leave them?'

The doctor shuffled back a step or two, her voice rising in pitch, no longer worrying about being overheard. 'I'll be ringing the police the second I'm back in my office. I'm heading there now. You've done the right thing, believe me. Had you digested any further anticoagulants, any more at all, you may well have died.'

40

Kesey finally found a free space in the busy hospital car park and ran towards the main entrance as crackling thunder threatened to transform intermittent spots of rain into a deluge. She stopped for a quick coffee in the small WRVS café on entering the building, glad of the caffeine's perceived restorative properties as she made her way along the long corridors towards the ward. Within five minutes, Kesey was standing alongside Ella's bed with a bag of seedless grapes in one hand and a triple folded statement form in the other.

The detective introduced herself and sat down in the only available seat, a hard wooden chair she didn't appreciate in the slightest. 'How are you doing, feeling any better?'

Ella popped a grape into her open mouth, relishing the sweetness on her tongue. 'Did Dr Thomas explain what's happened to me?'

Kesey nodded. 'She did, but I want to hear it from you. In your own words.'

Ella told her story, starting with the commencement of her health problems, followed by their likely cause, and then finally moving on to outline recent events relating to Mia, Isabella and her deceased parents.

'Just to be clear, you're telling me that your parents died in the fire?'

Ella wiped a tear from her face, her voice breaking as she spoke. 'Yes, both of them, that's what Mia said. I can't believe they're dead. My mum and dad gone, just like that when they should have years of happy life ahead of them. Life can be so horribly unpredictable. It still doesn't seem real. We were close, even if we didn't see as much of each other as we used to.'

'I'm sorry for your loss.'

'Adam tried to rescue them apparently, but the fire was too fierce. Mia said he was beaten back by the flames. It's almost too terrible to contemplate. I keep imagining my parents trapped by the fire and trying to escape.'

'And they suspected it was arson?'

'Yes, according to Adam, or at least that's what Mia told me. He claimed to have heard the same perpetrator in the grounds the previous night. He said he thought it was the same man who sent the emails. That whoever that was, followed them to Italy because of his obsession with Mia.'

'Did anyone else see or hear anything suspicious? Anyone other than Adam?'

'Not that I'm aware of. Or, at least I don't think so.'

'I want you to listen to me very carefully and to think about the answer and its implications.'

'Okay, I can do that.'

'Why would Adam try to kill you?'

Ella perceived a sudden coldness deep in her core, shivering despite the summer warmth. 'I wish I knew the answer. I've been thinking about little else since getting the results of the tests. Maybe he's fallen for Mia or her money. She's a lot better off than me.'

'Does he own a computer?'

'Yes, a laptop, we both do. What are you getting at?'

Kesey didn't reply, giving Ella time to join the dots herself. 'You believe it's Adam, don't you? I've been asking myself the same thing. Maybe he did it all!'

'What's his knowledge of computers like? Would you consider him an expert?'

'He says not. It's never seemed so... but I've only got his word for it.'

Kesey adjusted her position, shifting in her seat. 'How much do you know about him?'

Ella thought for a few seconds, searching her mind. 'Only what he's told me.'

'Have you met his friends?'

'No, I haven't. Adam's not the social type.'

'Workmates?'

'No, he's in personal protection. He goes off, does a job and comes back a few days later.'

'What about his family?'

'Oh my God, no, not a single one! He said they're all dead, other than a brother who lives in Australia.'

'How did you meet?'

'Online, he'd just moved to the area.'

'So, you really don't know much about him at all?'

'No, I guess not. He was in the army and grew up in a children's home, that's about it. He once said his mother rejected him at birth, but no more. I hadn't considered how little I know until now.'

'What regiment did he serve in?'

'He's never told me.'

'What about the name of the children's home?'

Ella felt her skin tingle, butterflies fluttering in her stomach. 'He never told me that either.'

'Bottom line, he could be anyone at all.'

Ella blew the air from her mouth. 'Yes, he could.'

'This may seem like a strange question, but have you ever seen items that could be used to disguise his appearance? Wigs, false facial hair, that sort of thing?'

Ella shook her head. 'No, never, nothing like that.'

'What does he drive?'

'A modern hatchback, why do you ask?'

'Not a dark-coloured estate car?'

'Not that I've ever seen.'

Kesey sighed, her shoulders slumping as another investigative door slammed shut. 'Have you got anything with his fingerprints on? Anything at all?'

Ella reached into her bedside locker and grabbed her handbag. 'There's a red leather card holder in the side pocket. I've never used it. He gave it to me at Christmas. It must have his prints all over it.'

'Can I take it with me?'

'Help yourself. Anything that helps.'

Kesey removed the wallet from Ella's handbag with metal tweezers she usually used as a beauty aid and dropped it into a clear plastic evidence bag. 'Has Adam ever been violent towards you, your suspicions regarding the poisoning apart?'

'No, never, I'd never thought of him as a violent man until now. I've realised he's not the man I thought he was. I didn't know the real Adam at all.'

'At this stage, he's a suspect, nothing more. Innocent until proven guilty.'

Ella's face reddened. 'Oh, come on, he cooked me food and I became ill, he stopped cooking, I got better again. And now I'm told I've digested rat poison after he's discouraged me from seeking medical help. It seems pretty conclusive to me. He wants me dead. How much evidence do you need before making an arrest?'

'Has he ever shown much interest in your sister, anything specific you can put your finger on?'

'Well, he read one of her books recently and asked a few questions about what was happening to her before volunteering to accompany her and Izzy to Italy. I thought he wanted to help because she was my sister. I didn't read anything sinister into it.'

'Going to Italy with your sister was his idea?'

Ella nodded, covering her mouth with the palm of one hand, her breathing becoming more laboured. 'You don't think he killed my parents, do you?'

'I'll be talking to the Italian police. It's something we can't rule out.'

Ella closed her eyes as a shooting pain in her head made her shudder.

'Just one more question before we make a written statement, if that's all right with you?'

'Go ahead. I'd like to get this over with.'

'Does Adam have access to any other buildings, another house, a flat or even a caravan, anywhere he could keep things or take someone he didn't want found?'

'I'm starting to question if I'd have known even if he had. I've lived with a stranger, a monster hidden in plain sight.'

'I'll take that as a no then.'

Ella lowered her voice to a whisper. 'I'm safe, I'm here, but what about Izzy? What about Mia? If Adam's a killer, they must be in danger.'

Kesey leaned towards her witness, gripping her hand. 'Let's get the statement written and progress matters from there.'

'What's that supposed to mean exactly?'

'The quicker I gather evidence and build a case, the quicker I can make an arrest. It's how the system works. There's no point in dragging a suspect in for questioning and then letting him go again without charge. When I make an arrest, I want to make it stick.'

'Will my statement help in that regard?'

'Yes, it could do, that and the fingerprints.'

'I'm ready, let's get it done.'

41

Mia stood blocking the doorway as Kesey, Best and two uniformed constables faced her. Kesey met Mia's confused gaze and took the lead. Her new rank carried responsibilities as well as privileges. 'We're here to see Adam, Mia. Stand aside, please. You need to let us in.'

Mia didn't move, her startled eyes flitting from one officer to the next before fixing on Kesey, desperately hoping for the best but fearing the worst. 'Oh no, has something happened to my sister? We've no idea where she is. We've been worried sick.'

'Have you reported her missing?'

'Adam said it was too soon.'

Kesey held a sheet of printed paper in plain sight. 'I've spoken to Ella, she's safe. We've got a warrant to search the property. You need to let us in *now*. I'll explain everything later.'

Mia stood aside, more confused than ever as Isabella appeared in the hallway, half-asleep and clutching a teddy bear. 'Come to Mummy, Izzy, everything's going to be fine. The nice police officers are here to make sure we're all safe. They need to talk to Uncle Adam, that's all.'

'There's not going to be another fire, is there?'

Mia shook her head, her heart sinking at the memory. 'No, Izzy, that's not going to happen.'

Kesey stepped into the hallway, the other officers crowding in behind her. 'Where is he, Mia?'

'Up the stairs and then it's the second door on the left, past the bathroom. But he's probably still asleep. We had a late night. Do you want me to wake him? It's going to be a bit of a shock if any of you lot suddenly appear.'

Kesey pointed at Best and then at one of the two uniformed officers, a heavily built rugby-playing man in his mid-thirties who seemed to fill almost the entire space. 'Go and get him, boys. Use the cuffs and keep a close eye on him. He's ex-military, he'll know how to handle himself. We can search the place as soon as he's safely in custody.'

Mia looked on incredulously, focussing on Kesey with pleading eyes as the two officers rushed towards Adam's bedroom. 'What on earth's going on?'

'Ella's in hospital, Mia, the doctors believe she's been poisoned. Adam will be formally interviewed later today.'

'Adam, poisoning Ella? Adam? That's ludicrous! I'd be laughing if it wasn't so ridiculous. You're arresting the one man who's keeping us safe.'

Adam was in the process of climbing out of an open window and onto a rickety, black metal fire escape when the two constables rushed into the room. The bigger of the two officers was quickest to react, his sporting instincts to the fore as he dashed forward and hurled himself through mid-air, grabbing Adam's ankle and dragging him back just as he was about to slink away to freedom. Adam kicked out with his free leg to no significant effect as the powerful man pinned him to the ground. He threw a single punch on freeing one arm, catching the second officer with a glancing blow to his chin that loosened a tooth. Both officers acted in unison, quickly overpowering their suspect, forcing him face down on the carpet and cuffing his hands tightly behind his back.

The bigger of the two men dragged his prisoner to his feet and punched him hard on the chest, sending him sprawling, after Adam head-butted the second officer, splitting his top lip and fracturing the bridge of his nose in the process. The startled officer raised a hand to his face and grimaced as the blood began to flow.

'Get him out of here, Dave, the bastard's broken my nose.'

The uninjured officer dragged Adam to his feet and shoved him towards the hallway as DC Best sauntered to meet them.

'For fuck's sake, you took your time.'

Best laughed. 'Oh, I knew you two could handle him. I'm the brains, not the brawn. I leave the rough stuff to you woodentops.'

Kesey placed a hand on Adam's shoulder, stretching out her arm as the big constable pinned him to the wall. 'I'm arresting you on suspicion of attempted murder. You do not have to say anything. But it may harm your defence if you do not mention when questioned something which you later rely on in court. Anything you do say may be given in evidence. Do you understand?'

'No comment, I've got nothing to say.'

Kesey took a backward step and smiled. 'Oh, it's going to be like that, is it? Have it your way. It won't do you any good. And no doubt we'll be adding assault on police to the charge sheet.'

Kesey grimaced as PC Benjamin Green joined them from the bathroom, dark blood still running down his chin and staining his shirt.

'Dave, you get the prisoner in the vehicle. Ben, we can drop you off at casualty on the way to the station. George, I want you to search every inch of this place, and let me know immediately if you find anything significant. You know the sort of thing you're looking for. And seize any computers, tablets or phones you come across for the tech team to have a look at. We won't start the interview until the search is complete and you're back at headquarters. Is everyone clear as to their responsibilities?'

The officers indicated their understanding as Kesey turned to Mia, who was holding her daughter. 'Please wait with Isabella in the lounge, Mia. It might be an idea to stay somewhere else once we're done here. Back in your own house, for example. I could arrange transport, if that helps. You'd be safe there now. I'll be asking one of my officers to take a statement from you later today.'

Mia ignored Kesey's impassioned plea. 'Why would you do that, Adam? Why would you hurt the officer like that?'

Adam shouted back on being pushed through the front door. 'Don't trust them, Mia! *He's* got to them. The bastard who killed your parents. I'm the only one you can trust. Remember that when you're interviewed. Don't believe a single word they say.'

'I want to see Ella.'

'Don't believe that bitch either. She's full of crap. She doesn't believe a word you say, so why should you trust her?'

42

Mia sat at her sister's hospital bedside and met her eyes. 'Hello, Ella, it's good to see you again. You had me worried for a while. What on earth were you thinking going off like that without telling me?'

'Where's Izzy?'

'A DC Bethan Williams is looking after her in the dayroom to give us time to talk. I think she's hoping you'll talk me into giving a statement.'

Ella sat bolt upright, adjusting her pillows. 'What, are you saying you haven't made one?'

'No, why would I?'

Ella's eyes flashed. 'Adam tried to kill me, that's why! He fed me rat poison. I was in agony. I would have thought that's a good enough reason, wouldn't you? For goodness' sake, Mia, just get it done.'

Mia looked away. 'I don't believe he'd do such a thing. He's one of life's good guys. Someone I can rely on. It's about time you understood that. I can't believe you're questioning his loyalty. If someone poisoned you, it wasn't Adam.'

'Then, who else was it? Can you tell me that? Adam's the only one who's cooked for me. He's got you conned. You need to open your eyes and see him for what he is.'

Mia glared at Ella, indignant as she jumped to her feet. 'Maybe Mattia did it. Have you considered that possibility? He's a far more likely suspect.'

'That's impossible, I only saw him the once before he was killed.'

'Killed? Are you telling me he's dead?'

'What, Adam didn't think to tell you? That seems a bit strange, don't you think?'

'He can't have known.'

'Oh, he knew all right! Mattia was run down in the street. Hit-and-run. Maybe Adam did that too. It wouldn't surprise me. I think he's capable of almost anything.'

Mia shook her head. 'Oh, come on, Adam saved me. He saved Izzy. He tried to save Mum and Dad! You should be grateful to him, not making wild allegations you can't substantiate. What use are the police? Where were they when the villa was burning down? If it wasn't for Adam, I wouldn't be here talking to you now. I'd have been burned to a cinder along with Mum and Dad. Why can't you see that? He's too good for you.'

Ella pointed her index finger, her frustration boiling over. 'Did he save you, Mia? Or did he set the fire himself? What if it was *all* him: the emails, the cat, the poison, the fire and even the missing women? Maybe he did it all. What do we actually know about him? Ask yourself that. Everything was fine before he entered our lives. Mattia's dead, poor Mum and Dad are gone and I've been poisoned. That's got to be more than a coincidence. Adam's the common factor. See what's staring you in the face before it's too late. Don't you think we've lost enough?'

'You're talking crap as usual! Adam told me what you really

think about me. That you don't believe a word I say. I really thought I could trust you, Ella. You've let me down. I don't know if I can ever forgive you for that.'

Ella drew a deep breath, releasing it before speaking. 'Talk to the police, listen to what they've got to say and then make your mind up. I'm begging you, Mia. Tell the police everything they want to know and put it in writing. If Adam's as innocent as you obviously think, he's got nothing to worry about. And if he's not, if you're horribly wrong as I know you are, at least then you'll find out the truth.'

Mia began striding towards the exit, her remaining tablets rattling in her pocket. 'Are there any depths to which you won't stoop? The police would twist my words, like you are. I'm telling them nothing, not a word!'

Ella called after her. 'Please, Mia, for old times' sake. Remember? Me and you against the world?'

Mia didn't reply as she reached for her medication. Ella was hateful, deluded, they all were. Ella hadn't been in Italy. She didn't see. Adam was the one person to rely on, her saviour in a dark and troubling world of woe. She'd be at his side every step of the way.

43

Kesey sat alongside Peter Best in the small Carmarthen Police HQ interview room and switched on the recording equipment as Adam, and his duty solicitor sat and waited for the questions to begin.

Kesey gave the time and date and then continued, 'My name is Detective Inspector Laura Kesey. Also present is Detective Constable Peter Best; the interviewee, Mr Adam Newman; and his solicitor, Mr Jonathan Webb. I need to remind you, Mr Newman, that you're still subject to caution. Anything you say could be used in evidence if the matter comes to court at some future date. Do you understand?'

Adam looked away and nodded.

'For the tape, please, Mr Newman. I need you to say it.'

'Yes, I understand.'

Kesey opened a thin cardboard file on the table in front of her and perused the contents, casually flicking through the pages for a few seconds before eventually speaking in her familiar Brummie drawl. 'Am I correct in saying that you haven't always been called Adam Newman?'

Adam clenched his fists, fighting to regain his composure. 'What's your point?'

'We've checked your fingerprints, Mr Newman, or should I call you Smith? We know exactly who you are.'

'I changed my name by deed poll. There's no law against it as far as I'm aware.'

The young lawyer, dressed in a cheap suit and overly bright orange-and-purple necktie, spoke up for the first time. 'Where's this going, Inspector? My client has a point.'

'I'm just trying to establish your client's true identity. I think that's in everyone's interests.'

Adam glared at his solicitor, losing patience. 'I've said I changed my name. It's all a matter of public record. Let's get this charade over with, shall we?'

Kesey couldn't believe her luck. 'You served as a lieutenant in the British Army Intelligence Corps.'

'So? I served my country. I would have thought that's something to be applauded rather than criticised. I'm a hero. They even gave me a medal.'

'You were stripped of your rank and dishonourably discharged after being convicted of assault by a military court. You also attacked one of my officers. You broke his nose. You're clearly a man with a violent temper.'

Adam gripped the edge of the table with both hands. 'The lying bitch made it all up. Women do that. They let you down. And as for the copper, he assaulted me, that was self-defence. I've got no case to answer.'

'Did you send her emails? The woman you assaulted. Did you send her threatening messages? We know someone did. I believe that someone was you.'

'I've got nothing to say. It's a fantasy, a figment of your imagination, nothing more.'

'Your accuser disappeared shortly after your return to civilian life. She hasn't been seen since.'

Adam sighed theatrically, making his displeasure obvious. 'I was questioned at the time. It didn't come to anything. I don't think they ever found the body. It seems the Bedfordshire police are as useless as you are.'

Kesey was quick to respond. 'Body? Who said anything about a body? Why do you assume she's dead? Do you know something I don't?'

'If she is dead, it's got nothing to do with me.' He grinned. 'Not that I'd mourn her loss.'

The solicitor spoke for the second time. 'Mr Newman's been arrested on suspicion of attempted murder. I'd be grateful if you'd limit your questions to that investigation, as opposed to going off on a seemingly random fishing exercise with very little bait. My client is here to cooperate within reason, but if you insist on continuing along your current tack, I'll have no choice but to advise him to remain silent. It's up to you.'

Kesey knew that some battles weren't worth fighting. It was time to move on. 'How much experience have you had with covert surveillance?'

Adam laughed, amalgam fillings in full view. 'I've had some experience. But then you already knew that. It's a basic technique. And a tad transparent, don't you think? You're asking questions you already know the answer to. You're going to have to do a lot better than that if you hope to catch me out. I've never heard anything more pathetic in my life.'

Kesey was beginning to wonder if she'd underestimated her adversary. 'There were covert cameras installed in every room in Mia Hamilton's home. She's your ex-fiancée's sister. That's too much of a coincidence. You put them there.'

The solicitor immediately objected to the line of questioning, but Adam interrupted him before he could finish his point. 'No, you're all right. I want to answer.'

Adam looked directly at the recording equipment with a smirk on his face. 'Did Mia say I'd fitted them? She must have seen whoever did the work. Do I meet the description, even slightly? Or perhaps you found fingerprints, my fingerprints, is that it? I think not, or I'd have heard about it long before now.'

'Why did you send Mia threatening emails? Did she do something to upset or irritate you? Rejecting your sexual advances for example. I'd really like to know.'

'Did you find any evidence of the relevant messages on my laptop? I know you didn't because there's nothing to find.' He paused, seemingly thinking things through. 'Unless I've got a second computer you haven't discovered. That's a possibility you shouldn't rule out.'

Kesey gritted her teeth. 'And, have you?'

'That's for me to know and you to find out.'

'That seems like a convoluted admission of sorts. Are you confirming you sent them? Maybe it's something you're proud of.'

'No, absolutely not! I'm merely highlighting the ludicrous nature of your approach. You're wasting your time, and mine too.'

'Ella is scared of you, Adam. She nearly died. You fed her rat poison. If she hadn't gone to the hospital when she did, we'd be investigating her murder.'

'How much longer is this farce going to take? I've got things to do.'

'You tried to kill your fiancée, any comment? You must have something to say in response. It's an extremely serious allegation. Don't you want to explain why you did it? This is your opportunity.'

'Did you find any rat poison at our house, even a trace? Or maybe you found it in my car. No? Nothing? Face facts, woman, if I had bought poison, which I'm not saying I did, I'd have bought it for cash and a long way from here. Or maybe I stole it. I could have stolen it. You've got nothing on me. You're pissing in the wind. Wasting your time interviewing an innocent man.'

Kesey played her next card, opening the file and sliding a six-by-four-inch photo of the severed hand across the table. She watched his unreadable face and thought for a fraction of a second that he may have flinched, just slightly. 'Any comment?'

'I hope the previous owner hasn't missed it too much. It must be something of an inconvenience. But not to worry, she's probably dead anyway. Not that that's got anything to do with me.'

'She?'

'Isn't it obvious?'

'You sent that hand to Emily Gravel.'

'Did I?'

'You froze it, packed it, and sent it by post.'

Adam laughed dismissively. 'Can you prove it or is it more wild speculation? Did you find my DNA or any other relevant forensic evidence to place before a jury?' He waited for a reply that didn't materialise and then continued, 'Oh, dear, why the silence? I suspect whoever sent it made certain there was nothing for you to find. Perhaps he's more intelligent than you are. It wouldn't take much from what I've seen. Women aren't suited to demanding jobs. You should leave it to the men.'

'You think you're very clever, don't you?'

Adam dragged his head back, snorting his amusement. 'I'm cleverer than you, that's for sure. If this is the best you can do, you've got no chance of a conviction. I'd give up now if I were you.'

Kesey loathed his attitude, she despised his demeanour, and most of all she hated the fact that he was right. She had all the suspicions in the world, she knew he was guilty, she had no doubt at all. But she had no evidence to prove it. 'Have you got any questions before we take a break, George?'

Best shook his head.

'Switch off the tape and put him back in his cell. We'll continue the interview in an hour.'

44

Kesey sat face to face with DCS Hannah Davies and grimaced. 'I've just completed the second interview with Adam Newman, ma'am. We've got nothing on him and he knows it.'

'Why arrest him when you did?'

'He posed a serious risk. The timing wasn't perfect, but I didn't feel I had any real choice. If I hadn't acted and he'd killed again, where would that have left me? We'd discovered his true identity and record. I thought I could use that to pressure him into implicating himself.'

'It clearly wasn't enough.'

Kesey avoided eye contact. 'Hindsight is an exact science. I made a call. It didn't seem nearly as obvious at the time.'

'What do you suggest we do now?'

'Let's charge him with assaulting Ben and then do all we can to ensure he's remanded in custody for as long as possible. I'm sure the CPS will go for it if I explain the circumstances.'

'Unless he pleads guilty.'

'That's not going to happen.'

The chief superintendent frowned. 'He'd be locked up for a matter of weeks at best.'

'I'm not saying it provides an ideal solution, but it would at least buy us some time. I may be able to persuade Mia Hamilton to make a statement. She could have seen or heard something that helps us. We've got nothing else to go on.'

'She still hasn't spoken to you?'

'Not since her initial statement at Grav's place. Newman's got her wrapped around his little finger.'

'Have you talked to the Italian police?'

'Yes, but no joy as yet. They've confirmed the fire was arson, but there's nothing to suggest who committed the crime. Enquiries are ongoing.'

'What of the other Welsh forces? Have none of the missing women been found?'

'I suspect they're all dead and buried, but no, they haven't been located.'

The chief superintendent picked up her reading glasses but didn't put them on. 'Very well, Laura, if anyone can persuade Miss Hamilton to talk to us, I feel sure it's you. Go and get it done. Hopefully, this won't come back to haunt both of us.'

45

Kesey glanced out of her lounge window as Grav downed another can of beer. 'He was given bail. Adam – he was given bail.'

Grav pressed the phone to his ear. 'What, after he broke an officer's nose, how the hell did that happen?'

Kesey stared at the car that had been parked opposite her home for most of the night. 'He pleaded not guilty after alleging police brutality. It was self-defence, apparently. He's got to report to a police station once a week pending a Crown Court trial... and that's it.'

'That wouldn't have happened years back. Everything has changed, and not for the better.'

'He's got a good lawyer. Some new bloke I hadn't met before. He looked like a kid straight out of college, but he knows the game. The less I see of him, the happier I'll be.'

'What's his name?'

'Jonathan, "please call me Jon," Webb.'

Grav laughed, beer spilling from his mouth. 'I don't know him.'

'I wish I could say the same.'

Grav took a breath. 'Thanks for keeping me in the loop, love, it's appreciated.'

'Who else should I talk to? Whenever I speak to the DCS, I end up wondering how long I've got left in the job.'

'Yeah, her majesty makes a habit of that.'

Kesey approached the window and peered out, staying half hidden behind the wall. 'He's outside the house now, has been for hours.'

'Who?'

'Newman, he sent me an email telling me he'd be there. In his own name. No effort to hide his identity this time. He's just sitting in his car staring at the windows through a pair of binoculars. Hopefully, it's a wind-up and nothing more. The quicker he pisses off, the happier I'll be.'

Grav felt his body tense. 'Why don't you go outside, bang on his car roof and tell him to fuck off? I can do it for you if you want me to. It would be a pleasure.'

'I don't want to give him the satisfaction. He's not breaking any laws, or at least, not yet. I can't nick him for parking in the street.'

'You've got to do something, love. He's a dangerous man.'

Kesey craned her neck and looked out on hearing a car door slam shut. 'He's out of the car. Oh for fuck's sake, he's coming towards the house.'

'Keep the door locked, love. I'm on my way.'

Kesey fell backwards, shards of glass striking her face as Adam hurled half a house brick through the lounge window. 'He's smashed the window, Grav, he's trying to get in!'

Grav grabbed his car keys as Kesey jumped to her feet. She fully intended to dial 999, but there was no time. Adam was stepping over the sill now, a knife in one hand. Run or fight, fight or run? Kesey reacted in an instant, leaping forwards on her well-toned legs and striking Adam with a powerful kick to his right temple, stunning him momentarily and sending him sprawling sideways into the nearest wall. Adam raised himself unsteadily to his feet with an animalistic snarl as Kesey struck again, but as she kicked out for a second time with all the force she could muster, he slashed her leg with the blade. She threw two fast punches, splitting his lip, and retreating simultaneously, warm blood pouring from her wound and filling one shoe. Kesey turned and ran towards the staircase, stumbling and dropping her phone as he rushed after her. She briefly considered stopping and picking it up, but he was almost on her now, slashing at her with the blade as she pulled away and climbed another step. Kesey moved as quickly as feasibly possible, adrenalin aiding her flight as Adam attempted to grab her and drag her down towards him. She turned and kicked him hard in the abdomen on reaching the landing, sending him back down three steps before he steadied himself, looking at her with cold, emotionless eyes that reminded her of a cobra about to strike.

As Kesey backed towards the bathroom door, Adam stopped suddenly, laughing maniacally on sensing his final victory.

'You've got nowhere else to run, Laura, it's over. You've wanted to know where I hide the bodies and now you are about to find out. You'll join them in the ground soon enough, but we'll have some fun before then. There's somewhere I plan to take you. Somewhere we won't be disturbed. Somewhere I can indulge my sadism to the limit. How does that sound?'

Kesey opened the bathroom door and took two backward steps. She was desperate to continue the battle. Keen to fight on. But she was weakening now, her eyes losing focus and blurring as her blood continued to flow. Adam approached her as she slowly slumped to the floor, a smile spreading across his face as he grabbed her by the hair and began dragging her back down the stairs towards the hall.

Grav brought his car to a screeching halt at the precise moment Adam carried Kesey's unconscious body out of the front door, held effortlessly over one muscular shoulder. Grav jumped from the vehicle, his chest tightening, then fetched a heavy metal wrench from the boot before striding towards Adam with a cold and determined expression on his face. 'You'll put her down if you know what's good for you, you vicious bastard.'

Adam dropped Kesey to the ground, her head cracking on the concrete path. 'What are you going to do, old man, are you going to try and arrest me? I'll deal with you, kill your little friend here, and then I'll go after your daughter. I've kept some particularly unpleasant means of torture in reserve only for her. She'll be begging to die long before the end. She's going to die a horrible death, and it's all your fault.'

Grav moved with surprising speed and agility for a man of his age and failing health. He threw himself forward, striking Adam a hefty blow with the wrench, breaking his left arm just above the elbow. Adam let out a visceral scream as Grav hit him a second time, virtually at the same spot. He tried to throw a punch with his uninjured arm, but Grav was quick to react, spinning his opponent, forcing him to the ground and handcuffing him with his hands rammed high behind his back. Grav dragged Adam to his feet, panting hard and purple in the face as he shoved him towards his car and into the front passenger seat.

Grav dialled the emergency services, summoning an ambulance for Kesey before driving away. She was going to be okay. That's what he told himself. Leave her to the experts and concentrate on what he did best.

Adam winced with every bend, and jarring pothole Grav negotiated, but he wasn't ready to let up. 'Don't go thinking you've won, old man. I may be locked up for a few years. I guess that's inevitable. But I'll be released sooner or later and then I'll kill your daughter. I'll have more than enough time to plan her demise in infinite detail. You can't begin to imagine the horrors

I'm capable of inflicting. I'll tear her apart, slowly, one morsel at a time.'

Grav didn't drive to the police station as he'd initially planned. He drove to the top floor of the town's multi-storey car park, where he dragged Adam from the car and stood him on the edge, staring down at the pavement three hundred and fifteen feet below.

'You can't do this, you're a police officer.'

Grav stood behind his prisoner, squeezing his broken arm tightly when he tried to pull away. 'I used to be a working copper, and a good one too, but all that's in the past. Every dog has his day. My luck ran out and now so has yours.'

'Okay, you've had your fun. Now, put me back in the car.'

Grav stared up at the grey clouds and saw Heather drifting towards him. 'Do it, Grav, you're doing the right thing. Kill the bastard. He threatened our little girl.'

'Are you sure, love? I'm an old copper, not a criminal, murder's a bit full on.'

Adam lost control of his bladder as he teetered on the very edge of the long drop, Grav nudging him forwards. 'Who the fuck are you talking to?'

'Ignore him, Grav, he's a lowlife, a scumbag, he deserves to die. Nobody threatens our little girl and gets away with it. You said that yourself. Send him to oblivion.'

'I could do with a drink, love.'

Adam tried to shake free, but he was frozen with fear of falling. 'You're losing it, old man, you're fucking mad! Put me back in the car!'

Heather shook her head as Grav looked up at her. 'Come on, push him hard, now's the time. Push the bastard off. Your days as a detective are done. There's nothing left to lose. It's Emily's safety that matters now.'

Grav leaned his weight forwards and shoved, the sound of

Adam's screams piercing his ears as he plummeted through the air and smashed into the pavement.

The big detective met his beloved sweetheart's eyes and held out a hand to greet her. 'I guess that's it, love, it's done. I've just killed a man. Prison is no place for a man like me. There's no explaining this one away. I'd be locked up for the rest of my life.' Heather smiled warmly in that youthful way of hers, the years melting away, as if she'd never died. 'Come on, my lovely boy, come and join me in the afterlife. We'll be together forever. What are you waiting for?'

'Kesey is going to be okay, isn't she?'

'Of course, she is. You've done your bit; it's her time now.'

'I'm going to miss the christening.'

'They'll be fine without you. The world will keep turning. No one's indispensable, not even you.'

Grav nodded his agreement, blowing Heather a kiss as he took a single step forward, smiling contentedly right up to the second he hit the ground.

46

Janet sat at Kesey's bedside, their son resting in the baby carrier alongside her, and wondered how she was going to tell her partner something she knew would break her heart.

'What is it, Janet? I know there's something. I can read you like a book.'

Janet looked away. 'Um... it's, er... it's about Grav. It's not good news.'

'Oh, no, he hasn't had another heart attack, has he?'

Janet reached out and held Kesey's hand. 'He's dead, Laura. He fell from a building after pushing Adam Newman to his death.'

'Grav? No! I won't believe it. He's larger than life. He can't be dead.'

Janet nodded. 'He's gone, Laura.'

'Oh God, why him? It's the end of an era.'

'There's a funeral at the crematorium in Narberth. I've spoken to your consultant. She says you're going to be well enough to be there.'

Kesey dropped her head, her eyes moistening. 'Poor Emily!'

'I called to see her. Her brother was there. He's visiting from Barbados.'

'That's good, Grav would like that.'

'That's what I thought.'

'I can't believe he's gone. He was almost like a father to me. I'm going to miss him terribly.'

'At least Newman's dead, I won't mourn his loss.'

'I can't say I'm sorry. We've got Grav to thank for that.'

Janet reached down, lifted the baby up gently and handed him to Kesey. 'You're going to be out of here soon. I'm hoping you're going to tell me you're not going to go back to the job. I don't know if I could stand it. You nearly died. I'd be worried sick every time you left the house.'

Kesey cuddled their son and met her partner's anxious gaze. 'I'm a police officer, Janet, just like Grav. You knew the deal when you agreed to marry me.'

'You won't even think about it?'

Kesey shook her head. 'I'm a copper. I'm always going to be a copper. I understand your concerns, really I do. But that's not going to change. It's what I was born to do. I'll be catching criminals until they pension me off. I'm already anticipating my next big case.'

47

TEN DAYS LATER

Emily and her brother sat hand in hand in the front row of the packed crematorium and watched as Grav's dark-oak coffin made its final journey into the all-enveloping flames to the sound of a rousing Welsh hymn. They rose to their feet as the furnace's door closed and made their way outside to share condolences with the many black-clad and uniformed mourners, who filed out after them.

Mia and Ella walked out together, hugging both Emily and Dewi with genuine affection, before giving their best wishes and strolling towards Mia's car.

Ella was the first of the two to speak as Mia manoeuvred out of the car park and into the road. 'Nice service. You know, for a funeral.'

'He had a lot of friends.'

'Yeah, he did. He was a popular man.'

Mia signalled to her right. 'Have you got time for a quick bite to eat before we head back to town?'

'What time is it?'

'Just after twelve.'

'Yeah, why not? How about that nice hotel in Saundersfoot, the one with the view of the harbour? It's about time we had a heart-to-heart.'

Ella adjusted her blouse, undoing and refastening a button. 'Sounds good to me.'

'Fancy some music?'

'No, let's take the opportunity to talk.'

Mia blew the air from her mouth. 'Okay, I need to say I'm sorry. I can't believe I fell for Adam's lies. I should have trusted you. I'm going to regret it for the rest of my life.'

'You mustn't be too hard on yourself. He was a good liar, one of the best. He had me conned for months. Think about it, I nearly married the man.'

'Am I forgiven?'

Ella reached out and patted her sister's knee. 'Of course, you are, goes without saying.'

'Thanks, sis, that means a lot.'

Ella took a tissue from her handbag and dabbed at her eyes as her tears began to flow. 'I can't believe Mum and Dad are gone and in such a horrible way. I just hope they didn't suffer, that would be too much to bear. I pray it was all over before they even knew what was happening.'

Mia braked, slowing the car almost to a stop in the narrow road. 'They didn't suffer. I keep telling you the same thing. I don't know what else I can say to convince you.'

'But what if you're wrong?'

'I was there, Ella. I saw what happened. It would all have been over very quickly. Don't torture yourself with what ifs. They don't serve any purpose. You need to accept what I've said.'

'You have told me everything, haven't you? You haven't held anything back?'

Mia eased her foot down on the accelerator as the driver in the car behind sounded his horn. 'Mum and Dad wouldn't have felt any pain, promise. You can take my word for it. I've thought about little else. I've dissected it in my mind. They died in their sleep. They wouldn't have felt a thing.'

Ella stared ahead, forcing unwelcome thoughts from her mind as the sea came into view. 'Are we going to the inquest?'

'Can you afford to?'

'To be honest, no. I was thinking of maxing out the credit card. It's not something I want to miss. It's too important for that.'

'How would you feel about me booking us a week's break? I thought we could go to the inquest together, give each other the support we need, and then arrange some form of memorial. A bench perhaps, or a tree, something along those lines? Mum and Dad loved Italy. It seems like the right place to do it.'

'Are you sure you don't mind covering the cost?'

'It's the least I can do. Don't mention it.'

The sisters sat in silence for the next five minutes or so, until Ella finally asked the inevitable question as they approached the entrance to the hotel car park. 'Are you doing okay?'

Mia raised a hand to her face. 'Yeah, I think so, all considered. I've cut down on the medication for Izzy's sake. I'll be stopping it altogether soon.'

'I'm glad to hear it.'

'What about you?'

Ella smiled thinly, wiping away the last of her tears. 'I've signed on with a dating website. One of the girls at work persuaded me. I've got to get back on the horse sometime.'

'You're a glutton for punishment.'

'So it seems. Hopefully, I'll strike lucky this time.'

Mia found a convenient parking space as the sun broke through the clouds and bathed the world in light. 'I don't think we're ever going to escape Adam, not completely. He'll always be there in our darkest hours. But we've got to get on with our lives. What other choice is there? Life has to go on.'

'Me and you against the world?'

'Absolutely! Let's go and enjoy some lunch.'

MORE FROM JOHN NICHOLL

We hope you enjoyed reading *The Dryslwyn Castle Killings*. If you did, please leave a review.

If you'd like to gift a copy, this book is also available as a paperback, digital audio download and audiobook CD.

The Doctor, the first instalment in John Nicholl's Galbraith series, is available to pre-order now.

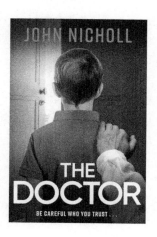

ABOUT THE AUTHOR

John Nicholl is an award-winning, bestselling author of numerous darkly psychological suspense thrillers, previously published by Bloodhound. These books have a gritty realism born of his real-life experience as an ex-police officer and child protection social worker.

Visit John's website: https://www.johnnicholl.com

Follow John on social media:

twitter.com/nicholl06
facebook.com/JohnNichollAuthor
instagram.com/johnnichollauthor

Boldwood

Boldwood Books is an award-winning fiction publishing company seeking out the best stories from around the world.

Find out more at www.boldwoodbooks.com

Join our reader community for brilliant books, competitions and offers!

Follow us
@BoldwoodBooks
@BookandTonic

Sign up to our weekly deals newsletter

https://bit.ly/BoldwoodBNewsletter